Unexpected Lovers

Work Husband Series

BLUE SAFFIRE

Perceptive Illusions Publishing
Bayshore, New York

Blue Saffire/Perceptive Illusions Publishing, Inc.
PO BOX 5253
Bayshore, NY 11706
www.BlueSaffire.com

Publisher's Note: This is a work of fiction. Names, characters, places, and incidents are a product of the author's imagination. Locales and public names are sometimes used for atmospheric purposes. Any resemblance to actual people, living or dead, or to businesses, companies, events, institutions, or locales is completely coincidental.

Ordering Information:
Quantity sales. Special discounts are available on quantity purchases by corporations, associations, and others. For details, contact the "Special Sales Department" at the address above.

Cover Designed by Natasha Snow Designs
www.natashasnowdesigns.com

Unexpected Lovers / Blue Saffire. -- 1st ed.
ISBN 978-1-941924-14-3

Not everyone is worthy of your love. If they can't respect you, respect yourself enough to walk away.

—Blue Saffire

Black Sheep's Sacrifice

Gio

"It's taken care of," Jace whispers in my ear.

I nod and narrow my eyes as my brother, Dante, stands before me at the altar. My little brother is making a mistake. I understand why. However, he's a grown man, so I'm going to allow him to make this decision on his own.

That doesn't mean I'm not going to cover him. It's only one more secret I'm going to own. As the oldest, I've learned some things he's yet to understand.

Life is about sacrifices. I've made many. I've been making sacrifices since I was told all the things I'll never be. In their eyes, I'm the weak one.

Funny, it's the weak hand that moves while the strong one strikes. In this life you need the weak hand to distract from the real power moves. I play the hand I've been dealt, but this isn't about me.

I'm getting ahead of myself. One day—and I say this with confidence—I'll right all the wrongs done to Ava Di Lorenzo's boys. All the secrets will be out and there won't be a weak link to be found.

First, my brothers have a few lessons to learn. For now, I'll leave our secrets to rest. Even my sister-in-law will be allowed a reprieve from the monster she has woken.

I'm patient. I had to learn to be. If nothing else I've said is remembered—remember this. When you bite a poisonous snake, don't be surprised when it bites back.

CHAPTER ONE

Trick or Treat

Lizzy

Laughter surrounds me and I roll my eyes. I'm at a great part in this book and all I want is some peace and quiet. Too bad all employees are required to come to these company parties. It's supposed to be a bonding experience.

For an introvert like me, it's like being boiled in hot grease. The only saving grace has been the fact that I get to dress up. Although, I had to dial back from the cosplay costume I had in mind as this is a work event after all.

Everyone already thinks I'm weird. I can only imagine what they would have thought if I showed up as Nubia. I sigh as I mourn not wearing my Black Wonder Woman costume. It would have been a representation of my hero. My big sister, she's the versions of me I wish I could always tap into.

"Happy Halloween, Lizzy." I look up and give a kind of grimace smile to one of my coworkers. I can't think of his name at the moment. He's one of the interns. He likes to talk a lot. I don't want to encourage that tonight.

I want to be left alone so I can finish this chapter. The main point of this costume was to be able to get away with reading with no one being the wiser.

As soon as I arrived, I found the first high boy not occupied by humans. I'd much rather spend the night with my book friends than these people.

They're not all bad. However, I don't like peopling. I'd rather stab my eye out than talk to people who look at me like I speak another language. I learned a long time ago; I'd rather not speak than be made to feel like I need to dumb down for others.

"Is this what I have my brother paying you so much for?"

I grin and get ready to say something snarky as I turn around. I freeze in place as I look up into the eyes of Gio Di Lorenzo. I'm startled at first by the white contacts he has in—they're such a stark contrast from his intense hazel eyes that always seem to be consumed by secrets. Even with the pale makeup, long blond wig, and fake blood dripping from his lower lip, he's still breathtaking.

All of the Di Lorenzo's are. However, this man has been a force from the first time I met him. Our meeting always brings a smile to my face. Gio lifts a brow and gives a dirty grin as if he's reading my thoughts.

"You and I both know this isn't what your brother pays me for," I say before leaning in to whisper. "Nor is he the one who pays me." I wink.

He winks back and places a finger to his lips, then glances around swiftly. "You look stunning. I don't regret a dime."

I laugh. "But that's not what you pay me for either and we know the pumpkin will return at midnight."

He frowns at my words and looks me deep in the eyes. I have to look away from his gaze as if I'm being burned. Gio is hot. I mean, melt your panties off hot, but I'm not a match for him or his tastes.

"It's always the treasures that don't understand their value," he murmurs.

"Whatever, my world is much more reality based than yours. This is why we're friends. I anchor you to the real world."

He rolls his eyes. "You're a brat."

My heart warms as he tugs me into a hug. It's safe and welcoming, like the first time he brought me into his embrace.

I pull away as I sense we're no longer alone. His younger brother, Dario now stands on his right. Next to Dario is Carleen. I laugh when I note they're dressed as Bonnie and Clyde.

"Good to see you again, Lizzy," Dario says, his hazel eyes twinkling as he looks between Gio and me.

"Nice to see you too. How's the restaurant?"

"No. Not tonight," Gio says sternly.

I'm not offended. I can be a bit of a workaholic. If I'm not doing my day job, I'm running my own thing.

Jace, Gio's right hand walks over and whispers something into his ear. I take the time to observe Carleen and Dario. As far as I know the two are best friends and business partners. Although, I've seen the way Carleen looks at Dario. Not to mention, he's hella protective of her.

I can't help but wonder if there's more there. The Di Lorenzo brothers have always made me weak in the knees from the sight of them. Nevertheless, even if I didn't think Carleen has feelings for Dario, he's out of my league. Gio and I will forevermore be nothing more than good friends—never to cross or blur the lines.

Then there's Dante, the third and youngest Di Lorenzo brother. Dario's twin, who's not only my boss, but he's also a married man. On top of being out of my league.

Gio reaches to close my mouth for me. "You're making a puddle, love," he teases.

I shake my head to clear it. My book is left forgotten on the table as I give the new small crew my full attention. My hands are suddenly sweaty.

I wipe them on my skirts and roll my shoulders. Dario drops his eyes to my cleavage and grins. Carleen looks between the two of us nervously.

"You look very nice, Lizzy. Wow, your corset is so detailed. Are those real book spines?" Carleen says.

"Yes, Vintage books that were going to be thrown out. I was able to turn them into a corset and had a friend treat the pages so I could use them as the fabric for the skirts."

"That's impressive." The hairs on the back of my neck stand up. I'd know that voice anywhere.

I turn to find my boss with his little girl in his arms. She has her tiny hands clenched against her chest with a beaming smile on her face.

"Bella wanted to come meet the Book Queen. I hope you don't mind."

I reach to brush my hand over the crown on my head. When I look into Bella's sparkling hazel eyes, I know I can't disappoint her. Taking in her cute little Princess Jasmine costume, I smile.

Giving a curtsy, I then say, "It's a pleasure to meet you, Bella."

"See, Daddy, I told you she's a real queen," she says to her father. She then turns to me. "I want to be just like you when I get big. Do the books speak to you? Do you have special powers?"

Bella's five going on six. I've been tasked with scheduling and planning her birthday parties for the last few years. It's been fun to plan them, although I'm always surprised by how much rein I'm given with the planning.

I remember being her age and believing in all things magical. Meeting a queen would have made my world. One with magic, well, let's say, I still believe in fairy tales for others. Which is why I smile and deliver.

"Oh, the books show me world after world. They play in my head like movies. Maybe I can show you how to see them too someday."

Her face lights up even more. "I'd like that," she says just above a whisper with awe in her eyes.

"That is if it's okay with you, Mr. Di Lorenzo." I clasp my hands in front of me and turn my attention to my boss.

He's dressed as a 1920s gangster. I can't help but wonder if he and his twin planned the theme. The Di Lorenzos Italian-Sicilian heritage is pronounced by their olive tanned skin, fleshy lips, and thick dark hair. I can't help drinking Dante in.

All three brothers have lashes so thick and long you would think they all wear mascara and eyeliner. Dante's hot on a regular day, but tonight I'd follow him in hopes of receiving a treat.

I snort at my thoughts. I'd more than likely get a trick instead. Gio raises a brow at me. I realize I'm letting my thoughts play out loud on my face again.

"Sure, it's okay," Gio says. "Uncle Gio will bring the queen to have tea with us."

In the last five years, I've gotten to know the Di Lorenzo brothers as I've worked for them. However, I know Dante the least. His wife isn't the easiest to stomach, so I tend to avoid her at all costs.

"Can we go now?" Speaking of the devil. Bethany steps up to Dante's side, whining like a brat. "I don't know why we have to be here in the first place. They work for us. We don't have to mingle among them."

"Bethany," Dante bites out.

"What? There were a plethora of events we could have attended tonight that matter. Such a waste of a good costume." She pouts.

I have to say, she is gorgeous in the adult version of Bella's costume. Her brown skin looks like silk and her dark-brown eyes are lined with black, setting off their large oval shape. She pulls off Princess Jasmine well.

I can totally see what Dante sees in her before she opens her mouth. From what I know, they were high school sweethearts. Gio has never been a fan of Bethany, but he tolerates her for his brother. That's love because I can't stand being around this narcissistic woman. She makes my gums itch.

"Oh, don't you look cute," she says dismissively to Carleen.

"Get your wife, Dante," Dario snarls.

Bethany rolls her eyes. "Don't worry about me. We're leaving."

"We aren't doing this for us. We're here for Bella." I notice Dante's cheeks turning red with his anger.

"I want to take a picture with the Book Queen."

This seems to bring Bethany's attention to me. She narrows her eyes before rolling them over me. Her features pinch as if she sees something disgusting.

What is it they say? Never judge a book by its cover. She'll be smart to choose her words wisely. This book has pages she doesn't want to read.

"Oh please, that's just Daddy's nerdy assistant. She's not even his executive assistant, let alone a queen. You don't need a picture with her."

"Why do you have to make everything about you and be rude to the people who help you live the life you're so privileged to live? Enough. Go wait in the car."

Bethany scowls at him and places her hands on her hips, looking as if she's about to go off. However, Dante places Bella on her feet and grabs his wife by the arm, tugging her a few paces away.

Bella moves to me and grabs hold of my hand. I look down at her and smile. Her eyes get as big as saucers. I give her a quick wink before I look back up at Mr. and Mrs. Di Lorenzo.

Dante has leaned into his wife's ear to say something that takes the wind out of her sails. She glares up at him before storming away. Dante returns to our group, placing a hand on top of Bella's little head.

She's had her eyes on me since her father put her down, totally unaware her parents are fighting. I lift my gaze to Dante's as he clears his throat.

"Before we go, will you take a picture with Bella? I think it will make her night. You're all she could talk about from the moment she saw you."

"She has better taste than you, brother," Gio says.

"Don't start."

There's so much bite in Dante's warning I flinch. He looks back at me and gives a weak smile. It dawns on me how unhappy he has looked in the last few months.

I bend and lift Bella into my arms. Dante takes out his phone, but Gio rushes to take it from him and pushes him toward me and Bella.

"You have to take this with them," he says.

I stiffen as Dante places his hand on my waist, drawing Bella and me into his side. He releases me as soon as we're closer to him. I feel like such a fool. He only wants his daughter closer to him and I have her in my arms.

"Look, Daddy. I kissed a queen," Bella says as she cups my face and kisses my cheek.

"Aww, that was perfect," Gio croons. "Two of my favorite girls and my little brother."

"Thank you," Dante leans to whisper in my ear.

He takes his daughter from me and turns to leave. Bella waves at me from over her father's shoulder. I smile and wave back. Once they're out of sight, I go to return to my book. However, Gio blocks my way and pinches my chin between his fingertips.

I search his face as he seems to search my eyes. When he finds whatever he's looking for, he nods.

"I was right. They belong with you."

He releases my face and turns to disappear with Jace at his side. A shiver runs down my spine. I'm left feeling like I just signed over my soul.

Dante

I'm livid. More and more I've been wondering what I see in Bethany and why I chose to marry her in the first place. We were young and searching for where we belonged. With all the traveling her parents did, she felt abandoned, and I knew the feeling well.

At the time, I wanted to be her knight in shining armor. Although her parents spent little time with her, she was no stranger to my family's world. It made sense for us to marry, I didn't see the red flags. I was too preoccupied with thoughts of someday taking over the family business, the one that wouldn't be passed down to Dario. Then there was the dark role I would also have to play at some point.

Bethany also showed me the face she wanted me to see. Never the mean, cruel, narcissistic side that flushes all her beauty down the drain. I've been a fool for this woman for years. Now, I spend long hours at work, so I don't have to deal with her callousness.

I keep my gaze forward as we ride in the back of the SUV. If I speak, I'm going to shout, and I don't want to do that in front of Bella. My daughter is the innocent party in all of this.

"We still have time to drop Bella off with the nanny so we can make George and Autumn's party."

I snap my head in Bethany's direction and glare. I work my jaw, trying to hold in my explosive rage. My employees work hard to keep my company going. Di Lorenzo Industries would be nothing but a racketeering ring without the people who keep it going day in and day out.

Lizzy is just one of the intricate parts of my staff. Of my three assistants, she's the one who oversees my schedule and keeps my life on track. She's shy and keeps to herself. She didn't have to pretend for Bella, and she didn't have to go through the trouble of wearing such a stunning costume in the first place.

Hearing her say she made it herself took me by surprise. Lizzy is quirky and always has the best gift ideas for clients and employees. The personal touch does it every time so I shouldn't be surprised by her talent, but that costume was out of this world.

Her face, I've never seen her with makeup on like that. Bella was right. She looked like a true queen.

I appreciate her efforts. A few weeks ago, I overheard her telling Gio she didn't want to attend in the first place. The office Halloween parties are a tradition passed down by my mother.

All the holiday parties are. No matter how wealthy they became, the workers had always been important to her and my grandfather. There was a time when my mother knew the name of every single employee.

"I've had enough for the night. I'll be putting Bella to bed and retiring myself."

"When did we become an old couple? This is what I've been talking about. All you do is work and spend time with Bella."

"That's more than I can say for you," I snap, trying to keep my voice down as not to wake my daughter who has fallen asleep against my side.

"What are you talking about?"

"Where is your brain? You ignore our daughter, treat everyone around you like shit, and you're spending has been crazy enough to get both my grandfather and our accountant's attention."

"It's our money and I play with Bella all the time."

"It's my family's money. And when was the last time you spent time with Bella without a nanny in the room to attend to her?"

"I don't want to have this conversation right now. Not with you like this."

"That's what I thought." I turn to look out the window again as I stew.

I need to figure out how to get my peace back without crushing my little girl's heart. I'm done with this marriage.

CHAPTER TWO

I'm Sorry

Dante

The elevator doors open on the floor of my office and Lizzy is the first person I see as usual. She stands with her tablet in hand and her glasses perched on her nose. She's back to her shy self. Not the majestic queen from last night.

"Good morning, sir. You have a full day ahead of you. I've placed the contracts you need to look over on your desk. Michelle has noted the changes you wanted to see happen. At noon, you have a meeting to discuss the turkey drive and the company Thanksgiving party. It looks like Gio has blocked out some time this evening to meet with you and Dario as well."

I listen as she continues. I know all of this, but this is our routine each morning. This is where I ask for changes to the schedule and cancel the appointments—I'm not in the mood to have or need more time to prepare for.

I run the corporate side of this family's business. We have a chain of restaurants, and we also mass-produce a few of our signature staples. Since I've taken over at the helm, we've moved from a multimillion dollar company to a billion-dollar empire, all started from one single little restaurant back in Italy.

I hope my mother would be proud of what I've done with her father's business. That is if she even cares. She's probably forgotten the business like she has everything else. However, my grandfather seems to be pleased from our conference calls and his visits.

"Thank you, Lizzy," I say as she gets to the end of my schedule, and we reach my office door.

She nods and turns to leave. I take in a deep breath. I'm still pissed about last night.

"Do you mind having lunch with me today? I'd like to make up for my wife's behavior last night," I say, halting her retreat.

She turns back toward me. Her lips parted and her eyes rounded behind her glasses. I force a smile.

"Th… that's not necessary. I have plans to have lunch with Gio today."

I frown, sometimes I forget Gio and Lizzy are such good friends. I've often wondered how they met and why my brother has only kept her as a friend and not one of his dolls in his collection. Lizzy has been around for years.

Gio isn't getting any younger. He's forty-two. Dario and I are thirty-four. Neither of my brothers has chosen to settle down. They may be onto something.

I don't know a lot about Lizzy. Yet as I think about it, my older brother may be too much for her. She's too quiet, I can't imagine her in his life. Whenever I see her, if she's not working, she has a book glued to her palms.

"I want to treat you to lunch. I can join the two of you. I'll text Gio and check with him."

"Um, oh, okay, but you really don't have to."

Before I can say another word, she turns and hurries off. I head to my desk to start my day. Instead of giving my attention to the contracts on my desk, I pull my phone out and send my brother a text.

While I wait for his reply, I open my pictures and look at the ones Gio took for me last night. I run my finger across my daughter's smiling face. Bella is my world.

I felt worse about Bethany's behavior last night after Bella spent the entire time at the breakfast table this morning gushing over the Book Queen. My daughter craves female attention.

Last night, Lizzy gave my little girl more than she knows and I'm grateful to her for it. My phone rings and I answer the call.

"Good morning, Gio."

"Good morning, brother. How can I help you?" His voice is the deepest of us brothers and rumbles with an authority only Gio can pull off.

"I was wondering if I could join you and Lizzy for lunch?"

"Really?" he says with intrigue in his voice. "What brought this on?"

"I want to say sorry for Bethany's behavior last night and thank her for making Bella's night. I don't know what she likes, so I figured I'd treat her to lunch."

"She loves books and she's a gamer. She has a YouTube channel and all that. Oh, and she's into cosplay. You can't go wrong with any of that, but I like the sound of lunch on you."

"A gamer? Really?" I say as my interest is piqued.

"Yeah, she's won all types of *WarZone* tournaments. Her Twitch is popular too."

"Her what?"

"Beyond your understanding. Never mind."

I clamp my mouth shut and note the information to dig for answers later. I frown and halt my train of thought. I'm still married to an overgrown baby.

I don't have time to think about or look into Elizabeth's life. Fuck, the fact that I know her real name makes me question myself. She has only ever gone by Lizzy here in the office. I roll my shoulders and toss my head back.

Bella needs her mother, so I have to try to make things work. At five, Bella is at a critical age. Although I'm not sure her mother is the best influence when I truly think about it—I would hate for my daughter to end up a spoiled brat. I want so much more for her.

I want her to have what we didn't. I never want Bella to know the pain my brothers and I knew.

"Dante," my brother calls, grabbing my attention. "Are you hearing a word I'm saying?"

"No, forgive me. My mind is all over the place."

"You know, you deserve better. So does Bella. People divorce all the time. You could be missing out on a connection with the right one while holding on to the wrong one."

I release a heavy breath. "I have to go."

"You always run when we try to tell you the truth. Listen, you have the entire family ready to support you in this. Bella will have all the love she needs."

"But no mother."

"If Bethany cares anything for her, she'll still be there."

I grow silent. This is my fear. My wife is there for our daughter now because she has to be. They live under the same roof. If we divorce, I have this feeling in the pit of my stomach that Bethany will be gone with the wind and Bella will be long forgotten. It has never been a question about whether I'll take custody.

"Just think about it, Dante," Gio says when I'm silent a beat too long.

"I will," I reply.

"No, you won't." He gives a dry laugh that lets me know he's frustrated.

I'm as frustrated as everyone else. I'm starting to feel caged in. If it weren't for Bella, I would have been divorced by now. It's bad enough Bethany refused to have a baby until she turned thirty.

"All the signs were there," I mutter to myself as I hang up the phone and toss it on the desk. "But the question is, what do you do now?"

I growl at myself and my lack of answers. Bella comes first, she will always come first.

Lizzy

"Lizzy, can you email those dates for the fair and charity event?" Michelle, one of the other assistants, asks, snapping me out of my fog.

I've been sitting at my desk in a daze. Dante wants to have lunch with me. Of course, I know it's nothing like the type of lunch I wish it could be. The man has no idea I've been crushing on him since I was hired.

I don't even know what I would say to him if we had lunch together. To be honest, I didn't take much offense from his wife's behavior. She's always been a bitch to me.

I once thought we could be friends. I'm a part of her husband's work life. I do more for their family than my own.

Her being a snob ruined that. She has always made me feel as if I'm beneath her. I may work for the Di Lorenzo's but I'm no stranger to wealth. I've never wanted for anything. I took this job as a favor to a friend. I have a certain set of skills Gio homed in on and wanted to acquire.

My phone rings on the desk, bringing me out of my reverie. I jump but rush to pick it up.

"Those dates," Michelle says as I put the receiver to my ear.

I nod at her before I speak into the phone. "This is Lizzy speaking. You've reached Mr. Dante Di Lorenzo's office."

"Hey, you. What have you done to my brother?"

I sigh in relief. "Nothing. He asked me to lunch, and I told him I had plans with you."

"Well, now you're having lunch with us both."

I look down at my clothes and groan. I may never have a romantic relationship with Dante, but that doesn't mean I want to sit across from him looking like this. I look like a goth kindergarten teacher.

There's nothing about my outfit that says twenty-nine and trendy like some of the others in the office. I look frumpy and twice my age. My sister would be so disappointed in me.

"Fuck," I whisper.

"Chill out. Dante doesn't bite. I think it's nice he wants to do this. We all know how grumpy he can be."

"He's not grumpy. He has a lot on his plate."

"Yeah, if that's what you want to call it. His ass is grumpy as fuck, and I'll call him on it any day of the week."

"Well, I like my job, so I'll keep my opinions to myself. Speaking of jobs. Where are you?"

"He can't fire you, remember and I'm getting out of the car now. I'll see you in a bit."

We hang up and I fall back in my seat as I think of what my life would have been like if I had more confidence in myself. My major in college was picked out of self-doubt, my living situation is one birthed from lack of confidence. I've been coming out of my shell with my gaming channel, but my love life still sucks.

When guys see me, they think nerd. When they find out I'm a gamer, it's like twice the turnoff. Why do guys assume female gamers are only into boring sex or don't have a sexual bone in their bodies?

I'd fuck the right guy's brains out. Like, I'd be a whole ho for my man. I like toys, playing dress-up, and I've been curious about a few different kinds of sexual play. Not to mention, for a woman my size, I've mastered some of the harder, more challenging yoga poses when it comes to flexibility and balance.

Gio would have been perfect. I snort at the thought. *You're not ready for that life.*

Apparently.

I have limits and it's been so hard to find someone for me. Online dating hasn't been so great. I make six figures, not counting the money I earn from my gaming channels and well, my extra business activities. You would think my financial independence was a plague to some. Others are deterred by my father's military background, although he made his fortune in tech and is a bit on the nerdy side.

"Lizzy, that email," Michelle huffs, losing her patience with me. That's a first. Clearly, I'm really out of it.

"Sorry." I find the dates and send her a quick email.

I take a breath and pull my shit together. I turn my focus back to the invites and requests for Dante's appearance, getting a document together with a list of events and dates to present to him to see what he will attend and which I'll have to send excuses for.

"Good morning," Gio croons as he walks through the main office heading for his door with Jace at his side. He turns to me with a smile on his face.

"You, bring all that into my office. We can go through them together."

I collect the basket with all the paper invites and grab my tablet with the emails and the scheduling system. Dante's usually booked solid this time of year.

Jace holds the door open for me as I scurry inside. Gio removes his suit jacket. The man looks as if he never misses a day at the gym. His hair is neatly blown away from his face showcasing his handsome features.

As I settle in, Jace takes a seat on the couch across the office in Gio's seating area. Silent as always. I can probably count on one hand how many times I've heard the man speak.

Gio comes around his desk to help with the paper invites. He will sometimes help out with the schedule as he handles blending Dante's life. He acts as Dante's executive assistant, but I know he's more to his brother and the company than that.

He frowns as he skims the invites. "No, to this. We're not going to waste his time with this. Hell no to this one. Honestly, why do they still bother with sending an invite every year? He never goes."

I snicker. "Some people like to hold on to hope."

"Well, at this point, they'll die holding their breath."

We both laugh. I look over a beautiful invite to a charity ball. "Does she know how lucky she is?" I murmur to myself as I note all the plus-one invitations I need to add to the list.

"Who's that?"

"Bethany."

Gio rolls his eyes and scowls darkly.

I bite my lip, not wanting to say what I'm thinking. However, he has become my best friend, if I can't say what I'm thinking to him, who can I?

"Dante sets the world at that woman's feet. All I want is someone to have a decent conversation with. I have no dreams of marriage or a family at this point. A nice boyfriend who can hold a conversation with me would be everything. Throw in some travel and I'm all over it," I blurt out.

"You turned down an offer of a lifetime. I treat my dolls like gold," he says and gives me a sultry look, then shrugs. "You will find the right one. Heck, would it really be illegal for me to push that bitch off a cliff? You would be so much better to my brother than she is. Fuck it, I'll put a bullet in her head and solve everyone's problems. He'll be all yours."

I lift a brow. He gives me a sheepish grin that belies the man I know so well. I laugh. "All of that is wishful thinking. I'd never have a shot with Dante. Every awkward bone in my body would ruin it."

What is it my Aunt Denise used to say?

I wish, therefore I am.

I used to think those were magical words when I was younger. Then I had my heart broken—again and again and again. Wishing has never changed a thing about me. Wishing gets you nowhere.

"Is it?" he questions.

"Give me a book, I'll take the guaranteed happy ending anytime. At least then, I know what's coming for me."

Gio only grunts.

My cell phone rings in my sweater pocket. I rush to check it. It could be my older sister. She travels a lot. I hate to miss her calls because I never know when the next call will be.

I haven't seen my sister face to face in so long. We FaceTime and talk all the time over the phone and when she joins me on my Twitch channel, but it's not the same. I miss sitting with my sister as she brushes my hair and talks to me in her soothing voice.

It's something she started doing when we lost our mom. Our world changed and she was there to make it all seem like it would be okay.

"Hello," I answer as I hold a finger up to Gio.

He winks at me and takes my tablet to start tapping away at it.

"What's up, sis?" Nyla says.

"Nothing, I'm with Gio working on my boss's schedule."

"Tell Gio I said hi. Are they still treating you well?"

"Of course," I reply. I cover the phone and lean in toward Gio. "Ny says hi."

To my surprise his eyes dilate and his lips part. I furrow my brows. The two have met once and for no more than a few seconds.

I dart my eyes over to Jace and he seems to be interested in the conversation. Something that's highly rare. I make a note to ask questions later. Gio quickly recovers and clears his throat.

"Hello, Nyla. Will she be home for the holidays?"

I place the phone on speaker. Peeking over at Jace once more. He's on the edge of his seat, his phone in his hands. If I didn't know better, I'd think his attention is fully on the device.

"Ny, Gio asked if you're coming home for the holidays? I have you on speaker."

"It depends. Am I wanted home for the holidays?"

"Absolutely, I miss you. I was hoping you would come home."

I glance at Gio and notice he seems to be holding his breath. I find myself mirroring him.

"I would like to get to know my friend's sister more. Come home. I'll send a jet to…"

Gio pauses to wait for Nyla to answer the implied question. She laughs. I can't help but feel like I'm missing something here. "I'll come home. I have to go."

Gio bares his teeth for a second before he quickly schools his features. Jace sits back in his seat with a tiny smile in the corners of his lips.

CHAPTER THREE

Lunch

Dante

I look down at my phone and nearly growl. The nanny has been texting me to inform me Bethany took off and left Bella hanging. They were supposed to spend the day together.

"Is everything okay?" Gio asks.

I look up and frown. I don't want to tell him the truth. He'll only gripe about me needing a divorce. I look to Lizzy as she busies herself with her phone. I can't help the smile that comes to my lips.

She's reading. I can tell by the concentration on her face. She gets that look a lot while at her desk. I make a mental list of all the things I do know about this woman from having her work for me over the years.

I clear my throat, drawing her attention. She looks up, a bit startled. While my brother fails terribly at hiding his chuckle, I force mine down. Lizzy's cheeks seem to glow as she looks between the two of us.

In this moment, I take in the differences between Bethany and Lizzy. While both are brown skinned. Lizzy is darker. She's more of a deep brown complexion. For lack of a better explanation, Hersey's chocolate comes to mind when I look at Lizzy.

Bethany, on the other hand, is more of an almond brown. Where they both have oval-shaped eyes. I think Lizzy's are a bit higher in tilt and more oval. Hers are definitely darker than Bethany's. Lizzy is taller than my wife, but fuller in shape.

I shake away the comparisons, to clear my thoughts. I'm not here to match my wife against my assistant.

"I hope I didn't interrupt a good part," I say, pointedly nodding to her phone.

"Oh, no. I hope you weren't trying to get my attention for too long." She gives a sheepish smile that lights her face.

Again, I can't help noting how different she is from my wife. Bethany has become like a dark cloud these days. It's always about her. My phone buzzes, pulling my attention from the woman sitting across from me. I scowl before looking down at the annoying device.

"Don't worry. You didn't miss much. His phone has had his attention since we arrived. I'm sure my sister-in-law is at it again," Gio says smugly.

I give him the finger and stand, smoothing down my tie and buttoning my jacket. "If you will excuse me, I need to make a call."

I move away from the table without waiting for a reply. Bethany is going to make me strangle her. I sent her a text to find out why she has, yet again, disappointed our daughter? Her reply, she needed to get her hair and nails done.

Hair and nails she had done yesterday. I should know. I had a team sent to her for the party. This is something that could have waited, or she could have taken our daughter with her. Bella loves to have her nails painted.

"Why are you testing me?" I seethe into the phone when I reach the sidewalk outside of the restaurant.

"Dante? Is that you?" Bethany replies.

"Who else would be calling you from my phone?"

"I don't know. I didn't think it was you because I know you haven't lost your mind talking to me like that."

I snort. "You're a funny one now? My daughter is at home in tears, looking for her mother and you want…what? Terms of endearment and sweet greetings?"

"Well, it would feel nice to hear you talk sweet to me."

"Fuck your feelings, just like you're fucking over our daughter's feelings. All she wants is to spend time with her mother and you're too much of a monster to care. Let me show you what a monster really looks like," I fume.

"You've done an amazing job of that."

I nearly stumble back. I can be an extremely cruel man, but I've never been unkind to this woman. I'm starting to question her sanity or if she's on drugs. She has to be on something.

"Excuse me?" I say in disbelief.

"Forget it, Dante. Look, I need to get in the chair to finish my hair. What is it you want?"

"Nothing, nothing at all."

I hang up and storm back into the restaurant. The sight of Lizzy laughing with her head thrown back brings me a bit of calm. She wipes at her tears and looks at Gio with such joy. I want someone to look at me that way. Bella hasn't seen what love looks like between a mother and father. I remember vaguely the way my father used to look at my mother.

I take my seat and the waitress comes to take our order. I'm not surprised when Gio orders for Lizzy. My interest is sparked. I have so many questions. Some I have no right to want to ask. Lizzy is my employee and I'm still very married.

"How did you two meet?" I blurt out, not able to help myself. "If I'm right, you did know each other before you applied for the job."

"Yes, we did," Gio says with a smile. I get the feeling there's more to it. Not in an intimate way. I know what Gio's dolls look like. It's hard to miss the relationship and bond my brother has with his collection.

"We met at a roller derby paintball event. Gio walked up to me after I slaughtered his team and told me I owed him twenty grand for beating the crap out of his girls. My options were to join his team or spend a night in his bed." Lizzy snorts and gives a small chuckle. "I clearly wasn't going to sleep with him, so I played a few games for him and the rest is history."

Gio winks at her and my blood starts to simmer. The thought of Lizzy sleeping with my brother induces anger I have no right to. Until last night, I never even thought much of my assistant other than being grateful to her for her hard work.

Lizzy was one of Gio's hires. I never know what my brother is thinking when he hires. What I do know is if he hires you, he trusts you.

The higher up he allows you to get, the more he trusts you. I'm sure Lizzy has been vetted and proven. Trust is everything for my brothers and me. We don't give it easily.

Gio tilts his head to the side as he takes me in. I try to ignore him as I watch Lizzy while her burger and fries are placed in front of her.

"Interesting," Gio murmurs before digging into his steak.

I reach for my bourbon and narrow my eyes in warning over my glass. I can see Gio's thoughts running across his face. I give a subtle shake of my head to tell him to drop it.

Whatever he plans to say will make this lunch uncomfortable for at least two of us. I'm not in the mood for it. I have enough on my plate, and I don't want to lose such a great assistant.

"This is so good," Lizzy moans and wipes her mouth with her napkin.

"I told you the chef here was great. Now you see why I want to poach him."

"When you promised me the best burger ever, I thought you were exaggerating."

"When have I ever exaggerated?"

"When Dario and I were like ten and you told grandfather you caught a ten-foot fish. It was more like five inches, if that," I reply and chuckle.

"Eat your pasta," Gio grumbles.

Lizzy laughs. "No, no. Keep going. What was it like growing up with this guy?"

My heart swells and sinks at the same time. I love my brothers and would love nothing more than to reminisce about our younger days. However, I'm not sure if Lizzy wants to hear this because of interest in Gio or interest in our past as a whole.

I'm starting to feel like an ass. I stab at my pasta and lift the fork to my lips, taking a bite. I'm not prepared for the explosion of flavor that hits my tongue. I swallow the story I had planned to share and turn to Gio.

"Who is this chef? Is it the one out of Boston you were telling me about? Why isn't he already working for us?"

"He hates your wife. She got him fired from his last job. She posted some rant on social media and it went viral. He was jobless by the next morning."

I bare my teeth and run a hand through my hair. I'm not going to miss out on a chef like this because of Bethany's tantrums. The chef is the heart of every restaurant.

"I want him on our team. Double the offer. Let him know Bethany has nothing to do with the business."

"I'm already on it. This was a planned lunch if you remember. I'm on my job, little brother. Look, here he comes."

I turn to find a tall guy in a chef's coat heading our way as he wipes his hands on a towel. The topknot isn't my thing, neither is the lip ring. I like my chefs clean-cut, with neat short hair. However, in a single bite this guy has impressed me enough for me not to care.

Gio stands and holds his hand out. "It's good to see you again, Jacob."

"Nice to be seen, Gio." He shakes Gio's hand before doing a double take as he scans our table. I stiffen in my seat as his mouth drops open when he homes in on Lizzy. "Holy shit, Izzy Gunz?"

Jacob wrinkles his brows and shoves his hand out in Lizzy's direction. Lizzy looks a bit startled—which is starting to become totally adorable, by the way.

"Um... ah—" she pushes up her glasses and cleans her hands on her napkin. "Yeah, I'm Izzy."

"You and Judge Sin are two of my favorite gamers. I watch whenever I have downtime."

Lizzy ducks her head and that glow returns to her cheeks. I'm now even more curious about her gaming and this channel. What did Gio call it? I'll have to ask him later.

"Cool, there's a lot of competition out there. I'm grateful for all the views."

"You guys are badass. I would love your autograph. I know you're eating, but if you wouldn't mind a pic, that would make my day," he says excitedly.

"How about you guys trade autographs? Izzy here has the contract for you to sign to come aboard and cook for us."

Jacob scoffs. "Dude, I was already considering your offer. That new place is going to be epic. A picture with a legend and an autograph and you have a new chef."

"Seriously?" Lizzy says with confusion written all over her face.

This isn't conventional, but that's Gio for you. He gets it done, by any means. He's calculated and methodical. It's something not enough people give him credit for.

"Yeah, totally, do you *know* know Judge Sin? Like really know her?"

"Yeah, I do," Lizzy says with a hint of pride in her voice. I can't help wondering who this Judge Sin is.

"What's the deal with the blacked-out screen? I heard rumors she's some type of model or actress or something. One forum said she's really some judge or something and can't be on cam. That would be totally cool, but I doubt it."

Jacob shrugs. Lizzy returns the gesture as a bit of mischief enters her eyes.

"She has personal reasons," she says shyly.

"If she's as pretty as you are, it's a total shame. I'd love to see you both on screen. Don't get me wrong, you guys game your asses off, but the view is worth the time as well. You know what I mean?"

Gio clears his throat. He looks cool and calm, but I, of all people, can tell he's pissed off and ready to blow. I'm feeling annoyed as well, but I can't allow this deal to fall through for a woman who isn't mine. I shove my jealousy into the box it needs to remain in.

"How about we stick to business? You can drool all over yourself when you're alone," Gio says tightly.

"Dude, I'm sorry. Are you guys dating?"

"No, no. He's…they're my bosses," Lizzy says.

"I'm her boss and this is a business lunch. Take your picture but respect my assistant as well."

I hope the words have come out as smoothly as I mean for them to. Is she interested in this guy? No, no, that's none of my damn business.

"Cool, cool, it's been a while since you've been on with Judge. Is she okay?"

"She's fine," Gio growls.

Interesting. I had assumed Gio's possessive reaction was about Lizzy. Clearly, it's not. It's about this Judge Sin. I note that information for later.

I have several questions. Gio never gets too possessive with his dolls. I narrow my gaze and truly study my brother. His jaw is still tight, and his fists are balled on the top of the table.

"Here, I have that contract for you. You sign, I'll take as many pictures as you like," Lizzy says as if sensing the tension around the table.

Jacob—totally oblivious to how close he is to losing his head turns and grabs a chair to pull up to our table. He sits much too close to Lizzy for my liking. I bite down my temper and focus on Jacob reading over the contract Lizzy has handed him.

"I'm sorry," Jacob says, holding his hand out to me. "I got so excited. It's nice to meet you. You're Dante Di Lorenzo, right?"

"Yes, I am. It seems my assistant is more famous than I am," I tease and wink at Lizzy.

She squirms in her seat. I shouldn't enjoy the response so much. However, I take it in like it's another bite of food. I eat it up, feeling like myself for the first time in so long, I can't remember.

"This is a dream come true, but…you're sure I'll never have to deal with that woman in my restaurant? No offense."

"My wife won't step foot in the restaurant. I'll make sure of it," I reply.

"If he fails, I'll handle it. You don't have to worry about her. You work for the Di Lorenzo family. We take care of our own," Gio reassures him.

"Cool, cool. I just want to look this over." He nods to himself and flips through the pages. The rest of us return to our plates.

Ten minutes goes by before Jacob signs and someone from the restaurant's staff comes to rush him back to the kitchen. I can't say I'm not happy to see him go. However, before he leaves, he pushes my buttons one last time.

"Hey, I have to go. How about you give me your number and we can have dinner. I'll get those photos then?" Jacob says as he stands.

Lizzy blushes. I hate that she's blushing for this guy. I'm tempted to grab the contract and tear it up.

Lizzy looks between Gio and me. I pick up my phone to busy myself so she can't read my reaction.

"I…um, I don't know if this is appropriate. I'm on the clock."

"Oh, cool, no problem. I follow you on the gram," he says with a nod and smile. "I'll drop in your DM and we can set something up there. My handle is Jacob eats."

He gives another crooked smile and winks. I throw back my fresh drink and stand, tossing a few bills on the table.

"Let's go," I say a little too sharply.

I've had enough of this. I don't care if Lizzy's dating life is none of my business. I have limits.

CHAPTER FOUR

Family

Dante

"It's good to have you back home," I say to my dad with a genuine smile on my face.

He arrived back home yesterday. I took some time off to bring Bella by to spend time with her grandfather. She's been talking her great-grandfather and great Uncle's ears off nonstop—Uncle Lucas isn't my real uncle. He's my father's best friend.

Dad and I were able to escape to his home office before she pulled us into her tea party with the new tea set her grandpa brought her from Italy.

"I wasn't sure if I would make it back in time for the holidays. So much going on back home. You know how things can get. If it weren't for Bella, I think I'd still be in Italy at this very moment."

"Yes, I figure it might have been Bella's phone call." I chuckle.

Bella found her way into my phone and called my father herself, begging for his return. She told him sternly she wanted his presence for Thanksgiving and Christmas.

"Ah, yes, did you hear the part when she threatened me if I didn't make it back for her birthday?"

"Yes, yes, I did." I laugh, lifting some of the stress off my shoulders.

"I missed you all. It was good to have some time away, but there's nothing like home and family. How are things going at the office?"

My father had his own business to run before he sold and retired, but he has always taken a vested interest in the Di Lorenzo empire, guiding me where he could.

"At the office, things are great. We just acquired an amazing chef. The newest acquisitions are going well. Things are looking great."

"Um, but at home?" he questions, seeming to pick up on my tone.

"He's still married to a troll," Dario says as he strolls into the room.

I sigh and push a hand into my hair. If I don't do something with my hands, I might choke my brother. I understand his disdain for Bethany. She verbally attacked his best friend, and he hasn't forgiven her for it. I can't blame him.

I blow out a breath and turn my attention back toward my father. "How did you do it? After mom left…" I pause for a moment as the bitter sting sets in. "How did you raise us and move on with your life?"

He sighs. "I know I made things look easier than they truly were. I was crushed after your mother left, but I had three boys to raise. I didn't have time to think about myself.

"I also couldn't afford to show weakness. I was lucky to have your uncle and grandfather there to support me. They stepped in where I needed and eventually, I realized focusing on you boys was the right thing to do."

He's talking about Uncle Lucas and my mother's father. Uncle Lucas has been in my life for as long as I can remember. If Dad couldn't be there for us, Uncle Lucas stepped in without question. At one point, my coaches at school thought he was my father.

I blow out a heavy breath and lean forward in my seat as I allow Dad's words to sink in while I run a hand through my hair. I remember how hard it was for my brothers and me after my mother disappeared.

I tried so hard to understand why. How could she? She was always so loving. It never made sense to me. I don't want that pain for my daughter.

"We were older than Bella. I don't know what something like this will do to her. I'm trying to prolong things to make it easier for her."

"Meanwhile, you're unhappy," Dario chimes in.

"Hello, kettle," I mutter.

"What's that supposed to mean?"

"You're in love with Carleen but won't tell her. You're not happy."

"Yeah, well, we both know why I can never go there. You, however, can set yourself free and find someone who makes you happy."

"If I do this, I'm doing it for Bella. I can wait to find someone new. That's not a priority," I say.

"It should be," my father says to me before turning to Dario. "And why are you avoiding love?"

"Come on, Dad."

"Don't come on me. This life is lonely as it is. A good woman keeps you grounded. You've been taking on more responsibility. You can lose your humanity if you're not careful."

"Why is *Nonno* passing it all to me? Why not Gio? He's the oldest."

My father sighs and purses his lips. "Son, we all know…to get respect, you can't have any weaknesses. Gio doesn't hide who he is, and that's…well, that's a weakness your grandfather fears will hinder him."

"You have to be kidding me, Dad," I bite out. "Who Gio is, is what makes him the right fit. Do you understand your son?"

He scowls and narrows his eyes. "I know my son is complicated, but his complications aren't meant to be in that world."

"You mean, you don't think a man like Gio can be alpha enough to run a crime family? Bullshit, Dad," Dario seethes.

"Gio has to be one of the most ruthless men I know. Half of the families we deal with go through Gio for everything they need or want. Gio fixes everyone's shit. If he took over, he'd already be a step ahead. Why force him to be my shadow?" I add.

"Why does everyone have to know? If he kept it to himself, your grandfather might reconsider. Yet he wears his lifestyle like a fucking badge."

"Because it's who he is. He's not embarrassed to be himself. Who he's fucking has nothing to do with how he would run the family. I don't understand shit that's coming out of your mouth." I clench and unclench my fist in agitation.

"But you will understand when I put you on your ass if you keep talking to me like this."

I take a calming breath. I've always known Gio's lifestyle makes my father and grandfather uncomfortable. I accepted who my brother is a long time ago. His partners are always consensual and cared for, for as long as they are involved.

Fuck, if Gio wasn't my brother, I'd fear him and Jace. Gio is a silent killer. He'd take care of some shit and you'd never be the wiser. I remember him stepping in to cover Dario a few times. To this day, I don't believe Dario has a clue.

"All I'm saying, Dad. Gio isn't the man you see him as."

"I'll do as I'm asked, but Gio would be a better fit," Dario finishes.

Dad grunts. "With those parties he throws. It would only take one enemy to catch him with his pants down and the Di Lorenzo name would be ruined."

I work my jaw. If I respond, we're only going to knock heads. I have enough on my plate. I don't need to start a war with my father.

"The Di Lorenzo name or Esposito? Your father is the only one who has ever had a real problem with Gio and his choices. You're spewing the same bullshit that comes from Papa Esposito, not *Nonno* Di Lorenzo. He has always accepted us for who we are," Dario presses.

I sense my brother's anger, but he has already stepped up. There's no need to keep knocking heads over this. Gio is happy with his life. I'm sure he's happy to wash his hands of all of this. I've tried not to get sucked too far in. When I was younger and reckless, it fed a need inside me. After Bella was born, I found a new peace and calm that caused me to release the darkness my family's name can bring.

"Dario," I say in warning. My twin can be hotheaded and stubborn.

"Grandpa," Bella squeals as she runs into the room.

Uncle Lucas ambles behind her. I pull a page from my father's book and act as if nothing is amiss. It's just another ordinary day. It's what we do.

Lizzy

"Hey, Daddy," I sing as I cup my father's face and kiss his cheek.

He's working on one of his classic cars again. Elijah Hemmingway is the best father in the world. I may not have his blood in my veins, but he has never treated me any different.

I never got to really know my biological father, Carl Manning. He and Elijah served together and were both engineers and techs. They had plans to start a business together, but my parents were taken from this earth much too soon. Elijah, like the kind and loving man he is, stepped up to raise his two goddaughters all on his own.

Carl was a brilliant man and built the company that made Elijah millions—leaving my sister and me to inherit fifty percent of said company. I wish I got to know my real father. His brain was amazing. However, I've come to know Elijah's genius firsthand. He can put anything together.

Once when I was about eight, he built me an operational wooden Ferrari as a go-cart to race the kids in the neighborhood. I think he was making up for my father not being around to do something like that. He said my father totally would have.

"Hey, sweetheart, can you hand me that wrench?" He points to his tools neatly lined up on his station.

"Sure, what's on your mind? You're only out here when you need to think or clear your head," I say, handing over the wrench.

"I'm thinking about your sister. She's been away for too long. Once you went to work for Di Lorenzo, she took on a lot more work. I'm wondering if it's time she takes a break."

"Why? Did something happen? Is she okay?"

My sister is badass. If my father is worried, something must have gone wrong. Dad shakes his head. He places the wrench down and picks up a towel to wipe his hands on it.

"When your aunt started to train you girls, it was never so that you would get into the business. She wanted you guys to be able to protect yourselves. It certainly wasn't for your sister to run out there chasing after ghosts and her personal demons.

"I wanted her to take the job with Gio, she was the one Denise assigned. I knew then she needed to be grounded, but she redirected him to you. I was so livid with her."

I take this all in as my mind races. Aunt Denise was a part of my father's team. He was both Elijah and Denise's commander. When Aunt Denise left the service, she started a business with my mom. Aunt Denise still has that side hustle, and Nyla and I happened to fall into it—the reason Gio sought me out, or so I thought. I never knew the job was meant for Nyla.

"But I like my job," I murmur.

He gives me a smile. "Yes, I know. I do believe you're better suited now, but back then I was thinking about your sister's safety. She can be so stubborn."

"We spoke a few days ago. I think she's on her way home for the holidays. Maybe you can talk to her then. Tell her how you feel. Make her see you could use some help around here," I offer, always wanting to keep the peace.

He goes to answer, but the door to the garage starts to open, which it shouldn't. Lightning fast, my father reaches for his guns mounted beneath the car he's working on. Why am I not surprised?

He aims for the garage door and that's when the stilettoed boots come into view. I know right away they belong to my sister.

"Jesus, Nyla," Dad breathes.

"What? Are you guys not happy to see me?"

I squeal and race over to my sister to wrap her in a hug. Her sweet scent is the first thing to greet me, bringing comfort with it. Dad comes over to wrap us both in his embrace as we remain in a tight hug.

"Look at you girls. Your mother and father would be so proud," Elijah croons.

Nyla pulls free and smiles up at Dad with sadness in her eyes. My sister was older than me when our parents died. She has taken it all so much harder.

Elijah's face crumbles as he seems to take notice of the tension his comment has caused. I reach to place a hand on his forearm. I know he means well.

"I'm sure they would be," I say. "As a matter of fact, I have a date this weekend. I think they would be proud I'm getting out of the house to interact with humans."

My words are teasing, but they do the trick. Nyla drops her bag and turns to me with her mouth hanging open.

"You have a date? Who is he? When is the date? Where are you going?"

"Whoa, killer. Hold your horses. He's sort of a fan of the channel. He's also a chef Dante and Gio just hired."

My sister turns her face away from me, but not before I spot the glow in her cheeks. For the millionth time, I can't help but wonder what I'm missing. I was sort of surprised by Gio's behavior the other day at the restaurant.

"Well, I'd like to hear more about him. How about you guys come hang out with me in the kitchen while I cook us something for dinner. I'd love to catch up on what's been going on with my girls," Dad says.

"Sounds good to me," I say happily.

"Sure, I just need a bath or shower and maybe a nap. You guys get started without me."

Dad nods, but disappointment shines in his eyes. Elijah has only ever shown he wants the best for us. When Nyla gets in her moods it can be hard to break through to her. Sometimes she can make you feel like the enemy when all you want is to love her.

"Take your time. I'll have beer and stew waiting for you when you're ready," Dad says.

"Thanks, Dad. As soon as I settle in, I'll be there." I give my sister a smile for reading the room and smoothing things over. She winks at me before she grabs her bag and heads into the house.

I can't help but smile. My family is home. This is going to be a great holiday season.

"Thanks." I look up from the book I'm reading on my phone as Dad places a beer in front of me.

"What's got your attention these days? Vampires, dukes and duchesses, or some detectives reluctant to fall in love?" Dad asks, nodding to my phone.

"He's a scientist and a werewolf. He's trying to figure out why his people aren't mating and creating offspring anymore. He's the first in a century to display signs of the mating call after a trip to the city and a run-in with a beautiful doctor at a convention."

"You know, I love when your face lights up like that as you talk about books. Your father used to get the same look when he figured out some great puzzle of his. You girls picked up his genius."

I smile. I love to read, if my father was as passionate about engineering, I totally get him. It makes me feel closer to him to know this tiny fact.

"Thanks, Dad. I know it couldn't have been easy to raise us on your own, but I appreciate that you try to give us pieces of Mom and Dad."

He swallows as his eyes tear up, he takes off his glasses to wipe at his eyes. Replacing them, he smiles. "I never forced you girls to start calling me dad, but when Nyla said it the first time, it broke my heart and made me proud all at the same time. Over the years, I've come to be grateful for the opportunity to stand in the gap for such amazing people. I hope I've done as they would have wished."

"I'm sure you have and more. I, for one, could never repay you. Although, I think I owe you thousands from the first year you started to buy me books," I tease.

Dad's laugh booms through the kitchen and I'm so happy to hear it. It's a far cry from the somber mood I found him in earlier and his melancholy mood that deepened after Nyla arrived.

I take a sip of the beer he gave me and return to my book as he moves around the kitchen to cook. The aromas filling the space have my mouth watering and he only has butter and shallots in the pan.

"So, a date?" I pause and look up. I knew this was coming eventually. "Tell me about him."

I bite my lip and screw up my face. I don't know what to say about Jacob. He's nice enough. I was surprised when he followed through on dropping me a DM.

I'm still a bit shocked he noticed me and made such a big deal during lunch. I know my channel has been growing but I'm still getting used to the emails and fandom.

"He's a nice guy," I murmur.

"He better be. You say he's a chef?"

"Yes, he's very good. Gio took me to lunch at his former restaurant. That's how we met."

"Gio, uh…has anything changed at work? Are you still working as Dante's assistant?"

I shrug and wrinkle my nose. "Yeah. Why do you ask?"

He shakes his head. "Nothing."

"Dad."

"Really, it's nothing. Gio came to Denise wanting a certain set of skills. I find it odd he's been using you as nothing more than an assistant for the last five years. His contract requested I not ask questions, so I'll leave it be for now."

I turn this over in my head. Gio is a complex man. However, if he had decided I should be his brother's assistant, it's for a reason. I trust Gio, so I shrug my father's concerns off.

"Well, back to this date. Where are you guys going?"

"He's taking me to dinner and a movie."

"Have you run his background?" Nyla says as she strolls into the kitchen.

I smile. She's dressed just like me in a pair of logo running shorts and my gamer logo tank top. The thigh-high socks are from the brand we started together after our channels took off and I got so many compliments on my socks. The black-and-white Adidas on her feet are the same shoes I bought her with my first check from gaming.

Dad looks up and grunts. I have to stifle a laugh. He is all for the business we're building, but he's not a fan of us modeling the gear.

"No, I didn't do a background check. I want to pretend we're normal for once. Maybe this is why I'm on my way to my thirties and still live in my father's house and don't have a boyfriend."

"Hey, I love having you as my roommate." Dad pouts.

"And your cooking is one of the reasons I'm not going anywhere, roomie."

He snorts and tosses a carrot at me. I catch it and pop it into my mouth. I release a hum as I chew.

"Seriously, Iz. You need to do a background check. If you won't, I will."

"Ny, if something was amiss, Gio would have found it in the hiring process, and I would have known because he had me work on the contract and acquisition of Jacob in the first place. Gio is beyond thorough."

My sister scoffs. I narrow my eyes at her. I go to say something about her and Gio, but Dad changes subjects on me.

"I've done the bookkeeping for you guys this month. Your numbers are looking great. When you two first started, I never thought socks and shorts would explode like this. And that's just your apparel numbers.

"You both can retire from the family business," he says and looks up through his lashes at Nyla. "At least slow down the travel assignments."

My heart aches from the sound of hopefulness in his voice. I look to Nyla and it's clear she's thinking this over. A mischievous smile comes to her lips.

"I'll come off the road when you start dating, Dad. We're all grown up. Don't you think it's time you start enjoying the life of a bachelor?"

I can't help but laugh. Dad's cheeks turn pink, and he drops his eyes back to the meat he's cutting. Nyla's right.

Dad does need to start dating. I can't remember the last time I saw him go on a date. He's a handsome man. Anyone to date my dad would be a lucky woman. He would treat her like a queen.

"I've been on a few apps. Lizzy set up a profile or two for me," he mutters.

I laugh loudly. "I did, but you haven't used them so that doesn't count."

He places the knife down. "Okay, I'll start dating if that means you'll stay home and stop taking so many assignments that take you away. Deal?"

"Deal."

"Why do I feel like I've just been hoodwinked?"

"Probably because I've been considering staying grounded for a while anyway." Nyla laughs and it's such a great sound to hear.

I look at Dad's face. His blue eyes shine with fatherly love. Elijah Hemmingway is truly handsome. He has model looks and the physique to match. At six-four he can be intimidating when he loses his temper, but he's one of the gentlest souls I've ever met.

Dad points the knife he picks back up at Nyla then me as we both laugh.

"You two are still little troublemakers. What you both should be worried about is making me a grandfather, so I have little ones to spoil for Christmas again."

"I'll leave that one to Ny," I scoff.

"I don't think that's going to happen."

I notice the faraway look on my sister's face. I'll have to spend some time catching up with her. Clearly, it's been too long.

"Is there one of those beers for me?" Ny asks.

"A fridge full," Dad replies, then turns to get her one.

I find myself lost in thought. What if Jacob is the one and I do fall in love and start a family? I shake the thought away. We haven't even gone on a date yet.

My attention is pulled away from my thoughts by my phone. It's the bakery for the cupcakes Dante wants for Bella for Christmas. I excuse myself to answer and tuck all thoughts of Jacob, kids, and love away.

I'm content with life the way it is. Work, books, and gaming.

CHAPTER FIVE

Nope

Dante

"I don't care if the entire fucking royal British family invited you to lunch. You won't disappoint our daughter again. Cancel your lunch and be a fucking mother," I bellow, losing my patience.

Bella's room isn't far from our bedroom. I should try to keep my voice down, but my anger has gotten the best of me.

"Dante, you must have lost your mind. Who the hell are you talking to? I've had this lunch on my calendar for months."

I fist my hands at my side, trying to hold on to my temper. Enough is enough. Bethany completely forgot about Bella yesterday while on a call with a designer or some bullshit.

"I'm talking to you. Do you have any idea how it feels to be a child who only wants their mother's love? Why can't you stop being so fucking selfish?

"She's the sweetest child in the world. She doesn't even require much. Give her a book and your time and she's happy."

This witch has the nerve to sigh and roll her eyes. How did I miss that this is who my wife is? I feel like such a fool and now my daughter is paying for my mistake.

"Oh please, Dante. Stop imprinting your abandonment issues on Bella. I'm not your mother."

I promise, I think my jaw just snapped. I told her those things in confidence, when I thought she cared for me. For her to throw them back at me now makes my stomach turn.

"You're right, you're nothing like my mother. She was kind and loving until the end. I only have good memories of the woman she was," I seethe.

"Whatever."

"You know what? None of that excuses how you keep harming our sweet baby girl."

"She's sweet until she asks you a million and one questions. My head hurts after fifteen minutes of that shit. You get to escape to your office and your restaurants. What do I get?"

"To spend the money," I snarl.

"Dante, I'm not going to keep going back and forth with you about this. This isn't what I signed up for."

"Trust me, I understand. Neither did I. Maybe it's time you leave."

The gasp that comes from her lips proves to me how delusional Bethany has become. If she didn't see this coming, she's truly in her own bubble, soaking in her own self-absorbed juices.

"You can't mean that. We're going through a rough patch. Fine, I'll cancel my plans. I can spend the day with Bella and tonight we can go out to dinner to reconnect. I heard you have a new chef at the new downtown location. We can go there."

The hell we can. Instead of growling those words at her, I turn toward my daughter as she peeks into the room, calling for me. The scowl on my face disappears. I squat and wave her over to me.

"Hi, sweetheart." I kiss her forehead and bring her into a hug.

"Hi, Daddy," she whispers and peeks over toward her mother. "Can I come to work with you today? Uncle Gio and Uncle Jace will play with me. They promised if I wanted, they would."

My heart feels like it splits in two. It's clear Bella wants nothing to do with her mother. Maybe I'm the one forcing something that will never be.

I bite back my anger and nod my head. "Sure, you can come with me. Daddy would love that. I'll text your uncle to let him know you're coming to check on him and make sure he's doing his job. You know he works better when you come to supervise him."

I place a finger on my chin, pretending to be in thought. "He has been slacking a bit. Maybe we can check on an update for your party. How about that?"

"Yay," she squeals. "I need to change. I have to look businesslike, you know?"

I chuckle at the serious look on her face. How can you not love this child? I kiss her cheek before I send her off to get ready.

"You spoil her. It's more than parenting. That's the problem."

I stand and spin on my wife. I point a finger at her. "No, I spoiled you. That's the only problem."

I storm from the room before I say something I'll regret. I text my brother because Bella will ask him if I did. Taking a deep breath, I pray for a better rest of the day.

Lizzy

"Dante's bringing Bella to work with him. Do you think you can help out with keeping her busy?" Gio asks as he appears in front of my desk.

I look up and smile. Dante had sent me a text to let me know he was running late, so I should move all his meetings back. He didn't mention Bella, but I'm more than excited for her to be here. I can pick her little brain on what she truly wants for her next birthday party.

Her mother is never very helpful. Dante always tells me to get creative and spare no expense. However, she's getting older and I'm at a loss for the direction I should take this next one in. I realized that after talking to the cake maker I usually use for her parties.

I was so concerned with Bella's peanut allergy; I was thrown when I was asked how I wanted the cupcakes decorated. That made me start to think about her party theme.

"No problem. She'll be some of the best company I've had around here in days," I say.

Gio narrows his eyes at me. I smile up at him. He knows I'm being cheeky, but it's so hard not to tease him. He can be so stern in the office at times.

He tilts his head as he studies me. "You're wearing makeup and that outfit is kind of sexy. Stand up."

I stand and do a little turn. Gio whistles, pulls a face, and nods his head. "What's the occasion?"

"I have a date," I say and shrug.

"Uncle Gio," Bella squeals and runs at Gio's legs.

From my perch on my seat behind my high desk, I can see the top of her head as she wraps around him and hugs his leg tightly. My heart melts. She looks so adorable. Stepping back, she tugs down her little blazer. I take in her shiny patent leather Mary Janes and pleated skirt.

"I'm here to make sure you get your work done. I'm dressed for business," she says and turns. "I dressed myself. How did I do?"

"You look like you're going to take this place over one day," Gio says cheerfully. "What's this about me getting my work done?"

"I told her you've been slacking," Dante says as he walks over to my desk.

"Good morning, Mr. Di Lorenzo."

"Good morning, Lizzy. You look nice."

"Oh, it's you," Bella says. She looks up at me dreamily. "But who's at the book palace watching over the books?"

I step down from my seat and round my desk to squat and get eye level with her. "Your daddy and uncle needed my help. The Book Court has the library covered. The books will be safe with them."

"Oh."

I have to stifle a laugh as her eyes round and she nods as if my explanation makes all the sense in the world. She runs her hand down the front of her little blazer.

"Can I help you help Daddy?"

"I don't see why not. First, we have to read your daddy his schedule. Wait right here." I stand and reach over my desk to pluck up my tablet.

As I'm reaching, a very deep, masculine groan fills the air. I look over my shoulder to find Dante scanning me from head to toe. Gio's cheeks are red as he looks like he's trying to hide his laughter.

"She has a date, brother. Doesn't she look stunning?"

"My schedule," Dante bites out.

I open the tablet, stand straighter, and reach my hand out for Bella's. She places her little palm in mine. I take a breath and start to read off the day.

"I moved all of your appointments back until afternoon. You have a conference call at one and two meetings. One at two thirty and the other at four."

"Can the meetings be moved? I want to have lunch with Bella."

"I think I can reschedule your four. I'll be happy to watch Bella when you're busy. I believe Gio needs to attend a few meetings, including your two thirty."

"I'll have lunch with Bella in my office around one thirty. Can you coordinate something for us?"

"No problem," I say and bend to hold my tablet out for Bella. "Okay, so we need to move a few things around for your dad. If you touch right here, we can block you in for lunch."

Bella's face lights up as she taps where I show her. "Good job. You may just take my job if I'm not careful. Here, watch this. We're going to cancel the meeting in an email."

"Oh, I know what we need to say. Dear…"

"Mr. Ambrose."

"Dear Mr. Am…Ambro, my daddy is spending the day with me. I'm sincerely sorry he has to cancel your playdate for ours. He'll make it up to you with lunch very soon. Thank you for your understanding."

I finish typing what the message will really say and smile at Bella. "Wow, you're so smart. I think that was an amazing email."

Gio chuckles. "Di Lorenzos are always ahead of their years. Come on, Bella. I have about twenty-five minutes before my next meeting. Let's go see what Jace is up to in my office."

"Bye, Book Queen. I'll see you in a little while," Bella says hopefully.

"I'll be right here when you need me, and you can call me Lizzy."

"Okay," she says excitedly as she waves and follows her uncle.

"I may need you to stay late today. How's the party planning coming along?"

I nearly jump out of my skin. I had no idea Dante had moved so close.

"Oh, um, I have a few questions. Is there a theme she would like? I'm a little lost for direction."

"Her interests change daily. At the moment, she'll probably want a Book Queen party. I think you should ask her. I've never seen her take to someone like she does you. Whatever you decide, I'm sure she'll love it.

"Do you have children of your own?"

"Ha, you'd have to date for that," I snort.

"But you have a date tonight, is that correct?"

"I did. I'll have to reschedule if you need me to stay late."

I honestly expect him to tell me I don't have to cancel. He'll ask someone else to stay, but he does no such thing. His expression is impassive. I feel like somehow I've done something wrong.

I shake the thought off. "Bella is a delight and so smart. I've taken to her too."

Dante nods. "You should join us for lunch. She would like that. Order whatever she wants. If you need anything for her while I'm working, have Michelle charge it to my black card."

"Okay, no problem. I've got it covered. I'll have plans to show you for the party by tomorrow."

"Take your time. I appreciate you doing this."

"No problem. It's my job."

His lips thin. "No, no, it's really not."

Dante

Am I a bastard for making sure Lizzy doesn't go on her date? Hell, yeah, but I'll be damned if she goes on a date dressed like that. The purple off-the-shoulder sweater dress fits her long curvy body like a glove. I even like her quirky vintage strappy '50s heels.

Her outfit is a far cry from the goth stuff she normally wears, at least that I've noticed. When she reached over her desk for her tablet, I thought I was going to burst through my slacks. Clearly, she either *A*, doesn't have on any panties or *B*, she has on a very thin thong.

Either way, her full, lush ass has the perfect shape and the right amount of jiggle. Her hips complement her long legs and the bubble seat of her backside. Bethany has done so much nip and tuck I don't think she even has an ass anymore. Not that I have a single desire to touch her at this point.

I don't know what turned me on more, the dress or how Lizzy handled my daughter. Bella soaked the attention up. It's hard having a daughter in a family full of men. Another reason I've been reluctant to divorce.

"Hello," I answer my cell phone and sit behind my desk.

"Mr. Di Lorenzo?"

"Yes, how can I help you?"

"This is First Credit Finance. My name is Keith, my ID number is three-seven-six-five-four-eight. I'm calling because there seems to be a charge that has triggered our fraud department."

"What's the charge and where was it made?"

"Mercedes Benz. In the amount of ninety-five thousand six hundred and seventy-five, sir."

I nearly throw my phone across the room. That's the same amount as the truck Bethany asked me for not too long ago. I priced it as I thought for a split second about purchasing it for her. Right before she started to work my last nerve.

"Decline the charge. As a matter of fact, freeze the card the charge was made from."

"I can do that for you, sir. I'll just need you to answer a few questions for me if you don't mind."

"Yes, but let's make this quick. I have a conference call to get to."

I spend the next ten minutes closing Bethany's card and making plans to cut her off from a whole lot more.

CHAPTER SIX

I'll Be Good

Lizzy

Oh my God. I love this little girl, she's so stinking cute. She's taken off her blazer and has taken a seat in the accent chair, mimicking my posture as we all eat lunch in Dante's office. Gio and Jace have joined us, so we're sitting in Dante's lounge area.

The guys have taken up all the couch space after I insisted. They're all over six feet tall. Gio and Jace have to be at least six-four, six-five and Dante is a good six-six. I opted to sit on the floor even though Jace and Gio did try to make room for me on the couch.

I allowed Bella to sit in the only accent chair left. However, she still sits with her legs tucked to her side. I wasn't sure if she was modeling after me until I switched sides and she did as well.

"Lizzy, are you going to finish your egg roll? Daddy keeps looking your way like he's still hungry," Bella says, and both Gio and Jace burst into laughter.

I look to Dante, but he clears all emotions from his face. He clears his throat and tosses his napkin onto his plate.

"I've had more than enough to eat, Bella. Allow Lizzy to eat her food in peace."

"She's not bothering me. I'm going to eat this egg roll though," I reply.

"Here, Daddy. You can have the rest of my rice. I've had enough," Bella offers.

"I'm fine, Bella."

"Here, I'll take that," Gio says, taking the plate to place it on the coffee table before Bella spills it.

Instantly, she scoots from her seat and comes to sit beside me on the floor. I grin as she watches me, scooting closer to see how far I'll allow her to get. I chuckle and wrap an arm around her to pull her into my side. She gives me the biggest smile ever and leans her head against me.

"You smell nice," she says.

"Thank you."

"Bella, why don't you tell Lizzy what you want for your birthday party? She's helping me to plan it and we could use your help," Dante says.

I wipe my mouth as Bella gasps, pulls away slightly, and looks at me excitedly. My heart swells. I have to make this the best party ever. This little girl deserves it.

"I want a superhero party. I want to look like the pretty girls on Uncle Gio's phone," Bella says.

I look to Gio and lift a brow. His cheeks turn red. I cover my mouth as I try not to laugh.

"What is she talking about?" Dante asks.

"I have a picture of Lizzy on my phone dressed as Nubia," Gio mutters. "Bella was playing a game on my phone earlier. She must have seen it then."

"Nubia, as in the Black Wonder Woman?" Dante asks.

"The very same."

Oh my God, the picture of my sister and me from Halloween last year. How the hell did Gio get that photo?

"Do I even want to know how or why you have that picture?"

"Not really," Gio mutters.

"Let me see it," Dante says. "I mean, I want to know what we're talking about here for the party."

"Sure, that's why you want to see it. Google Nubia and that will give you plenty of an idea."

"Gio, let me see the damn picture before I kick your ass," Dante growls.

Bella gasps at my side. Dante seems to remember himself and shifts in his chair as he adjusts his tie and then his cuffs. I pause to think all this over.

Why is seeing the photo so important to him? Gio is right, he can Google Nubia. Bella wraps her little arms around my neck as she sits up on her knees.

"Never mind. We don't have to have superheroes. I'd like to have a skate party and books. I love books. Maybe we can give everyone a book to take home so their daddies can read to them like mine," Bella says softly.

"I'm sorry I lost my temper, princess. You know Daddy and Uncle Gio can get into it sometimes. That doesn't mean you can't have your superhero party."

"In fact, I think I have enough to throw you the perfect party. I know exactly what to do," I say.

"Really?" Bella says with big eyes.

"Absolutely."

"I'm sure she will do her best, Bella."

"I think it's going to be awesome. She's the Book Queen, she can do anything. I'm going to be a good girl. I promise. If I'm good, you'll stay my best friend, right, Lizzy?"

I'm taken aback by the question and the tension that fills the room coming from all three men. I search Bella's hopeful face.

"You could throw an entire tantrum and I'll still be your friend, love. We all have moments, real friends don't leave because of them. You don't have to worry. I'm not going anywhere," I say and run a hand over her hair.

Dante clears his throat. I look to Gio and Jace and they look as if they're going to explode. Bella wraps tightly around my neck and squeezes.

"I'm so happy I met you. This has been the best day ever," she says in my ear.

"Fix it, Dante or I finally will," Gio says through his teeth.

A shiver runs through me. Again, it's like I'm caught in the middle of something I know nothing about.

CHAPTER SEVEN

Lies & Manipulation

Dante

"You mistake my kindness for a weakness," I roar into the room as Bethany strolls into our home after midnight.

She jumps as she startles. I've been sitting in the dark waiting for her arrival. With each hour, my blood has been boiling. I can't comprehend why I'm going through this shit. Women would line up to take Bethany's spot.

A ring on my finger has never stopped the advances. I know I would have no lack of company. I frown at the thought. I'm not looking for someone to warm my bed. I need someone I can trust.

"It has been brought to my attention that I can no longer trust you," I seethe.

"Me? Do you know how embarrassed I was today?"

"You weren't too embarrassed to call my father. Now, were you?"

"What else was I supposed to do when my husband cut my card off in the middle of a purchase?"

"The purchase of a ninety-five-thousand-dollar truck you did not need. Did I not just give you a Range Rover? No, that wouldn't matter. You just keep taking and taking and taking.

"You know what kills me? You walk around like you run this fucking company or as if you're the head of the family or some shit.

"You think I don't have eyes and ears?" I take a calming breath before tossing a drug test at her feet.

"What's this?"

"You've been acting as if you're on drugs, so before I take your ass to a psychiatrist, I want to know if you're using. I can't have you placing my daughter in danger."

She scoffs. "Fuck you, Dante. I'm on drugs because I'm using retail therapy to deal with my husband telling me he wants a divorce? You won't even touch me anymore. If I were on drugs, you drove me to them."

"I won't touch you because you're an evil bitch. I saw that video of you pushing Bella away from you. I know you've been taking money from her account." I have to pause to get the rest out. "Do you know she thinks you treat her the way you do because she's a bad girl? I know what that feels like, Bethany. I'm not going to allow you to do this to her."

Guilt covers her face. She takes a few steps toward me. Ducking her head as if she's truly remorseful. If this was five years ago, I'd believe the act.

"Dante, I...I planned to put the money back. Daddy needed some help. I thought I could help him and put it back before you noticed. I've been so stressed out. I may have lost my patience with Bella, but I would never hurt her."

"Why didn't your father come to me? It wouldn't have been the first time."

I call her on that bullshit lie because I know her father has come into a new lucrative investment. It's a rumor I've been meaning to look more into. Man, this woman can lie through her teeth. How am I just seeing her for who she is?

"He was embarrassed. I found out by accident. He made me swear not to tell anyone."

I don't have it in me to call her on her shit. I'm exhausted. I've been living this nightmare for longer than I care to admit. If not for our daughter, I would have had the guards at the gate turn her away.

I inhale deeply and drag my tired body up to my secret place. I can sleep in the bedroom up there. I need a break from my lying, manipulative, selfish wife. A moment to think clearly and make some real decisions.

"Dante," she calls after me. "I still love you."

"You have a poor way of showing it," I mutter and keep walking.

Lizzy

"And who has you smiling like that?" I say as I walk into the kitchen.

Nyla looks down at her phone with an uncharacteristic goofy grin on her face. Something has changed about Nyla. I just can't put my finger on it.

"No one," she says quickly and puts her phone on the counter face down.

I shrug it off and go to the refrigerator. I'm hungry. Since I didn't go on my date, I didn't eat dinner.

"Hey, what happened to your date?"

"My boss needed me to work late. I had to cancel."

"That sucks. You want to get some content in? It's been a while since we've gamed together. We can push some product too." She's right, it's been almost six months since we've played together.

"That sounds good. I'm not going to get any sleep. Besides, the sponsors are going to be after us if we don't post something new soon."

"Yeah, I know. Not that we need them. Our merch and subs are keeping us afloat," she says.

"Afloat, I was thinking of taking a long vacation or buying a boat or something." I chuckle. My sister bursts out laughing. We both know I would never.

Although, she's right. Our merchandise and subscriptions to the Twitch channel are keeping our accounts very healthy.

"Yeah, I can finally let go of my harem of sugar daddies." She snorts and slides off the stool she has been perched on.

I tilt my head at her. Something in her words jumps out at me. I get ready to pry, but her phone rings.

"Hey, I'm getting ready to jump on for some content. I can't really talk right now," she says into the phone.

After a pause, she speaks again. "Does he know you're calling?" I watch her face closely as she frowns. "Why is it so hard for him to tell me he wants me? Yeah, I know that, but even that wasn't done right."

The person on the other end replies while Nyla looks up to find me staring at her.

"He has to call for me. Look, I have to go." She takes a pause. "Yeah, I want to see you too, but this is on him. I'll text you later."

"So you're seeing someone?"

"Lizzy, you're not ready for me to share my life."

"What makes you say that? I miss our talks. What happened to us?"

"You're still my baby sister. My life has just become more complicated over the years. Trust me, one day, all the secrets will come out."

"Are your secrets why you're back and thinking about sticking around?"

"Not mine exactly, but they're twisted up in it all." She purses her lips and looks like she's going to say more. "Come on. We have an audience who awaits."

I know right away the conversation is closed. She has that look in her eyes. I'm a little taken aback. That look usually appears when the topic centers around Mom and Dad.

CHAPTER EIGHT

Subs

Lizzy

I had to double back to the kitchen for some popcorn. After I changed to cam up for my Twitch channel, my stomach started growling so loudly. Meanwhile, Nyla worked on getting our moderator to join at such a late hour.

"Hey, Aunt Denise," I sing through a mouthful of popcorn.

"Hey, girls, it's good to have you together again. We have to do lunch sometime."

"Absolutely, thanks for doing this, Aunt Denise. You know how we get. I don't think I'm going to get much sleep tonight," Nyla says.

"I hear you. I can't get my brain to shut up. Hopefully this popcorn will quiet my stomach."

"You girls know I don't sleep. Especially since Martin passed. You girls keep me young and give me something to do. Besides, I love watching you work. I'd swear you girls have been on tour before."

"I, for one, can't wait to get at this new map," Nyla says, quickly changing the subject. Probably because, like me, she can feel the mention of our parents coming.

From what I know, my parents were super tight with both Elijah and Aunt Denise. I guess that's why they have never left our lives.

Luckily, Aunt Denise is a night owl. I guess it comes with her PTSD. We call her Aunt Denise, but she's our godmother. She stepped up to help Elijah with the girlie stuff when he stepped in for our parents. Aunt Denise was who he called when I started my period and she took me for my first bra.

I always wondered why Elijah didn't marry her and make her our mom. I was so young I didn't realize she was already married. However, she has remained in our lives nonetheless—now as our admin for the chats on our channels.

"Let's get this show on the road," I say into my headset and pick up my controller.

"All set," Nyla says.

"I'm in both chats and ready to go," Denise says.

"Cool, Judge Sin, I'm bringing you in now."

I read the chat and it goes crazy at the mention of Judge Sin. It's been so long since Ny and I have been able to play together.

"Hey guys, this is Izzy Gunz. I'm so glad to be live and playing tonight. You know, it's always good to take a bit of a break, but I've missed you guys."

I read to myself some of the comments coming in. Jacob_eats grabs my attention as the comments roll by. I can't help but to smile.

"Aww, Rajaz, you miss being here too? Thanks for the love."

"Hey, guys. You're all making me feel so special," Nyla says. "Dude, I'm excited for this new map."

"You love my tank, Ponygirl? Thanks. These are actually new up on the site." I push up my glasses and focus on the game as we're about to be dropped onto the map. Nyla and I zone in and start our first battle royal.

We crush our first round and, of course, the trolls jump into the room to call us hackers. My sister and I are just that damn good at this. We make it look so easy. A few rape and death threats come through, but Denise is quick to block and handle those.

While we wait in the lobby for our next deployment, I start to look through the chat once again.

"Thanks for the love, Kimmie, Broc, Ahsha."

"No, guys. I'm not going to cam up," Nyla says. "Nothing has changed."

I murmur to myself as I read. "I loved the blue and gray braids, Izzy. Will you do them again?" I laugh. "I'm thinking about it. I loved them too."

"Am I looking forward to the holidays with my loved one? I don't know, Doll Collector. I'm just getting settled in. I'm waiting to see if a few friends will reach out," Ny replies to the comment she reads.

I continue to read the chat before I glance at the incoming donations. "Thanks for the six months, Hellon. Thanks for the year, Goliath. *Awww*, Jacob_eats, thanks for the hundred subs. That's so sweet."

"Wow, Iz. He's asking for a date in the chat. I don't know Jacob_eats. Maybe if you donate another hundred subs she'll think about it," Nyla says, sometimes we pull up an extra screen to be able to read each other's chats. I'm not surprised she has mine up since she has her home set up.

I try not to laugh but fail. Jacob replies, *done*, in the chat and my cheeks heat.

"Whoa, he did two hundred."

Nyla laughs so hard she snorts. "I think this guy really wants a date, sis."

"Hold on, guys. I know Jacob. We were supposed to go on a date, but I had to cancel for work. Please don't start donating subs thinking you're going to get to shoot your shot." I'm holding my stomach at this point as I laugh.

"Thanks, Nay-nay for the six months." I pause and my mouth drops open as the next donation comes in.

"Are you kidding me?" I breathe. "Holy shit, bro. I don't know who you are, Doll Collector, but thanks for the hundred thousand gifted subs."

Nyla goes completely silent. All I hear is her breathing in my ear and it sounds more like panting. Suddenly my chat is flooded as if someone has started a raid. Everyone's typing in Judge Sin.

I assume whoever this Doll Collector is, they're the one who sent this raid and the donation was meant to get Ny's attention as well. This person has to know we share everything and that what happens for my channel happens for my sister's and makes her happy that I'm happy.

I pause the game. "Guys, I need a bathroom break. Give me a bit."

I get up and go down the hall to where Nyla is set up in her room. When I open the door, she startles and drops her phone. Her face is drained of color.

"Hey, you know who this Doll Collector is?"

She only nods as she licks her lips. She shrugs and gives a sheepish smile.

"I guess someone has a little more swag than Jacob. This was his way of calling me. You might want to step up the guys you're dating," she teases.

"Don't try to distract me. Who is he?"

"Avatar and Goliath are asking to play a thousand-dollar wager. You down?"

"Some guy just dropped two hundred thousand dollars' worth of donated subscriptions to *my* channel, not yours and you just want to gloss over it? Did you not see all the people who just raided the chat as well? Some guy knows the way to your heart is through your sister and in order to know that he has to know you."

"Drop it, Liz."

"Ny," I growl.

"Let it go. Let's get this money, sis."

Something in my head clicks into place. "Oh my God, Doll Collector," I gasp, putting the pieces together.

"Liz," Ny warns.

"I'm going to slowly back out of this room because I know you're not that crazy. There's no way you're that crazy."

"Don't knock it until you try it," she says with a trembling grin.

"How do you even know him? You barely spoke when you guys met?"

"I've known him for much longer than you know. I knew him before that day. Before you did."

It all clicks into place. Dad said my assignment was meant to be hers and she redirected it to me.

"Wow," I breathe.

"Can we drop it?"

"You're not happy, though, are you?" I inch back toward her.

She shakes her head. "Don't...let's get our heads in the game. Having this business and the gaming will allow me to come home. It's my ace to keeping myself in all of this."

I bite my lip against all the questions I have. I'm stunned, but my sister is a grown woman. She can handle herself. I have my own life to figure out.

CHAPTER NINE

From The Heart

Lizzy

"Thank you." The small child with the huge grin on his face says as I place mashed potatoes on his plate.

"You're welcome."

I might not like being around people, but I love to give back. I want to see people happy. I was honored when Dante asked me to help out for the annual Thanksgiving turkey drive they put on for the less fortunate.

It's an all-day affair at one of the larger restaurants here in the city. The Di Lorenzo's have several New Jersey–based locations.

This one has been closed for the day just for this event. First thing in the morning, Dante's wealthy friends and connections came in to donate turkeys and money. This year there has even been a toy drive to gear up for the Christmas party Dante has planned for the kids at the children's hospital.

From afternoon to evening, we've given away turkeys and served hot meals. The fixings all come from the Di Lorenzo restaurants around the city.

The little boy looks up at his tired-looking mother and gives her a heart-melting smile. "See, Mama? I'm going to eat, and you can rest. Everything is going to be fine."

She squeezes his shoulders and returns his smile, but not without sadness in her eyes. I place a good helping of mash on another plate and a big piece of chicken and greens before handing it over to the mother.

"Eat up. If you want, he's welcome to come play with me and some of the kids in the tent out back. There's a magic show happening in about twenty minutes," I say with a warm smile.

"Thank you."

"No problem. We're happy to help in any way we can," Nyla says beside me.

She, Aunt Denise, and Dad volunteered to help. It feels good to have my family here with me. I peek down the table to see Gio, Dante, and Dario horsing around. When I don't see Carleen, I turn to find her biting her thumbnail as she stares at Dario. She's sitting on a crate in the corner, off to herself.

Nyla bumps me with her hip. I return my attention to scooping food. As I focus my gaze before me, I find a smiling Jacob.

I can't lie. He looks good. He has on a tight-fitted T-shirt and well-worn jeans. His hair is gelled into a stylish mohawk.

I'm digging the lip ring. I hadn't noticed it before. However, I'm paying more attention this time, and the fact that he's biting his lip at the moment draws my attention to it.

"Hey." He winks at me as he looks me over. I'm glad I dressed nicely for this, even if I'm in all black.

The shear top is still modest, and the black jeans look tight but are flattering to my hips as my sister put it. However, I look like a saint next to her.

It's hard for Nyla not to look sexy. Although, I haven't for a second missed the skintight liquid-leather leggings she's wearing with ridiculously high heels. The off-the-shoulder gray sweater dials down the pants a bit, but she looks gorgeous. I stop comparing myself to my sister as Jacob draws my attention.

"You look great."

"Hi, Jacob. Thanks. You look nice too. What are you doing here?"

"The guys forgot a few trays at the other location. I had to rush them over. You guys seem to have a great crowd going here."

"Oh, that was sweet of you to bring them over. Are you on shift tonight?"

"No, I'm thinking about sticking around to help out here."

"Oh, okay." I bite my lip. I'm still not sure how I feel about Jacob. He's handsome enough, but I don't get butterflies from him.

At my age, I should probably give up on butterflies and signs. Although, for me, you have to hold my attention. I'm not sure there's enough spark for Jacob to do so.

"I've been texting you. Do you think we can reschedule for next week? I'll shoot you over my days off on Monday." He lifts a brow with a hopeful expression on his face.

"Why not? I'll let you know when I'm free."

"Cool, I can't wait."

I give him a shy smile that's wiped away in seconds. My gaze lands across the room and my eyes connect with a sight that boils my blood.

Bethany is bent at the waist, pointing a finger in Bella's face. It's clear that Bella is crying. Although I'm not sure why, from the way she's shrinking back and drawing her body in, I can tell whatever Bethany is saying has something to do with it.

Normally, I'd mind my business when a parent is chastising their child, but something isn't right. Bella is a good child. I can't see a reason for Bethany to have to yell at her or correct her to the point of tears.

Not to mention, I saw Bethany hitting the glasses of wine heavily when the big donors were here earlier. I haven't missed the fact that she's been avoiding being in the same area as Dante.

Which he hasn't seemed to mind as he's played the gracious host all day.

Bella's gaze seems to scan the room. I assume, looking for her father. However, I note the moment she finds me. Her chest rises as if her breath hitches.

Faster than I can blink, she darts around Bethany and bolts for me. I move through the gap between the tables to meet her.

"Lizzy," she cries out as I squat, and she flings herself into my arms, her little body trembling. I hold her tightly and start to rub circles on her back.

I've been spending more time with Bella as I've been planning her party. Dante has brought her into the office a few times in the last few weeks. I love the time she has dubbed our *playdates*.

When I rise with Bella in my arms, Dante towers over me. I look up into his eyes and find a storm brewing. Bethany comes running over and shoves me in the shoulder.

"Get your hands off my daughter," she shouts.

I bite down on my words and hold on to Bella tighter. I have to chant to myself to keep from waxing this chick's ass the way she deserves.

Not in front of Bella. Not in front of Bella.

"Bethany, have you lost your damn mind?" Dante says tightly.

"I'm sick of hearing about Daddy's assistant this and Daddy's helper that," she says as if mimicking Bella's voice.

Bella turns in my arms and leaps into her father's. "What's the matter, princess?" Dante coos more gently to his crying daughter.

"I only asked to play with the other kids. She yelled at me."

"No, I didn't, you little liar."

"What the hell is wrong with you?" Dante snarls.

"She's lying."

"Why can't I play with the poor kids?"

"I didn't say it like that."

"Oh, really? Then where did she get that from, huh, Bethany?"

Dante tightens his hold on Bella and steps closer to Bethany as he lowers his voice. "How old are you? Who's the five-year-old here?"

"Why'd I even come here?"

"I have no idea. I didn't invite you."

"Well, maybe I should go."

"Don't do me any favors."

I start to fidget, feeling like we're all witnessing something very private. My family has moved closer. I know it's probably because Bethany put her hands on me.

"What are you saying, Dante?"

"I'm saying we're both happier without you. Do whatever you want. We'll be fine."

Dante pauses as if to take a calming breath. "It's time you get some help. Talk out your issues and pull it together. Whatever you need to do, but you're not going to subject Bella to this any longer."

"Subject her? Subject her? What about me? She's the issue. I never—"

"Finish those words and I'll have you dropped right here where you stand," Gio seethes.

Dante

I stop breathing. My brothers and I have been fucked up since we were younger and our mother left us. To have my wife fix her lips to tell this amazing little girl in my arms she never wanted her is like an arrow through the heart.

I would never put my hands on a woman, but I can't say I don't have the urge to slap the shit out of Bethany, especially when the alcohol on her breath singes my nostrils.

"You should be careful who you threaten, Gio."

"I don't make threats. You don't even know how close you are to taking your last breath."

Lizzy's sister appears behind Bethany at that moment. I don't question my brother's words. I learned not to a long time ago. Not to mention, I caught Gio and Lizzy's sister in a heated conversation earlier that told me this isn't their first time meeting.

I brushed it off at the time, but now as my brother looks at the gorgeous woman communicating with only her eyes, it's clear to me there's a lot here I probably don't want to know.

"This is your fault," Bethany snarls in Lizzy's face.

I expect Lizzy to shrink back. I get ready to snap out of it to defend her, but she shocks me. Bethany goes to slap Lizzy, but Lizzy catches her hand midair.

Nyla grabs Bethany by the back of her hair. "You must have lost your drunk ass mind. I ought to beat your ass for making that baby cry," she hisses down into Bethany's face.

"Ny, don't." Then in pig Latin Lizzy says. "She's not worth it."

Nyla shoves her away. "I'll see you again soon."

"You're all going to regret this. I hope you have someone to look after that brat once you're gone."

"Now who's slinging threats," Dario snaps. "You're playing a dangerous game, Beth."

"You've all hated me from the beginning. You think I'm not prepared? I knew you'd turn him against me."

I scoff. "As if you needed help?"

She bursts into fake tears that put my five-year-old's tantrums to shame before she storms off. When I gaze around me, embarrassment starts to set in. All eyes are on us.

I turn to head back toward the offices, so I can tend to Bella. Gio places a hand on my shoulder. He leans into my ear.

"That's a problem."

"I know. What would you have me do?"

He looks me deep in the eyes before he nods. "Nothing, do nothing." He kisses the top of Bella's head. "Uncle Gio will make this better. Promise."

CHAPTER TEN

Normalcy

Lizzy

The event has wrapped up, and I told my family I'd find a ride home. I wanted to stick around and make sure Bella was okay. She has been upset since her mother stormed out. Not even the magic show could cheer her up.

I knock on the door to the back office. The door swings open to reveal Dario, Gio, and Dante huddled together. Jace peers out at me, then steps back to allow me in.

The three brothers embrace and murmur to one another before breaking apart. The twins tower over Gio, bringing a smile to my face. Gio is larger than life and is such a protector when it comes to these two, so it's cute to see. One thing I've learned about Gio is that he loves these two men fiercely.

"Call me if you need me," Dario calls over his shoulder as he goes to leave.

Gio pats Dante on the back and moves toward the door. I look over at the couch in the office to find a sleeping Bella. She looks so peaceful.

Gio stops to pull me into a hug as he exits. "We need to talk. Everything is about to change. Now is when I need you," he whispers in my ear.

I nod my understanding as he releases me. I've never fully understood why Gio wanted to hire me. However, I'm always ready for anything. Especially if it means helping this family.

Jace closes the door behind him after everyone leaves. Dante moves to the couch and scoops Bella into his arms, taking the place she had lain.

"Is she okay?"

He blows out a breath. "She will be."

"I'm so sorry if I've caused a problem."

"Come, sit."

I move closer and sit beside him and Bella. I run a hand over her hair. She stirs and burrows closer to her father. She's a lucky little girl. It's so clear to see how much Dante loves her.

"When I was about eight, my mother abandoned us. She just left. Not a word. I spent years feeling like it was something I did."

He takes a pause and sighs. "I didn't want that for my children. When I found out Bethany was pregnant with Bella, I was so happy. I had all these plans. I was going to be the best father and husband. We would have a boy next after a year or two.

"Then Bella was born. Bethany became someone totally different. She started to treat the staff like shit and her spending got out of control. I hated her treatment of the staff, but I was willing to overlook the spending."

"You don't have to tell me all this," I say as he stops talking to stare down at Bella.

"No, I need to get this off my chest before I explode. She wouldn't even feed our daughter. I thought maybe it was postpartum depression or something. I wanted to give her time, I tried to get her help.

"Then, it dawned on me. She was full of shit. She doesn't love me, she loves what I can do for her. She can't love anyone other than herself. Bethany doesn't have a single motherly bone in her body. It had nothing to do with depression, she gave me a baby because she thought it would appease me, keep me feeding her lifestyle and vanity.

"I don't even recognize the woman I married. She should be given an Oscar for the act she has put on over the years. That woman played to all my weaknesses. My need for a family, my need to protect and please. My hate for who I had become."

He chokes up. "My father can be stern. I can't help thinking my mother left because she needed to be safe. The older I got. I couldn't make sense of her leaving us otherwise."

"She never tried to reach out, not even after you got older?"

"No," he says tightly.

I wipe at a tear. "I was only three when I lost my parents. They were killed. Nyla was older, so she remembered more about them. I never got to know the love of a mother. Elijah has been a great stand-in, but I've always felt like a part of me is missing. A part he could never stand in for," I blurt out, not knowing why.

I've never told anyone about my parents. I always simply say, they passed away. The pain seems to sear deeper as I try to understand a parent not wanting their child. I may not remember my parents, but I know I was loved. They didn't up and leave, they were taken away without a choice.

"And that's why I've warred with divorcing my wife. She's toxic, but she's Bella's mother. I can't replace that. It feels like whatever move I make, I'm hurting my daughter. I won't even talk about the secrets Bethany has that I never should've allowed her next to."

"I can't tell you what to do, but this isn't okay either. The look on Bella's face. Bethany's behavior toward her and in front of her. Sometimes, we have to take the lesser of our evils.

"I get where you're coming from. You don't want your daughter to hurt the way you did. But she's smart, Dante. She sees what's going on and now she's experiencing her own type of hurt." I pause and purse my lips.

"I think I've said too much. I don't know all the details, so I'm going to mind my business."

"You have been more of a help than you know. This is above and beyond your job description." He chuckles. "Do you need a ride home?"

"No, I'm going to order a car."

"Don't be silly. We'll drop you off."

"Oh, okay. Thank you."

Dante

Yes, Bella has been my main reason for my indecisiveness with Bethany. However, in truth. My wife knows too much. Given her father's ties and connections, I never saw her as a threat.

However, even now, her words ring in my ear. Bethany's vengeful spirit is a problem. I can't have her take me away from my daughter and I can't lose my brothers. They're all I have.

My mind weighs heavy with all of this as I ride in the back of my SUV. Despite my loathing for my wife, I would never cheat on her. No matter how hard it is to sit here with Lizzy beside me, smelling like sin.

"I saw Jacob. Did you guys have another date?" I ask to distract myself from my thoughts.

I look away from my window to find Lizzy lifting her head from her phone. I smile. She's reading, always reading. Her nose wrinkles a little.

"Jacob? Oh, no. I didn't know he was coming. He said something about bringing over forgotten trays or something. We haven't rescheduled our date yet."

"Um." That's a little surprising. He keeps sniffing around her. I was sure he weaseled his way into a date by now.

"I've been busy. It will happen."

Not if I can help it.

I'm thrown by my possessiveness and thoughts. Lizzy is free to date whoever she likes. It might be the way he looks at her. As if he's waiting to taste the menu of the day. I hate it.

"Why haven't you applied for any of the promotions? I've been through a few assistant-executive admins because of Bethany. I've never seen your resume for the position."

She pushes her glasses up her nose. "To be honest, I have a business I run outside of working for your company. I wouldn't want it to interfere with giving my all to the position. The travel could prove difficult for my business."

I grunt and nod. Against my better judgment, I did dig into her gaming channel. I watched once. It's the reason I'm a bit surprised she and Jacob haven't been on a date. He practically tried to buy a date.

"What would you need to facilitate both?"

"I'm a professional gamer. I work long hours creating content. I'd need to be able to record no matter where I am, and I may not be the most useful some days. My position is perfect for that lifestyle. I'm able to keep you, my fans, and my sponsors happy at the moment."

I think over her words. I crave normalcy for myself and Bella. Lizzy could help with that in so many ways. It's only a thought, but I wouldn't mind promoting her. She works well with Gio and that means he trusts her.

"Think about it. If the position opens up again, I'd like you to at least apply."

She bobs her head before dismissing me and going back to her book. The SUV falls silent. I slump down in my seat and try to relax.

When we pull up to the gates of a rather impressive home, I sit back up and duck to get a better look. Well, no wonder she doesn't care about the promotion.

I pay well, but not this well. The gates open and Oliver begins to roll in. I look over to Lizzy, but her face is still in her phone.

"My birth father, he was an engineer and tech genius. He built a multimillion-dollar company before he was killed. Elijah was his partner. My sister and I inherited everything, including Dad's half of the business. Our gaming business is our third successful venture," she says without looking up.

"Third?" I say with a smile.

"Yeah," she says nervously, finally looking up from her book. "We...um...well—"

Her words are cut off by the ringing of my phone. I pull it from my pocket to see it's Bethany. I can't help the scowl that comes to my face.

"Thanks for the ride," Lizzy says as the door is opened. She jumps out before I can respond.

She's forgotten as I take the call. I know something is wrong from the moment I pick up. I can hear Bethany sniffling.

"Hello?"

"Dante?" she slurs.

"Where are you?" The protector in me comes out.

"Don't act like you care now. You canceled all of my cards and froze my accounts." I knew this was coming. I confirmed the process was completed after the scene she made at the restaurant. "You turned him against me. You turned everyone against me."

"I told you to stop running to my father in the first place."

She laughs manically. "Your father? I'm not talking about your father. You know what's the worst part? I should have married him, not you. My father was so hell-bent on a marriage between us and the sex was amazing, but I never loved you. Not like him."

"What the fuck are you talking about?"

"The man I was forced to give up, the one I should have had a child with," she slurs. "He was going to help me. I told him everything about you and your family. He was going to make sure you all went to jail, and I could be free.

"Now, he won't even take my calls. I'm ready to leave and he doesn't want me. Don't act stupid, Dante. You know what you did."

"Listen to me, I don't give a fuck about who you're fucking. And I have no clue what the hell you're talking about, but you're done fucking me and my daughter over, you self-absorbed bitch."

"Your daughter, what about me? I'm so tired of everything being about her. You know that's what sent me back to him, that little girl."

"Fuck you, Bethany. I hope you burn in your selfishness. Do me a favor. Go somewhere and die, we'd all be better off."

"Daddy?"

I look down at Bella and the sad, anxious look on her face breaks my heart. I try to reel my temper in. I shouldn't have said that.

"Oh God," Bethany slurs before a shrilling scream comes through the line.

"Bethany, Bethany," I yell into the phone.

I'm met by the sound of glass shattering and more screaming. My heart races. I have this burning sensation in my gut. I know something bad just happened. The look in Bella's eyes is one I don't think I will ever forget.

CHAPTER ELEVEN

Work Wife

Dante

Thanksgiving is a time to be grateful for what you have. To celebrate those you love. However, as my feet pound against this treadmill belt, I can only focus on my losses.

Do me a favor. Go somewhere and die, we'd all be better off.

Those will forever be the last words my daughter heard me say to her mother. Not, I love you. Not, I'm sorry we lost our way, let's fix this. Not, you took my breath away the first time we met.

I think I've hurt the one person I tried to protect in all of this. I gasp and push myself harder, trying to outrun my demons.

I should be happy. My family's secrets are safe. At least they are once we find this guy Bethany was fucking. We need to silence him. I can't have this hanging over our heads.

I focus my gaze on the mirror as my brothers and Jace appear in my gym. Pulling the earbuds from my ears first, I then hit the brake on the treadmill. I roll my neck as I come to a stop.

"Man, I'm so sorry," Dario says as he pulls me into a hug.

"Thanks. I'm okay."

"What happened?" Gio asks. "What are the police saying?"

"She was run off the road. A pickup slammed into the side of her truck and ran her into a ditch."

Gio pulls a hand down his face. "Wow, I hate to say it, but karma is a bitch. Do they have any leads?"

"No, but I need this to stay out of the media. Bethany's blood-alcohol level was twice the legal level for her to have been operating a vehicle. That's why I called you, Gio. See to it this stays away from the news."

"I'm on it. Tell me about this other driver. What do we know? Were they drunk too?"

"We would have to know who they were to know that. They were gone by the time the emergency responders arrived. The vehicle had no plates, and the VIN was removed. Unless they can lift some prints, there's no way to know who did this."

Gio nods. I wish I had something to give him to help find the person who did this. Maybe getting revenge for Bethany would lift some of this guilt I have.

I continue as I think of everything that happened that night. "They wanted to question Lizzy about my alibi until my phone records and Oliver cleared me. So you guys might want to make sure you're ready to be questioned. You know, since they'll be grasping at straws. The accident was around eleven, up in the hills, near her dad's."

"I was home with Carleen all night. We ordered Chinese around just before eleven, eleven thirty. Carleen got sick two minutes into eating, and I went next door to get Doctor Brown," Dario says.

I lift a brow. "She's staying with you, right?"

"Yeah, something happened with the contractor for her place, and she had to move out for a while. She's been with me for about a month now."

"How about you two?" I look to Gio and Jace.

"I had a doll party last night," Gio says.

"So, I guess that covers you both."

"No, I wasn't there," Jace says. "Well, not the entire time. I went out to eat with a friend. We joined Gio later. However, we were ticketed for public lewdness. We weren't anywhere near the site of the accident."

Gio looks at Jace and his jaw tenses. I don't have time to figure them out. I have all I need to know. My brothers had nothing to do with this.

"Let me know if there's anything I can do," Gio says after a beat.

"Actually, there is. There's another reason I called. Bethany was on a drunken rant before the collision. She said something about some guy she was fucking. She said she told him all about us. He was going to help her take us down or something. I need to know who he is and make sure whatever she told him is never breathed to a soul," I say tightly.

"I'll handle that," Gio says. "You need to focus on burying your wife and taking care of Bella."

I stumble a few steps and flop down on the weight bench. I blow out the breath I didn't notice I was holding. Bella, I haven't told her, her mommy isn't coming home ever again.

I had Oliver take her home after he dropped me at the station, it's why they questioned my alibi at first. Again, my last words to Bethany ring in my head.

Shit.

"What am I supposed to do? Bella has already been craving female attention. This will be devastating for her."

"Will it?" Gio lifts a brow at me.

"I don't know. Lately, she's seemed to be more and more afraid of Bethany. Thank God for Lizzy. Bella seems to smile the most when she's around."

"And there's your answer. Hire Lizzy as your live-in PA, promote her. She's been running your life like your office wife for three years now, whether you realize it or not."

I blink a few times. Guilt consumes me. I was with Lizzy only seconds before answering Bethany's call. Maybe if I had been out looking for my wife, she'd still be breathing. At least, then my daughter wouldn't see me as the monster who told her mother to go die. A monster I never wanted her to see.

"That's a complicated relationship. I don't want to confuse Bella. There's already so much on her little shoulders," I say.

"You mean you want to fuck Lizzy," Dario says.

"Is your dick still leaking for your best friend? Don't judge me until you've finally gotten that nut out of the way."

Dario gives me a smug smile. "Again, it's only complicated because you want to fuck her. I said what I said, asshole."

"About time," Gio croons and slaps Dario on the back. "You two deserve to be together."

"I didn't say we're together. I leave for Italy after the New Year. Nothing has changed."

The smile falls from Gio's face. He looks to Jace and gives a subtle nod. I would have missed it if I weren't paying attention. Gio narrows his eyes on me when he sees me staring at him.

"Promote Lizzy. It will work out in the end. Bella is attached. Lizzy cares about her. You can trust her. I promise you that. Lizzy will always protect Bella with her life. It's who she is," he says in that big brother tone that tells me his word is final.

"Her nose is always in a book. She has a business to run. She can't drop her life for mine."

"It's already done, Dante. Promote her or I will."

"This is my daughter, my life, Gio. I have to think about her feelings and what's best for her. Lizzy already told me her business is more important to her. She won't want the job." I stand and shout.

Gio gets in my face and looks into my eyes. His chest heaves. He cracks his knuckles at his sides.

"When have I ever led you wrong? When have I ever not been ten steps ahead in life? I see what you all don't. My niece is my top priority. Get over your bullshit. This is the right thing to do. I have you covered. Lizzy's life will work out to fit yours. It's already done."

With that, he turns and leaves. Dario tosses a thumb toward an exiting Gio and Jace.

"And *Nonno* wants me," he snorts, then turns to leave me with my thoughts.

CHAPTER TWELVE

Crushed

Dante

"Daddy, are we going to Grandpa's for Thanksgiving dinner?" Bella asks with her big hazel eyes trained on me.

"No, sweetheart. I don't believe we are. We need to have a talk."

She tilts her head to the side as she watches me take the seat beside her on her bed. "Oh, I wanted him to see my new dress. Maybe I should save it for my next playdate with Lizzy. I can come to work with you next week to see her, right?"

"Well, princess. I don't know if that's going to be a great idea. A lot will be going on around the office, it might be better if you stay away for now."

"But...does that mean I can invite Lizzy here? She can come when Mommy goes out, so Mommy doesn't get mad again."

"Bella, that's what I need to talk to you about."

I pull her into my lap and embrace her tightly. I swallow hard, trying to find the right words. No matter what, I'm about to change her world forever.

I kiss the top of her head. It smells like the coca butter Bethany used to use. I close my eyes and try to think of happier times. I picture the fresh-faced Bethany who ran up to introduce herself to me in high school.

She was gorgeous. Her face was hers, no shoots, no surgery. I loved the glow on her brown skin. It was a week later when my father introduced me to Bethany and her parents at dinner. I thought it was destiny. I was in love.

I now regret my stupidity. I should have seen so much. "Daddy?" Bella cups my face, bringing my attention back to her.

"I love you, Daddy. I'll be good, so Mommy will stop being so mad at us. I promise."

I grit my teeth. "You have never been a bad girl. Your mother wasn't mad at you. She was upset with Daddy. Princess, I'm so sorry, Mommy's not coming back. She was hurt and had to go with the angels to live with them. It's now just you and me."

"Oh…" She pauses and I can see her thinking. I hold my breath. "Like Ralphie?"

Ralphie was my and my brother's hound. He died two years ago. It was the first time I had to explain death to my little girl. She cried for about two weeks.

"Yes, like Ralphie."

Her eyes become sad and she looks down into her lap. "You won't go with the angels, will you? I don't want you to leave me."

I tighten my embrace on her. "Baby, no, I'm not going anywhere. I plan to be in your life for a very, very long time."

"That's good. What about Lizzy? Is she going away too?"

"No, not if I can help it. I think we need her."

"Yeah, I think so too. She's magic. When she's around, everything is better. She makes me happy."

Damnit, Gio.

I kiss Bella's forehead. "And that's all I want."

CHAPTER THIRTEEN

What Did I Miss

Lizzy

I never thought I would say I'm happy to be back at work. Nyla insisted I unplug during the small break. No phone, no social media, no TV. The only thing I was allowed to do was read and game a bit. Not that I would have done much of anything else.

However, I wanted to get out of the house. I love my family, but I have my limits. Listening to Dad's dry-ass jokes can only last but for so long before you're ready to put a gun to your head and pray for forgiveness.

I step off the elevator at work with a sigh. Finally, a place where I can be quiet and fade into the background. I think that's why I love it here. I can come out of my shell when I want to, but it doesn't have to be often because I'm not always needed.

"Hey, Lizzy. I wasn't expecting to see you here today," one of the interns says. Peter, that's his name.

"Why not?"

"Well, for starters, I saw your position pinned to the board. I thought your channel blew up during the vacation and you were finally leaving us commoners behind."

I cringe at his acknowledgment of my channel. I'm not embarrassed by my following. However, I'm still getting used to people recognizing me.

I remember when it was only Nyla and I playing for hours. I had been doing what I love. I wasn't ready for the fame that came along with it.

"Wait, my position has been posted? That must be some type of mistake," I say, opening my emails to see if I was fired or something and missed it.

Surely not, Gio would have called me himself. Dante may be my boss for all outward appearances. However, Gio is my real boss. My directives come from him. All my promotions in the company over the years have come from him.

There have only been two before I was placed as Dante's third assistant. While I was honest with Dante about why I wouldn't want to apply for a promotion, the real reason is that Gio hasn't told me to do so.

Suddenly Gio's words come back to me. *Everything is about to change. Now is when I need you.*

Peter reaches to scratch the back of his neck. "Well, I sort of brushed up my resume and was going to apply. I think it would be pretty cool to tell my friends I took over Izzy Gunz old job and I get to sit in her seat every day."

I can't help gawking at him. No way he's serious. My phone vibrates in my hand, pulling my attention.

It's Gio. I start to freak out. He wants me to meet him in his office.

"Do you have plans for the Christmas holiday? I can't imagine things are going to be too festive around here."

I look up at Peter with my brows drawn. He tends to ramble a lot, and most times, I zone out. I try really hard not to do that to people, but sometimes I give up. Peter is one of those people

I've given up on. He takes too long to make a point and he's honestly weirder than I am.

"Why wouldn't things be festive around here?"

His eyes widen and he looks at me as if I'm crazy. He goes to lean in. On instinct, I draw back and clench my fist.

He purses his lips but starts to whisper anyway. "Wow, you must have been gaming the entire break. I know you zone out. I guess that's why you're so good. So, I guess you didn't hear about the boss's wife?"

"No, what about her?"

"For some reason, they're keeping it hush-hush, but she was killed over the holiday. Someone ran her car off the road. When I saw your position was vacant, I thought you were quitting because of your channel, if not, then because of the scandal."

"Scandal? What scandal?"

"They don't know who ran her off the road. Why keep something like that quiet? I say something fishy is going on."

"You don't know that. You can't just go around damaging people's names for gossip."

Peter throws his hands in the air. "Hey, I'm only sharing what I heard. I meant nothing by it," he says.

"Well, brush your resume up for a new job, not a promotion if you're going to spread speculations. A part of the job is discretion."

"Izzy—" I glare at him. I don't care if he knows my alter ego from my channel. At work, I'm Lizzy. I haven't made friends with anyone here to make them comfortable enough to call me Izzy.

"I'm sorry. Lizzy. I meant no harm. You didn't know, so I thought I was sharing something you needed to know."

"It is my job to know Mr. Di Lorenzo's schedule. Nothing more, nothing less."

"I hope this doesn't keep me from getting hired full-time. I…I also sort of wanted to ask you out sometime. Me and my big mouth."

"I don't date coworkers. And as I'm only the schedule keeper, I have nothing to do with hiring. If you don't mind, I need to find out *if* I even work here anymore."

I march off without taking a glance back. I shouldn't have been so short with Peter, but my heart is breaking for Bella. Her mother was taken from her. The poor little thing has been so starved for attention from her mom, now she will never get it.

I pause outside of Gio's office and swipe at the tears that slide down my cheeks. I take a calming breath before I tap at the door. A muffled voice comes through the barrier.

I turn the knob and stick my head in. Gio sits behind his desk. I peek in farther and find Jace. He gives me a nod.

"Come on in, Lizzy," Gio says as he flips through papers on his desk.

"Did you fire me?"

"No." Gio chuckles. "My brother wants to promote you. Current circumstances will call for a new type of assistant. A position I can't fill for him myself. We both thought you would be the best fit."

"Fit for what exactly?"

"Dante will need a live-in, traveling, executive assistant who can help balance his office life and help with Bella as she adjusts to the changes."

"A nanny? Doesn't she already have a few of those?"

"Yes, she does, but none of them have your skills. You probably haven't heard, but Bethany was murdered. We don't know by who. My brother now has to worry about the safety of his family. You're the best choice for this."

"So, he knows about me?"

"No, I've continued to omit this fact. He knows I trust you and that I feel Bella will be safe and cared for around you."

He steeples his fingers in front of his mouth and sits back in his chair. I roll my shoulders. It's always been understood that I would be activated in Dante's life. However, I've never known what for or why.

"Are you sure he will be okay with who I am when he finds out?"

"He will have to be. Honestly, the only reason he hasn't figured it out already is because he's been under so much emotional stress."

I snort. "And because I look nothing like what I am. Why me, Gio? Why not Nyla or one of your own?"

"I know every one of my dolls for who they are and what they are capable of. I didn't possess a doll fit for Dante before you. You have come to know me. You know I have a plan for my plans. You're perfect for my plans concerning Dante and Bella. This situation only makes everything more convenient."

I sag my shoulders. I knew this was coming, so why am I so... I can't explain it.

"Have a seat. I need to know how we make this convenient for you. What do you need to keep your business running and to fulfill your contract? I'm a man of my word. You will have both. I know the sacrifices made to do this for me."

I lick my dry lips. I'm going to be living with Dante. We should start with a chastity belt or at least a vibrator and a lifetime supply of batteries.

I shake that thought away. Nothing has changed, he's my charge, therefore, he's off-limits. Not to mention, the man is grieving and has his little girl to worry about.

"I need a space to game. I'll need a rig to play and record. You've seen my setup.

"Someplace to keep my products for when I need to push them live. I game at night, that has to be okay. If I'm going to travel, I need to be able to create content on the go. Lighting, cams everything to keep up to standards with my channel's quality of content. You make that happen, I can do what you ask."

"It's already done. Keep Dante and Bella safe and happy and you'll have a friend for life. Anything you want, Izzy, ask and it's yours."

"But I have to keep my mouth shut about who and what I am?"

"This should always be implied and understood," Jace says from the couch.

I turn to look at him. He never speaks. Given that he has chosen to now drives home how important it is for Dante to never know who I truly am.

"Got it."

"Would you like to help us pick your replacement?" Gio says and lifts a brow.

"Definitely not Peter." And then it hits me. A smile comes to my lips. "They will work closely with you, like I did, right?"

Gio narrows his eyes, but nods.

"I think I know the perfect person."

Jace chuckles. I turn to look at him and catch a smile on his lips. Yup, I have the perfect replacement. It will benefit us all.

CHAPTER FOURTEEN

Cruel Women

Dante

"What is it you wanted to talk to me about?" Gio asks as he takes the seat in front of my desk.

"Do you trust Lizzy? I mean, in terms of our family. The truth."

Gio tilts his head to the side. "I thought I made myself clear. Why are you stalling? You should have announced her promotion and given her the details of her new position by now."

I rub my hands up and down my face. "I'm moving her into my home. With my daughter. I need to know this is the right thing to do. I just buried my wife. Forgive me if this wasn't on my list of priorities."

He bares his teeth at me. "Do I trust her? I do. You know she wouldn't be this close if I didn't. It's the right thing to do, Dante. Go out there and call her in for the promotion."

"I will, but not for the promotion. Just to talk, this needs to be something she wants to do. She'll be dealing with Bella. She has to want this. I can't have Bella thinking she's responsible for another adult's unhappiness."

"Do what you feel you must, Dante. I assure you, she will take the promotion. I hired her for a few reasons. She'll be a great addition to your travel team and executive staff. Bella is already important to her."

I wrinkle my brows. Nothing is ever as it seems with my brother. I go to zone in on his words, but my phone grabs my attention. I hold a finger up to let Gio know I need a second.

I open the text message from the unknown number to find a picture of my dead wife. She's in the arms of another man. His back is to the camera, so I can't make out his face. However, I know it's Bethany because of the clothing. I remember the day she wore the outfit as if it were yesterday.

I scroll to the next picture, and this time I still can't see the man's face, but I can look right into Bethany's eyes. I bring the photo into focus, trying to get a better look at the man.

This has to be the guy we need to silence. I need to know who he is. And why is someone sending this to me now? Could this be her killer?

"What? What is it?" Gio says.

I toss the phone across the desk. He catches the phone and looks down at it. I don't know if I want to toss this desk or sag in relief that we have a lead, at least.

She hasn't been in the ground for four full days and Bethany is still fucking with my life from the grave. It's like I was never meant to be happy.

"Don't worry about this. I told you, I'll take care of it."

"Should I feel this numb? Why do the women in our lives want to hurt us so much? First Mom, now Bethany. I don't think I want to get into another relationship. My life can't take it."

"Listen to me. You're right. Life has been fucked up for us. We got the short end of the stick. However, there're always the demons playing in the background. You don't know who they are, but they are there. Don't allow them to win. You deserve to be happy, not bitter. Let the past go. Good things are coming your way, Dante. I promise, little brother. If it takes my last breath, this I promise you."

In the back of my mind, I know I should ask my brother more questions. Why is he so sure of his words? What does he know that I don't?

However, the sad look on my daughter's face pops into my head and the last words I spoke to my wife, who was about to die, play in my head. Happiness isn't meant for me.

All I can do is nod. I will never allow another woman to get close to me, for Bella's sake. I'll swear off the opposite sex. They're all evil and aim to tear out my heart.

CHAPTER FIFTEEN

Point Made

Dante

I sit in my office looking into the eyes of the detective who's leading the investigation into Bethany's murder. He looks as if this is the greatest inconvenience he has ever had.

"There are no leads, no prints, nothing. I think we're looking at a lost cause. A part of me wonders if your wife drove out in front of them in her drunken state and caused the accident. Maybe they freaked and ran after," he says dryly.

Right, because some random person was driving around with no plates and a scraped VIN. I bite back my frustration. They've been dismissing this case because of Bethany's alcohol levels. I know she shouldn't have been driving under the influence, but that doesn't mean she doesn't deserve justice.

"Well, thank you for coming to get us up to speed," Gio says as he pats me on the back from where he stands beside me.

The detective nods. "Sure, no problem. You folks have a happy holiday. Oh, and Mr. Di Lorenzo. I'd keep an eye open, maybe get some security for your little girl, we still don't know why your wife was targeted. A wealthy man like yourself, I'm sure you have some enemies you might not be thinking of.

"I know what you guys told my partner. You can't think of anyone, but this came from somewhere and they were smart, so I'd say to watch your ass."

He gives me a stern, knowing look. I have to wonder if he's on the payroll and is taking the chance to give me a real warning or if he's talking out of his ass.

I wait until he leaves and look up at Gio. He shrugs and rounds the desk to take the seat the detective had been in. My mind races. Could this be connected to the family? Is Bella in danger?

"Relax. I would never allow harm to come to Bella. You know you're always guarded. I'm not worried about this. However, I'm questioning why Lizzy hasn't moved into your place and why she's still sitting at my new hire's desk?"

"I'm not ready," I mutter.

"Ready for what?"

"It's only been a week since the funeral."

"You have a trip coming up. You need to make the transition soon. The holidays are here and if she's settled in the house, it may lessen the blow for Bella."

"The trip isn't until after the New Year. I have time. I'll have Bella so busy with Christmas gifts, hopefully she won't notice Beth isn't there."

He glares at me and tucks his phone into his suit pocket after finishing a text. "All bullshit and you know it."

He crosses his leg over his knee and sits back. I lift a brow. He's making himself pretty comfortable.

I don't know why. He was only here for moral support while I spoke with the police. A knock comes at my office door.

I frown. No one should be knocking unless it's one of my assistants with paperwork for me. Michelle is supposed to be on a break.

"Come in," I call.

The door inches open and Lizzy pops her head in. I look to Gio to see a grin on his lips. Before I can speak, he beckons Lizzy in with two fingers.

"Come, have a seat, Lizzy. My brother has been so busy in his grief he has forgotten to have an important conversation with you."

"Gio," I growl.

"No worries, Dante. As your executive assistant, I'm on top of this. I have it all handled."

Lizzy pushes her glasses up her nose and ambles over to the seat next to Gio. She sits and looks at me expectantly. I clench my teeth tightly. I'm going to kill Gio.

"Wait, maybe I need to handle this too. Lizzy, how soon can you move into Dante's estate? I've secured a room on the first floor for your gaming studio.

"Your rig is set up and waiting. I had built-ins put in for your merch. The lighting was designed just for you, I hope it's to your liking.

"It's out of the way, so you don't wake Dante or Bella when you're recording, and they won't disturb you either. Your bedroom, however, will be next to Bella's."

"That's next door to mine," I grunt.

"Yes, I'm aware. However, now that Bella will be relying on Lizzy as well as you, I thought it best to place Lizzy in the room between the two of you," Gio says with a smug smile.

"I can move in as soon as I call the movers. It will depend on how soon they can get my things there, but if you need me sooner, I can take the things I'll need for now," Lizzy says, looking between the both of us.

"You're sure about this? Bella needs to come first. There's travel involved. I plan to bring her along with me for a while."

"I'm ready to do my part. How is she? This must be so hard for her, for both of you."

"She's doing as best as can be expected."

"You can have the rest of the day off to oversee the move of your things," Gio says as he taps his phone against his knee. "They'll be there around three."

Lizzy pulls her phone from her pocket and frowns. "That gives me four hours. Okay, I can make do with that."

"Gio, don't you think you're moving a bit fast? I haven't mentioned this to Bella. Slow down. Allow me to think."

He snorts. "I tried that."

Just then, another tap comes at my office door. It opens and Jace comes through the door with a sad-looking Bella in his arms. She has her head against his shoulder. When Jace steps all the way into the office, he taps Bella on her back and nods toward Lizzy.

Bella lifts her head and her entire face lights up. She jumps from Jace's arms as he lowers to place her on her feet. Like a bullet, she runs for Lizzy and hops into her lap. Her arms are around Lizzy's neck just as fast. Lizzy hugs her back and I swear I see the moment my little girl's body relaxes.

"I missed you. I need my best friend so much," Bella says, breaking my heart.

I look at Gio and nod. He's right. He gives me a stern look but nods back, standing to leave with Jace.

"If you don't mind, I can take her with me. I only have to instruct the movers. I've been packed for days."

I rub the back of my neck. Yeah, Gio is always a step ahead. One of these days, I'll learn. However, has he taken into consideration how attracted I am to this woman?

Why would he have to? You're not going to pursue her. Women are the devil. You're done with them.

"This is a fact," I mutter.

"Excuse me?"

"Nothing, it's fine if she goes with you. Just make sure one of my guards joins you. Gio will tell you who to take. Thank you, Lizzy."

"You're welcome, Mr. Di Lorenzo."

I go to correct her and tell her to call me Dante but change my mind. I need the formality to remind me she's off-limits.

Lizzy

"Dad, stop feeding her ice cream. You're going to give her a tummy ache. She needs to eat some real food. Are you trying to get me fired on my first day?"

"Sorry, honey. You and your sister ate ice cream for like a month after…"

There's a pang in my heart as his words trail off. After my parents were killed. I can't believe Bella has learned that pain. No one should know what this feels like.

I see she's not the same little girl I once knew. Something like this changes you forever. Yeah, I never liked the woman, but I wouldn't wish death on her. Not really.

"Thank you, Mr. E," Bella sings happily. "This ice cream is melting my sads away. It and my best friend Lizzy moving in to play with me."

She gasps and her eyes get big. "We can have sleepovers in my room, and we can do each other's hair. I can paint your nails. Daddy lets me paint his but never with color. Sometimes Uncle Jace and Uncle Gio will let me do theirs black.

"We're going to have so much fun. You never yell at me. Not like…"

My dad shows how he earned the title of best father ever. He rounds the counter and runs a hand over Bella's hair.

"I'm going to need some of that ice cream too. You're taking my buddy with you. Lizzy will do all of that and teach you to play games. Whenever you're sad, you look for her. She's magic when it comes to healing feelings. Just you wait," he says and looks at me with a wink.

Thanks, I mouth.

Bella's smile has returned and she's back to eating her ice cream. She looks up thoughtfully.

"Don't worry. I won't be selfish. I'll bring her back to visit. Then you'll have someone to eat ice cream with," she says with her adorable smile.

Dad laughs.

"I think that's more for you than my dad," I tease.

"Sounds like a win-win to me. So, you all set?"

"Yeah, I think so."

Dad nods. "I'll drop your car off in the morning. Your aunt wanted to leave you a gift before you take it."

I grin. Aunt Denise's gifts always pack a powerful punch. I'm not complaining. My phone rings, pulling my attention.

"Hold on, Dad, this is my boss." I pick up, knowing Dante is probably concerned about Bella. "Hello."

"Hi, Lizzy. I'm pulling into the house now. I don't see the truck. Is everything okay?"

"Yes, my Dad has cooked dinner for us. The movers are packing up the last of my things now. He can pack dinner to go, and we'll follow the truck out."

"Can I speak to Bella?"

"Sure, one sec."

I hand Bella the phone. She takes it from me like a little lady. I lift a brow and stifle a laugh when she places the phone on speaker and holds it in front of her mouth. "Hello, Daddy?"

"Hey, sweetheart. How are you?"

"I'm having such a good time with Lizzy and Mr. E. Mr. E helped me with my sads. We have to get him something nice for Christmas. I'm taking his Lizzy with me. Now he's going to have the sads."

"We'll find him something nice. I promise."

Bella gasps and her eyes brighten. "Oh my goodness, Daddy. We have to go shopping. I need to get a gift for Lizzy too. How many sleeps do I have? Is there time?"

"We have time." Dante chuckles.

"Okay, listen. I want to eat the food Mr. E made. I'll talk to you when we get home. You want to talk to Lizzy again?"

Dad and I cover our mouths as Bella dismisses her father. This girl is too adorable. I take the phone off speaker and bring it to my ear.

Dante's warm chuckle greets my ear. I'd be lying if I said my belly doesn't drop. I remind myself I need to give Jacob a call or text. If I'm going to be living with Dante, I need to have some type of social life with a male outside of work, or I might rub my clit raw.

"I guess that's settled. You guys go ahead and eat. I'll handle the truck when it arrives. Gio, Jace, and Dario plan to stop by to help me wrap gifts. We all suck at it, but I figured we might figure it out as a team." He snorts.

"Or...you can leave it for me. I don't mind. I love gift wrapping."

He's silent for a second. I chew on my lip, hoping I haven't overstepped. I don't know if maybe that was Bethany's thing. Not that I believe she would have chanced a paper cut that didn't come from spending cash.

"I might take you up on that offer. We can work on the bike and dollhouse instead. Thank you, Lizzy."

"Please stop thanking me. These are things I want to do."

"I'm going to have to get used to that. You and Bella have fun. Ride safely. See you when you get home."

"See you, boss."

CHAPTER SIXTEEN

Failure

Dante

"Daddy, we're home." Bella's little voice sings through the house.

I rub the back of my neck as I look around Lizzy's new studio. Gio and Jace helped me open and sort out the boxes she had so well labeled. I didn't want to go through her things, but Gio was right. She'd probably be exhausted by the time she arrives, and I want her to feel at home as soon as possible.

Home.

I didn't miss how she threw out there that I'm her boss when I mentioned this place as home. I wonder if she's thinking the same way I am. We need to keep this professional. I'm now a widower and she's my live-in PA.

Besides, I'm unlucky in love. Wait, I don't even know if I've ever known love. I haven't cried once since Bethany's death. I wonder if I'm emotionally closed off altogether. It would make sense to the man I have become.

"Daddy," Bella squeals as she jumps in my arms. "Wow, is this Lizzy's new room?"

"One of," I say and kiss Bella's cheek.

"Wow, can I come in here with you sometimes, Lizzy?"

"Now, Bella. Lizzy needs to work when she comes in here. We can't bother her. She'll be on camera talking to her gaming friends."

"It's cool. She's welcome to come in when I'm not recording. Sometimes, I just game for pleasure." Lizzy pushes her glasses up her nose and gives me a small smile.

"As long as you ask first, Bella. I don't want you to disturb Lizzy. I promised this would be her room to have time to herself."

"Okay, I'll stay out."

"He said you have to ask first, not stay out. I don't want my best friend thinking we can't hang out," Lizzy says and taps Bella on the nose.

"Daddy, we have to be good hosts and give Lizzy the rest of the tour of the house." Bella yawns. "Can she help me with my pajamas and read my bedtime story tonight?"

I make a sad face at her. "But those are my jobs. What's your daddy supposed to do?"

Bella giggles. "You can help her this time. To show her where my things are, but she'll need to know for when you work late. Lizzy said she'll be your work helper, but she's here for me too."

Gio chuckles. "I think that's my cue. The real boss has arrived."

He and Jace start for the door. "What about what you guys came to help me with?"

"You said Lizzy offered to help. We're all thumbs when it comes to that stuff. Lizzy's got this."

"Whatever," I mutter.

"Call you in the morning. Don't make her quit on the first night." Gio winks.

I roll my eyes. Gio can be a dick. From the look on my daughter's face, I'd have to keep one eye open when I sleep if I made Lizzy quit. Bella eyes me warily after her uncle's words. I kiss her cheek and tickle her.

"Come on, I'll show you to your room and then I'll show you Bella's nighttime routine. We left your personal things for you to unpack. I hope you don't mind us taking care of this room for you," I say and hold my breath.

I mentally chide myself for being so tense as I wait for her answer. Lizzy gives me a bright smile as she looks around the room.

"Honestly, I wasn't looking forward to unpacking this room. You guys did a great job. I love the shelves."

"That was all Gio. He had guys in here all week to get this room ready."

"Thank you. This all must be an inconvenience to you. I plan to stick to weekend content, so I'm focused on the weekdays."

"We can work on scheduling as we go. Bella does have nannies on staff already. I'll need you more for travel and for when she needs…" I pause and look down to find Bella knocked out in my arms. I can speak more freely. "For when she needs someone to connect with. You know, when this all gets hard for her."

"I understand. After my parents…you know. Dad says I whimpered for months when it kicked in they weren't coming back, but that took a few months to set in. I'll be here when she needs me."

I nod and grunt. I can only hope things don't get that tough for Bella.

I curse as I look down at the wrapping paper and the gift I'm trying to wrap. Once we got Bella in her pj's and put her to bed, I allowed Lizzy to go get settled. I thought I'd try to wrap some of these gifts on my own.

These shits look horrible. Bethany used to get things wrapped at the store. I think she even hired a professional gift wrapper one year.

"Fuck," I grunt as I fail at ripping off a piece of tape and getting it on the wrapping paper to keep the ends closed.

I lift my head as snickers float my way. I look up to find Lizzy in a pair of yellow-and-white knee-high socks and tiny yellow runner shorts. Her tight T-shirt has a doll's face on the front. The eyes on the face of the doll are buttons and her mouth is sewn shut.

I have to tear my eyes away. Lizzy is about five-ten, maybe a little bit taller. In all that length is a curvy body that would make you sell your own body parts to have a single taste.

I try to look anywhere but at her. I mean, I can see this woman's ass from the front. What has my brother gotten me into?

"I texted Gio to find out where you were hiding the gifts so I could get them done for you. He sent me here," she says.

"Thanks, but if you want to go game, you can go ahead. This can wait. It's late."

I hate that my voice comes out so husky. I clear my throat and roll my shoulders.

I want to tell her not to walk her ass around my house like this, but she's doing me a favor. Not to mention, I take note of her ogling me shirtless, in sweats. Sweats that aren't doing shit to hide how stiff she has me at the moment.

"I don't sleep well. I'll be up most the night. I don't mind getting that handled for you."

"Oh, okay. Have you always had trouble sleeping?"

"Yeah. I used to fear Elijah and Nyla would disappear if I went to sleep. The insomnia kind of stuck with me through the years."

"Fuck." I run a hand through my hair. "That's tough."

She shrugs before walking over to me and the unwrapped gifts surrounding me. I stifle a groan as my gaze locks in on her thick thighs rubbing against each other as she walks and the fat pussy print between them. I have to remind myself lust doesn't equate to love, and since I have a daughter to think about, I can't afford lust because Bella needs love.

Lizzy looks at the gifts I tried to do on my own and shakes her head before she laughs. She's extremely pretty when she laughs.

Her wild curls dance around her face as she does. Those full lips call out their own siren song.

Fuck, Dante, get it together.

"You know. I might just fire you on your first night if you keep laughing," I tease.

She rolls her lips and mocks locking them shut before she throws away the key. I ball up a piece of wrapping paper and toss it at her.

"Are you going to show me how to do this or not?"

She lifts a brow. "I thought I was going to work on this alone."

"I want to feel like I'm a part of more than paying for the gifts. You know? I want to make this Christmas special for her."

She nods. "I get it. No problem. Welcome to Christmas Gift Wrapping 101."

"You're a lifesaver. Now, if you tell me you know how to put that bike and dollhouse together, I'm giving you a raise."

"Is my dad an engineer? You go ahead and call HR. We'll have that bike and dollhouse done by morning."

"Thank God, I swear the instructions for neither are in English."

She releases another of those gorgeous laughs. I find myself chuckling a little. Her laughter is infectious. Over the next few hours, I find myself wiping at my eyes a few times as she makes silly jokes and laughs at herself.

"What got you into gaming?" I ask when we have a brief moment of silence.

She looks up as if I've pulled her from her thoughts. "Nyla got me started. I've always wanted to be like my big sister. One day she was playing with a friend. When he left, I sat next to her and picked up the controller. I've been hooked since."

"I'm guessing you two are close?"

"We are. Same as you and your brothers, I think it's safe to say."

"My mother's father made sure of that. That we all looked out for each other. Watched each other's backs. I wanted that for

Bella. You know? Someone to watch her back and for her to watch theirs."

"You're attractive and Bella is amazing. You can totally still find someone who will fall in love with you both and expand your family."

All of the Italian in me raises up. "Fuck outta here." I catch myself after the words are out of my mouth. I look away, chiding myself for the harsh response. Lizzy has been nothing but nice to me.

"Aww, come on. There's someone for you. As long as you don't try to wrap gifts for her."

Her laughter pulls my gaze back to her face. She has a heartwarming smile in place. Not the scowl I thought she'd have from my harsh words and harsher tone. For the first time, I notice she has an adorable dimple in her right cheek. Suddenly, the bands around my heart start to loosen and one falls away.

CHAPTER SEVENTEEN

For Me

Dante

"So, how has it been living with Lizzy?" Dario asks as he sips from his coffee cup.

"Remember that time we ran into the shed back at Nonno's in Italy?"

"The time you stepped on that nail?"

"Yes, that would be the time. It feels sort of like that."

Dario winces. "Dude, they had so much trouble getting that thing out. I thought you were a goner, or at least the foot was."

"I've never known pain like that in my life. Nonno wouldn't let me cry either."

"No, but you got your first taste of whiskey. I was so jealous. Anyway, back to your PA. You're telling me, living with her"— he points in Lizzy's direction—"equates to the greatest pain you have ever known. How?"

"How did I not realize how gorgeous she is before I hired her to live with me? I mean, sure, I was aware that she is attractive, but I don't remember her tits being that perky and her smile being so breathtaking."

"So, what's the problem?"

"Women aren't for me. My poor choices affect Bella. At the moment, Lizzy is Bella's anchor. She's more off-limits than any woman there is," I say.

Dario grunts. "After the level of fucked up my life is, I'm going to mind my business."

"What does that mean? Where's Carleen?"

My brother pulls a hand down his face. "We had a fight. Don't ask me what about. I still don't know."

"What? You guys never fight."

"Tell me about it. I never should have read her diary and I sure as hell shouldn't have given her that wish."

"What wish?"

"Long story, bro. I sort of—"

"Daddy, Uncle Dario. Let's go. It's time to open up presents."

"We're coming, munchkin," Dario croons. "I can't deny Bella seems happier. How about you? How are you holding up?"

"I'm fine."

Dario heaves a breath. "I know we've been taught to hold our feelings in, but I see this shit eating at you. If you're not going to deal with it by releasing some sexual tension, find something. Bella needs you as much as a substitute mother."

My twin's words burn right through my chest. A substitute mother? Is that what I've done?

I'm not sure how I feel about that idea. No, I haven't dealt with my emotions or grief. All in one night, I found out my wife was cheating on me and she was then murdered. We couldn't even have an open casket.

A week after burying my wife, I had to move in a live-in PA. Lizzy and Nyla have been questioned as suspects. Apparently, someone told the police about the altercation at the restaurant during the Thanksgiving dinner.

They were both cleared, but there are still no real leads as to who could have done this. I don't have time to fall apart about my losses. Day by day, my focus has been on Bella's happiness. She's my priority.

I walk into the sitting room where the tree and gifts are. Gio sits in my throne chair, looking as if he's the king of my house. I shake my head and go to take a seat in front of the tree on the floor next to Bella.

I laugh to myself when I notice Bella has her mass of curls pulled up on top of her head the same way Lizzy does. They're in the matching pajamas Bella insisted I buy for them as we shopped for Lizzy's gift.

I can't help but wonder who's idea the hairstyle was. Most likely Bella's. I decide in this moment I'm doing the right thing. I'm going to ignore my assistant and treat her like any other employee.

Besides, it's too soon for me to get involved with anyone. The last thing I need is to create motive, so the police turn their attention back our way.

"Merry Christmas," Lizzy says with that bright smile.

"Merry Christmas," I murmur.

"Who is this one from? That's my name, it's for me," Bella says as she places a gift between herself and Lizzy.

"It's from your Uncle Gio."

"Thank you, Uncle G," Bella sings as she tears away the paper.

"You're more than welcome, princess."

Bella gasps and squeals as she gets the box open. I look between Gio and Lizzy. I honestly don't think we need to bother with the rest of the gifts.

"It's almost exactly like mine. Your Uncle asked me to see if the Book Court would honor you with a gown and crown of your own. As Book Queen, I didn't see why not," Lizzy says.

The little dress looks just like the one Lizzy wore for Halloween. The only difference is the tulle skirt. I look to my brother and give him a nod of gratitude. In a single gift he has made my daughter's day.

Gio has a habit of doing that. Making things better even when you don't know you need him to or how you need him to. I look to Lizzy because I have no idea when she had time to do this.

Thank you, I mouth.

She gives me that gorgeous smile, and those bands around my heart loosen just a bit more, and another breaks and falls away.

Lizzy

I know Dante wanted this to be a great Christmas for Bella to distract her from her mother not being here. I'd say mission accomplished. Bella has been all smiles this morning as she has opened present after present.

I love how Bella's happiness is so important to all four of these men. Her uncles love her as much as her father does. I've wished for family connected to my mom and dad a million times throughout my life. Not that Dad and Aunt Denise haven't been great to us.

How can I explain it? I've never felt connected to anyone other than my sister. There's nothing like blood. I look up at Dante and his brothers as they tease and rib each other.

Dante looks up as I lock eyes on him. He gives a small smile. It's the first I've seen in weeks other than the ones he gives Bella. He moves away from the group and retakes his seat beside Bella.

"Can we give her our gift now?" Bella asks.

"Yes, go ahead."

Bella grabs one of the few gifts left. Her excitement is so adorable. She turns and hands me the small box.

"You guys really didn't have to," I say.

"I think we did. Go on, open it. Bella picked it herself."

I open the box and smile so hard my face hurts. Inside is a charm bracelet with books and crowns hanging from it. I look closer and notice the crowns all have different color stones set in each, making the bracelet sparkle in the light. I clench the bracelet to my chest.

"I love it. Thank you so much."

"See, Daddy. I told you." Bella leaps to throw her arms around my neck.

I hug her close with one arm as I hold tight to the bracelet in my other hand. I love her scent. It speaks to her innocence and sweet personality. She smells of cocoa butter and strawberries. It's her shampoo and body cream. I have used both on her in the last week.

Dante clears his throat. "I...um...I have something for you too."

I release Bella as Dante places a box in front of me. I'm a little thrown off. I did get him something, but I didn't think he would get me a gift outside of what he planned to get me with Bella.

"I have one for you too. Hold on." I move to grab the box I wrapped for him.

I already gave Dario, Gio, and Jace the gifts I purchased for them. Dante takes the gift hesitantly. I'm a little nervous for him to open it.

"Should we open them together?"

"No, you first," I say.

He nods and opens his gift. I watch and hold my breath. He chuckles and looks up at me with suspiciously moist eyes once he has the box open.

"A race car track?" Gio says with amusement in his voice.

"It's the exact one you guys broke," Dante says after swallowing hard a time or two.

"The one mom got you before...how did you know about that?" Dario asks.

"I told her," Dante says.

"I know you're not eight anymore, but I just thought you would like it." I shrug.

"Thanks so much. This means a lot. Why don't you go ahead and open yours?"

I lift a brow at Dante. He returns it with a small grin. I lift the lid from the heavy box after I try to give it a shake.

I fight not to cry when I see the box full of books. I look up at Dante and blink a few times. Not only has he bought me books, but they are my wish list. I pick one up and inhale.

"Thank you. Thank you so much."

"I noticed you still have a blank shelf in your studio. I thought they would all look perfect there. You're welcome."

I stand to give him a hug. Dante stands and wraps me in his embrace. He smells so good. There's cologne that makes you do a double take and then there's cologne that makes you stop in your tracks and lick your lips. Dante's would be the latter with a side of melt off your panties.

Now these…these are the butterflies, the sparks, the tummy-warming sensations I've been searching for. Too bad they're for a man I can't have.

"Grandpa, *Nonno*, Uncle Lucas," Bella squeals.

I turn to see three older men enter the room. One with thick dark-brown hair and bright hazel eyes like the brothers. Another with salt-and-pepper hair and another with thick, jet-black hair. Bella runs into the arms of the man with the thick dark-brown hair. The other two men are loaded down with gifts.

To my surprise, they aren't the only new arrivals. I lift a brow just as the man with the dark-brown hair speaks.

"Gio, look who I found pacing outside of the front door. When I asked you about her, you said you didn't know where to find her. You wouldn't lie to your *nonno*, would you?"

I look to Gio to find him staring at Nyla with so much heat in his eyes I start to squirm. Jace places a hand on Gio's shoulder and leans in to whisper something to him.

"I wouldn't lie to you, *Nonno*. I didn't know her whereabouts when you asked. Ny, it's good to see you well and in person."

"Gio," she says sharply.

I'm so confused. Gio and Nyla saw each other about four or five weeks ago for sure, as far as I know. Nyla is scheduled to start as my replacement in the New Year. So, I know she went in for the interview. However, I keep my lips sealed. There's something going on here I know nothing about.

Gio turns his gaze to me and nods me over. I hesitate for a moment before my sister gives me a subtle nod. I move over to Gio's side and push my glasses up my nose.

"*Nonno*, have you met Dante's new personal assistant and Ny's little sister?" Gio says.

The older man turns his sharp eyes on me. They brighten and he moves across the room. I feel a little self-conscious as I stand in my pajamas Bella asked me to wear before asking for me to fix her hair like mine.

"You must be Liz. I've heard so much about you. You're the only weakness I know your sister to have," the man says.

"If you think so," Jace snorts under his breath beside me.

At this point, I have so many questions. Clearly, my sister knows this man. He has called us both by our family nicknames and he speaks with such endearment for my sister.

"I'm Grandpa Di Lorenzo, but you, my dear, can call me Giuseppe."

"He's my *nonno* G," Bella says proudly.

He places a hand on top of Bella's head. "Yes, I am. Did I miss you opening all your gifts?"

"No. I didn't open yours and Grandpa's."

Nonno G chuckles. "No, you haven't."

The other two men carry the gifts they're holding over to the tree. The salt-and-pepper–haired man comes over and looks at me with an appraising eye. I give him a nervous smile and he holds out his hand to me.

"I'm Frances Esposito, Dante's father."

"Yes, we've spoken on the phone before. I'm Lizzy M—"

"Hemmingway," Gio cuts me off.

I cover my shock quickly. I actually go by Manning. My father's name.

"Lizzy Marie Hemmingway," I say when Mr. Esposito looks at Gio questioningly.

"Lizzy Marie, what a beautiful name for a beautiful woman."

"It's actually Elizabeth Marie," Dante says.

I look to him with wide eyes. I didn't know he knew my real name. Again, I find myself smiling at him.

"Well, it's nice to finally put the face to the name," the last man with the jet-black hair says. "I'm Lucas. They call me Uncle Lucas. Bella talks so much about you. You're quite the star around here."

I look down at my feet. I don't feel like a star at the moment. Not with my sister looking like she's going to perform a full concert. Her hair is flawless, as is her makeup and sweater dress.

"Come on, Bella. Why don't we go change for the day and then you can come back and open the rest of your gifts," Dante says.

"Okay, Lizzy, will you help me put on my new dress?"

"Sure, sweetie. Come on."

I rush from the room, breathing a sigh of relief once outside of all the tension.

CHAPTER EIGHTEEN

Clean up

Dante

I stroll through the house to make sure all the lights are out. I notice the sound of movement in the sitting room and head that way. I turn the corner to find Lizzy in those damn shorts again.

This time a black pair with white trim. She is wearing a pair of those knee-high socks as well. This time she has on a pair of shell tops.

I bite my lip as she bends to pick up and rearrange a few of Bella's new toys. I fold my arms across my chest and take her in for a moment.

"You don't have to do that. The staff will handle it in the morning," I finally say.

She jumps and drops the jump rope she just picked up.

"Sorry, I didn't mean to scare you." I start to move farther into the room. "Come sit. It's been a long day."

I take a seat on the couch and pat the space beside me. She saunters over cautiously, her eyes roaming over my bare chest. The shy look that comes to her face makes me smile.

"I wanted to at least make it look neater, so the staff doesn't freak in the morning."

I nod. "I appreciate that. You've done more than enough for today. My grandfather took to you as much as Bella has. You have to be exhausted."

"He was nice. I didn't mind. He just wanted to talk."

"I appreciate it. I think I noticed today we can all be a demanding bunch. If my nonno didn't talk your ear off, I think my uncle was going to feed you to death." I chuckle.

She laughs. "And Gio and Dario planned to tease me until the ground opened and swallowed me up. We can't forget that."

I laugh louder. "You're officially family. We always wanted a sister."

"You know, I think that's why Gio and I clicked. He became like a big brother to me."

I pause to think on that. "I can see that. I wonder why he never introduced you to Nonno before today."

She snorts. "But my sister seems to know him pretty well."

"You caught that too?"

"Yeah, okay, so I'm going to ask because she won't say a word. Do you know what's going on with Nyla and Gio?"

"Haven't a clue. He treats her like one of his dolls but…" I stop to think of what the difference was that I picked up on. "Better, he treated her…I don't know it was different. I've never seen him like that."

"Okay, I'm not losing my mind. I was thinking the same thing."

"I can't blame him. You two are stunning women. Your parents had some stellar genes."

Her lips part and she looks at me with awe. I'm so tempted to lean in and kiss her soft-looking lips. She has to know how gorgeous she is.

She looks down into her lap. "I don't think your other grandfather likes me much. What's that about?"

I've noticed she changes topics when she's nervous. It's cute. However, once Papa Riccardo arrived, I did notice his attention to Lizzy and his seeming disapproval. I ignored it because I bump heads with the man naturally. We've never been close.

"Ignore him like I do."

"Bad blood?"

I shrug. "Believe it or not, he used to be Nonno Giuseppe's adviser."

She tilts her head at me. "You mean, his consigliere."

I grin and look at her through my lashes. "What don't you know about my family?"

She shrugs. "Gio and I are good friends. I know quite a few of his secrets." She narrows her eyes as if trying to see deeper into me. "I'm still learning about you."

"They were best friends and yes, he was his consigliere."

My phone rings in the pocket of my sweats. "Excuse me," I say as I pull the device out to check it.

It's my father-in-law. I bare my teeth, not wanting to deal with this conversation, but I guess it's just as well before I do something stupid.

"I need to take this," I say and stand.

Lizzy

I want to kick myself. I was in a trance the moment Dante said Nyla and I are stunning. Yeah, I think my sister is, but I wouldn't place myself on the same pedestal I put Ny on.

My phone buzzes, pulling my attention. I look down at it and see it's a text from Jacob. I smile and call instead of texting him back. I need to have a dose of reality.

"Hey, you."

"Merry Christmas, gorgeous."

Ugh, why doesn't it feel the same? My entire body hummed when Dante was sitting here.

"Hi, Jacob. Have you closed down for the night?"

"I'm locking up now. I wanted to catch you before you got on to game. How was your Christmas?"

"It was great. Bella was happy. That was the most important thing for me. I got to spend time with my sister as well."

"That's great."

"How was yours?"

"Things were busy. I'm dead on my feet. I can't wait to get home and have a beer. I wish I had a pretty face to greet me at my place."

I think about taking the trip across town to make that happen. However, we haven't been on a date. My gut is telling me to take my time with this.

"Aww, I wish, but I need to get this content done. Judge and I usually do a huge giveaway for the holidays. The sponsors have sent some things for us to giveaway," I reply.

"It was wishful thinking. Listen, I'm about to get on my bike. I'll text you when I get home."

"Okay, I'll talk to you later. Get some rest."

"Thanks."

CHAPTER NINETEEN

Skill Set

Lizzy

"Hey Jacob," I say into the phone as I make my way to the kitchen.

I've been living with Dante and Bella for about three weeks now and it has been interesting, to say the least. Jacob calls almost daily now. However, I haven't had the time to go out on a date with him.

Dante and Bella keep me pretty busy. Although, I've been making it a point to text and talk with Jacob at night while he closes up the restaurant.

"Hey, gorgeous."

"What's up?"

"I was hoping you would be able to find some time to have drinks. I'd love to see that gorgeous face in person."

"I don't know. We're getting ready to head out this weekend. There's so much to get done—"

My words are cut off as a yelp escapes my lips. I run right into a hard body and almost drop my phone from my ear. I tilt on my heels and curse Nyla for suggesting the black four-inch patent leather stilettos.

I look up as my body is drawn into the one I crashed into and lock gazes with hazel eyes. It's the intensity for me. My brain scrambles and my nipples tighten against my bra.

Dante's hand on my back is so warm it's almost a distraction from the hard hot body at my front. Gah, this man is too sexy for words. His warm, minty fresh breath fans in my face.

"Lizzy, you there?" Jacob calls, bringing me down from the cloud I'm floating on. I clear my throat and take a step back. Running my free hand down the front of my black pencil skirt, I try to find my voice.

"Hey, Jacob. Let me call you back. I have to go," I breathe into the phone.

"I'm looking forward to it. Later, baby."

I wrinkle my brows. That's a first, but I'm not totally turned off. Jacob is growing on me.

"Later."

I hang up and look up into Dante's eyes. In my heels, he's only a few inches taller than me, but I still feel so small in front of him. Dante is built like *I spend time in the gym and will crush you* built. It works well with his height. I tug at the yellow silk blouse Bella picked out for me last night.

"Sorry," I murmur. "I was distracted."

Dante snorts. "We leave in fifteen."

I feel the loss of his hand on me. I nod and rush to get Bella a bowl of cereal. As I place the bowl in front of her and pour her cereal into the bowl, Dante finishes his coffee and moves to place a hand on Bella's back before he kisses her nose as she looks up at him.

"You look nice," he says.

I look at Bella and smile as I notice she's wearing a yellow top and black skirt. Her little Mary Janes are on her feet. However, when I turn my eyes to Dante, he's looking at me.

"Oh, me?"

"Yes, you. Yellow is your color. You should wear that color more often. It places a glow on your skin."

"Thanks," I say and duck my head.

"Things seem to be getting serious with Jacob," he murmurs.

"Not really. I mean, we talk a lot, but neither of us has found time to go out on that date. I'm feeling things out, I guess."

"Bella's grandfather wants to spend some time with her. Her maternal grandfather. He'll come by the office to pick her up today. Once she's gone, I need you to sit in on some meetings with me. We'll be working late tonight."

"Oh, okay, should I pack anything special for Bella?"

"No, her LeapPad is all she needs. She has clothes and things already there."

"Okay. I emailed you the updates to your meeting and those contracts you want to look over. Some samples of the new sauces are coming in today. Gio sent me a few potential locations for the new Chicago store and restaurant," I rattle off.

"You took care of those gift baskets we talked about?"

"Yes, Bella and I made sure those were taken care of yesterday."

"Is that right? I think I need to give my little assistant a raise," Dante croons in Bella's ear as he tickles her.

"Daddy, I don't get paid." Bella giggles.

"What? Really? You should. I'm going to talk to your supervisor."

"I don't have a supervisor. I have Lizzy and Daddy." Bella's eyes shine as she looks between the two of us.

"Finish your breakfast, sweetheart. I'll be in the car."

There…that's what has made the last two weeks interesting. Dante can be playful and open one minute and cold and closed off the next. I never know what I'm going to get.

I'm starting to get whiplash. God, I need to get it together. Nothing is ever going to happen between us, so there's no need for this burning disappointment.

Dante

I think I'm making a mistake. I've watched Bella grow more and more attached to Lizzy in the last three weeks. It's only been three weeks. What's going to happen in a month or a year?

God, I don't think I can keep this up for a year. When Lizzy ran into me this morning, I wanted to hold her to me and finally sample those full lips.

However, guilt consumed me as the thought crossed my mind—they still don't have any leads on Bethany's killer. Although, I've been questioned again.

I wish I knew who did this so I could have some closure. I'm tired. I can't bury myself in my work like I would normally try to do because Bella needs me.

I take a calming breath and scroll through my phone. I'm a bit on edge as it is. Bella's grandfather has been insisting on spending time with her. I wouldn't have a problem with that if I didn't think there was an ulterior motive.

Bethany wasn't just born conniving. She learned from the best. However, the man did just lose his only daughter and his granddaughter is all he has left. My mother-in-law, on the other hand, seems to have her daughter's disposition. She clearly doesn't give a fuck. I haven't seen her since Bethany's death.

"Daddy, I have my new cell phone Uncle Gio gave me. You can call me later. I don't have to use Grandpa's phone. Do you have my number? I have you as Daddy," Bella rambles as Lizzy helps her into her booster seat.

"I have your number. You have to make sure you take good care of your phone and don't lose it."

"I have my purse. It straps across me. I'll have it with me all the time."

I turn to see her holding up her little purse with a smile on her face. Gio and Dario really did help me to spoil her. It seemed to work. She made it through the holidays without crying over Beth or asking about her.

Not that I think I'll be able to avoid it forever, but I wanted her to have this. A time to be a kid. She is still my baby. I'll shield her from as much as I can.

Lizzy gets into the car beside me and hands me what looks like something wrapped in a paper towel. I lift a brow as I take it.

"You left your bagel in the toaster. If we're going to work late, you need to have your energy throughout the day."

"Thank you. I forgot I put it in there."

"No problem."

With that, we ride to the office in silence. Both Bella and Lizzy lost in reading as I run through a few documents, making notes. I can't help thinking to myself, I can get used to this.

We ride up in the elevator once at the office. I stand behind Lizzy, taking her in. It's not lost on me that she has changed her hair. It's in long braids, today she has them pulled up on top of her head.

I'm a fan of the sexy ass heels she's in. They draw attention to her long legs. I love that she's a tall woman. Yet, I still tower over her. She still seems so much smaller in comparison to me. For all her curves, I have bulk to match.

I drop my eyes to her full ass. I imagine shoving my hand in her hair and stepping up behind her to feel that lush ass against me as I grow hard to show her what she's in for.

"Daddy, will we have lunch before I leave?"

I move to place a hand on the small of Lizzy's back as Bella holds her hand. Lizzy turns to look at me with surprise in her eyes. The doors to the elevator open and I lead them both out.

"Can we make that happen, Liz?"

Lizzy's lips part as she searches my face. I liked the comfort my nonno had with calling her Liz during Christmas. I've been thinking about it since. I don't know what makes me call her the nickname now.

"I think I can make something happen. I got the email with the list you want me to cover for today. I think I can fit your lunch in before she leaves," she replies softly.

"Move anything you have to."

"Lizzy, what's on our agenda for today?" Bella asks.

I snort with laughter before I catch myself. Bella looks up at Lizzy expectantly.

However, I answer for her. "Today Lizzy will be going through the list of curricula I sent her to pick the best one, so she can start your homeschooling."

I look at Lizzy and see she's chewing on her lip. "I noticed on your resume; you have a master's in education. You have a great skill set. I thought since she'll be traveling with us, you wouldn't mind, but if I'm asking too much, I can get a list of traveling tutors."

"No, it's fine. I can handle it. I saw the list, but I wasn't sure what it was for at first. We'll get right on it."

"Thanks." I almost lean in to peck her lips but bend to kiss Bella on her cheek instead. "Be a good girl for Lizzy. When you come back from Grandpa's we'll do something fun before we have to go away."

CHAPTER TWENTY

Forgot Who I am

Dante

I smile as I chew on the chicken I just dipped in one of the new sauce samples. Bella's excited talk about her morning with Lizzy makes me chuckle. Instead of ordering lunch from somewhere random, I had it brought in from one of my restaurants to see if this sauce can hold up to our standards.

You always lose quality with mass production. However, it is my job to make sure we keep things up to *Amore Domestic* Standards. Our family's flagship restaurant in Italy is the bar we set for all of our restaurants and products.

Dario has already sent over his notes and opinions on what needs to be changed. He's right, these flavors are lacking.

Bella dips her nugget and takes a bite. She pulls a face instantly. I burst into more laughter. Lizzy quickly holds a napkin up to Bella's mouth.

"I don't like that one."

"We have our first veto from the young Di Lorenzo." I wink at Bella and toss the sauce into the bin. "Here, try this one. You might like it."

I hand her the sauce that has piqued my interest the most so far. She dips another nugget after taking a sip of water. This time her eyes light up.

"Good?" I ask with a smile.

She nods and holds the cup of sauce out to Lizzy. "You have to try this one. It's delicious."

Lizzy dips her chicken into the sauce. I watch her sensual mouth as she chews. She bobs her head and covers her mouth. I'm disappointed to lose my view.

"I do like this one. It has a little kick to it, but not too much. It's smoky too."

"I was thinking the same thing. Come here, taste this one. I think it's too much for Bella's palate, but you might like it."

I hold my fork out to Lizzy. I could have very likely handed over a little cup with the sauce, but I'm going with my gut. I want to see her mouth wrap around my fork.

She stands and leans over my desk. Like when she's on her channel gaming, she doesn't realize how sexy her simple gestures are. The only things that could pull my attention from those full lips are her perky, plump breasts. The top buttons of her blouse are open and reveals just enough to commit me to this chair until I can calm this mass growing in my pants.

"Mmm," she moans. "That one is amazing."

A throat clears, pulling my attention from the view. Lizzy straightens and turns. I look to Bella, who's happily finishing her nuggets. When I do look to the door, I find my former father-in-law.

The scowl on his face says it all. I pick up my napkin to clean my mouth, then toss it onto my finished lunch. I stand and smooth a hand down my tie.

"Lizzy, this is Mr. Kumar, Bella's grandfather. Can you take Bella to get her things?"

"No problem. Come on, Bella."

"Wait, I'm not finished." Bella pouts.

Lizzy goes to collect the rest of Bella's food and takes her hand. "Come on, you can finish at our desk."

"Okay," Bella whines. "Hey, Grandpa," she says as they walk by him to leave out.

"Hi, Bella."

I don't miss there isn't the same warmth between them that Bella has with my family. I've never picked up on that in the past. Bethany was the one I was concerned with as Bella's mother. The door closes and Kaling starts in.

"My daughter has been in the ground for all of, what? Four and a half weeks. Twenty-six excruciating days," he chokes the last part out. "Who is that woman you're playing house with? You have Bella sitting in here as if her mother is forgotten filth beneath your shoe."

I close the distance between us before I can hold myself back. I get right in his face and look down at him like the scum I've come to know him as.

"I believe you've forgotten who the fuck I am. Who I spend my time with is none of your fucking business. You've come to pick up your granddaughter. Shut the fuck up and do that," I seethe.

"I will not forgive this. You...you know what happened to Bethany. You're behind this somehow. I will not rest until—"

"You can rest with your daughter if you like," Gio says as Jace holds a gun to the back of Kaling's head.

"I never should have gotten her involved with your family. That was my mistake," Kaling says as his eyes fill with tears.

"Spare me the show. I don't know what you planned to gain, but you had a motive for pushing our marriage. You can go. Jace, will you accompany Bella? She is to return home this evening. There will be no sleepover," I say sternly.

"You will deny me this?"

"Until you show you can be trusted, this is how it will be. You want to spend time with Bella, she will have an escort. Again, take some time to remind yourself who you're dealing with."

"Oh, and so we're clear. I know nothing about what happened that night. Direct your attention and ire elsewhere. I never cheated on my wife. I'm respecting her memory even now, although I know for a fact she was having an affair. Find out who she was fucking, he may be the one with the answers you're looking for."

I tug at my cuff and move back around my desk to have a seat. Jace sees Kaling out and I sit back in my chair, steepling my fingers in front of my mouth.

"I told you he was going to be an issue," I say as Gio closes the door behind Kaling and Jace. "He's been calling and asking a million questions."

"I heard you when you said it. It's why Jace and I were awaiting his arrival today. I had a feeling you would need to make your message clear."

"What now?"

"You finish your day, get ready for your trip. Leave the rest to me."

I purse my lips and nod. My temper still simmering right beneath the surface. I work my jaw and seethe. The nerve.

CHAPTER TWENTY-ONE

Travel & Stress

Dante

I push the door open slowly. Steam rolls out of the bathroom as I step in. I know I should turn around, but it's as if I'm being pulled into the room by an invisible force.

Lizzy's scent fills my nostrils. I lick my lips and move toward the shower. The glass is fogged, I can only make out her silhouette. I reach for my shaft and palm it. She's been enticing me for weeks.

Those blouses that stretch across her breasts. Her fat ass. The way she looks up into my eyes. I only want a taste. One taste and I'll be able to get this under control.

"Dante," she gasps over her shoulder as I open the shower door and step in behind her. I reach for her arms and pin them to the wall in front of her.

"Don't you know how much I want you?" I say in her ear as I glide my palms down her wet arms.

She pants and shakes her head. I allow my hands to keep traveling down her body until I palm her fat mound. Her whimper is like sweet music to my ears.

I kick her feet apart to widen her stance slightly. She pushes her ass back into me, bumping into my erection. I bite down on her shoulder as I push two fingers into her wet heat.

"Dante," she moans.

I groan as I work my fingers in and out of her. I lose all focus as I thrust into her and her tight walls suck me in. I grab her throat and pump my hips into her, going as deep as I can at this angle.

"Daddy, Daddy," I pop up, startled from the heated dream. I've been having them more often than not.

"Bella, what's wrong, sweetheart?" I say through my sleep-heavy voice.

God, I'm exhausted. Meeting after meeting for six weeks, compounded with the travel and lack of sleep. I rub at my eyes as Bella flings herself onto my chest.

"I had another bad dream," she whimpers. "Lizzy's door is closed. She's recording."

Yeah, she was recording before I fell asleep. I think that's what prompted my dream about her. Her nipples were poking through the fabric of her tight T-shirt. I tuned into the channel, unable to help myself.

"It's okay. I'm here, sweetheart. You're safe and everything is going to be fine."

"Can I sleep in here with you?"

"Of course."

When we arrived at the first hotel, Bella insisted on sleeping with Lizzy. Since Lizzy uses the attached suite for gaming, we didn't see a problem with it. Lizzy doesn't sleep much as it is.

"Daddy?"

"Yes, sweetheart." I run my hand through her curls and stare up at the ceiling.

"I know Lizzy is working hard on my birthday party, but I don't think I want it. Can we have it next year or something?"

I sit up and look down at Bella. I'm not sure what has brought this on, but the sad look on her face gives me pause. The party is next month.

"Whatever you want," I say sincerely. "Do you want to tell me why the change?"

"I don't feel like it will be fun. Grandpa K is always sad. You're not happy either." She shrugs.

"Okay." My heart sinks. I didn't know my own displeasures had been showing on my face. I try my best to mask my pain. I've been questioning myself more and more.

Lizzy

I panic the moment I walk into the room and notice Bella is gone. I stayed on pretty long tonight. There weren't a bunch of hackers on, and we took advantage of the play.

Hackers can really ruin the experience. Dante doesn't need me in the morning, so I enjoyed their absence. Bella will usually sleep in with me.

"Bella?" I call out as I check the bathroom attached to our room.

I don't find her in there and my heart starts to race. I rush out to the common area. I check the front door and the lever is still securely in place.

"Bella?" I whisper out as I move to Dante's room.

I hold my breath as I hear giggling and the rumble of Dante's voice. I release a breath of relief and tap at the door and wait for an answer.

"Come in," Dante calls.

I push the door in and pop my head inside.

"Everything okay?"

Bella sits up in the bed. "I had a bad dream. I didn't want to disturb you, so I came to Daddy."

"Oh, I'm sorry. We have to come up with a secret knock so you can let me know you need me."

"It's fine. We're getting a chance to catch up anyway. Bella has requested to postpone her party until next year."

"Really? That means I now have time to teach you how to skate since you want a skate party," I say.

Bella's entire face lights up. I just learned she doesn't know how to skate. Something I should have asked from the beginning. I fully intended to throw the party at a skating rink. I called in a few favors already.

"Yes," Bella cheers and fist pumps the air.

I look down at my watch. "I'm going to try to get an hour or two of sleep. I just wanted to make sure Bella was okay."

"Wait, I'm coming with you," Bella says and hops from the bed.

Dante gives an exhausted chuckle. I wish there were more I could do for him. I make a mental note to book him for the spa before we leave. Two more days before we head out and this time we're heading home.

CHAPTER TWENTY-TWO

Relief & Guilt

Dante

"So, what are you telling me, Gio?"

"One situation has been taken care of, but it has led me to some facts about another. The police will finally stop sniffing around you. They have found a suspect and it looks like this is all wrapped up," he says.

"What? Who was it? Do they have them in custody?"

"Unfortunately, that won't be possible. It was a murder-suicide. The guy from the picture."

I suddenly feel cheated. I don't get to absolve my guilt through revenge. *It's guilt you shouldn't have, Dante.* My brain chides.

Gio continues on the other end of the phone. "I think we need to bring in a forensic accountant. It seems Bethany and Daddy dearest were digging further into our pockets than we thought. I want every dime found."

"So do I. Call in Lance and Summer Anderson, their firm is the best. And if a single penny was moved or touched by Kaling—"

"No words needed, little brother. I'll keep you posted."

I grunt and end the call. Why must I keep getting pulled back into all this? I've gotten my hands dirty for years, but when Bella was born, I needed a break. I didn't want to take a life after watching it being given.

Yet it seems my vacation from being a true Di Lorenzo is over. Today hasn't gone the way I'd like. I need to get laid and soon. Those dreams are fucking with my head.

I check the text message Lizzy sent while I was on my call. She and Bella have gone to one of those bear-building stores nearby. That gives me time to have a drink at the bar. However, I'm stopped in my tracks as I go to head for it.

"Mr. Di Lorenzo, your assistant made an appointment for you at the spa. If you would follow me," the woman from the hotel staff says.

Again, Lizzy takes care of my needs as if reading my mind. A good massage will help with this building tension. I can get that drink after. I grin to myself as I think of my assistant. She's turning out to be worth her weight in gold.

Now, if I could figure out how to get her in my bed without fucking everything up, I'd be a happy man. I shake that thought away. I may have to settle for the first willing, warm body at this point.

Why does that thought leave a sour taste in my mouth?

That hit the spot. I've never had a masseuse so thorough. I'm not sure if I want that drink after all. I'm tempted to drag my tired body up to my room and pass out.

I check for a message from Lizzy, but I don't have one. I shoot her a quick text to check in. She replies to let me know she and Bella are still having fun and plan to stop and play some games and get a bite to eat.

I go to tell her I'll join them, but my attention is pulled by a stunner who walks into the hotel bar. "I guess I'll get that drink after all," I mutter to myself.

I saunter into the bar and take a seat a few stools down from the gorgeous woman who pulled my attention. She's not as dark as Lizzy or as tall, but she's still very attractive.

"A double of your best tequila."

The bartender nods and pushes away to get my drink. I pretend to scroll through my phone, not acknowledging the woman only two seats away.

"Hard day?" she says in a sweet voice.

I look up and give her a smile. "Something like that." I keep it short and simple.

She gets up and moves closer. Her perfume isn't my favorite, but she looks like she takes good care of herself.

"I'm here on business. You?"

"The same."

"Wow, you're not much of a talker."

"I'm not in the mood to talk," I reply.

"Oh no? What are you in the mood for?"

"I'm a recent widower. I've had a tough day. In all honesty, what I need is a good blow job and to fuck your brains out."

I take a sip of my drink as it arrives and allow my words to sink in. She gives me a slow smile as she looks me over. I haven't lost my touch.

She leans into me. "That's big talk, I hope you can make good on it."

"I make good on everything I say."

"I'm Arizona."

I snort and start to second-guess this. The last thing I want is some dry ass pussy. I need to get into something wet and tight. I haven't had sex in so long, I deserve true pleasure.

"I'm...you know what? I'm not into this. Thanks for the conversation." I stand and throw a couple of hundreds down. "Have a few drinks on me."

I finish my drink, then turn and head upstairs. I'll take that nap so I can play with my daughter when she gets back. Damn, what has my life become?

Lizzy

I took Bella out to get out of Dante's hair for a bit. I wanted him to enjoy his spa time and get some rest. The man works so hard.

We push into the room and it's so quiet. I place a finger to my lips to quiet Bella once I see Dante passed out on the couch. I notice the empty bottle of tequila hanging from his fingertips.

"Rough day," I murmur.

I get down to eye level with Bella to distract her. She's bursting at the seams to tell her father about her day. Her hazel eyes are filled with curiosity as she looks back at me.

"How about we let your daddy sleep? You can come with me in the game room, and we can watch some cartoons."

She clasps her hands together. "Can we watch your cartoons? The old ones?"

I chuckle and tap her nose with my finger. "*Care Bears* and *Gargoyles* it is."

Since we have the attached suite, I can close the door, so we don't disturb Dante. It must have been a rough day. In the six weeks we've been traveling, I've never seen him drink and not to the point of passing out.

I hope everything went well with the spa. I stand and take all of our things into the bedroom before changing into sweats to lounge and watch cartoons with my little friend. I can't help but laugh when I find Bella looking down at her street clothes and then back at me.

"Would you like to change into something more comfortable?"

"Yes, please."

"Come on. I think I have some nail polish in my bag. Would you like to paint our nails while we watch cartoons?"

"Yes, yes, please."

I laugh at her excitement. I wish everyone were as easy to please as Bella. I find her some lounge pants in her suitcase and a T-shirt.

"Can you brush my hair after we paint our nails? It always feels nice," Bella whispers as I help her get dressed.

"Of course. You know, Nyla used to brush my hair when I was little. I loved it too."

"I like Miss. Ny. She's nice and so pretty, like you. I think Uncle Gio and Uncle Jace do too."

I bite back a laugh. I guess Dante and I aren't the only ones to notice something was up at Christmas.

I wink at Bella. "I think my sister likes you too."

"Do you miss her?"

"Yeah, we've been gone for a long time, and she only just returned home from traveling. I miss her a lot."

"Can I tell you a secret?"

"I don't see why not?"

"I miss my mommy. She was mean sometimes, but I miss her."

I pull her into a hug and hold her tight. I know I can't replace Bethany like everyone seems to be trying to make me, but I can fill in the gap as much as I can, like Elijah and Aunt Denise did for Nyla and me.

"It gets better. I promise."

"You make it a lot better. I always wanted someone to spend time with. I hope you never leave."

I squeeze just a bit tighter as my heart breaks for this little girl. A throat clears and I lift my gaze to find Dante leaning in the doorway. He rubs at his jaw, bringing attention to the five o'clock shadow he's sporting.

"Hey," I say.

Bella pulls away and turns to look at her father. "Lizzy is going to watch old cartoons with me. Care-a-Lot and the stone people."

Dante lifts a questioning brow. "She means Care Bears and Gargoyles."

"Oh, two of my favorites. Can I join you guys?"

"I don't know, Daddy. We're going to be painting our nails."

"Good, Lizzy can do your fingers while I do your toes."

"And I can do Lizzy's fingers while you do her toes."

"Deal," Dante says before I can refuse.

CHAPTER TWENTY-THREE

Let's Talk

Dante

I place Bella in the bed and kiss her forehead. She fell asleep halfway through having her nails painted. After she told me about all the excitement from her day, I'm pretty sure she was fighting to stay awake, to begin with.

Lizzy goes to climb into the other queen-size bed in the room. I know I should leave her to it, but I want to talk to her. I heard the things Bella said. I want to discuss them with someone who may be able to help me sort things out.

"Do you mind coming back out with me? That's my favorite season of *Gargoyles*."

Lizzy looks up from her phone and that shy look takes over her face. I want to make her cheeks flush and her face sweaty as she looks at me with that shy look in her eyes. However, I know that can never happen. Bella's words cemented that this evening.

"Okay, hold on a sec."

"Trying to get in one more chapter?" I chuckle.

"Actually, yes and Jacob has been texting. We're going on our first date when I get back."

Why does this knowledge piss me off so fucking much? I have thought about making Jacob disappear a few times. However, his restaurant is doing great at the moment. Numbers have soared since he's come aboard.

I grunt in response and head back to the room we were watching cartoons in. There was a time when I was always in control of everything. Before becoming a father, I was a different man.

I wouldn't say Bella softened me, I just changed priorities and thought I could change who I am with them. The old Dante would have found a way to make Lizzy forget all about Jacob. I'd once been ruthless in all aspects of my life.

"Sorry, did I miss much?"

"No." My words come out harshly.

You're not going to keep her away from Jacob like that.

I sigh. I can't sleep with Lizzy, but I need a friend as much as Bella does. I swallow my shit and tap into the old Dante. I reach for Lizzy's legs and pull them into my lap.

She looks startled at first. I reach for the nail polish. Allowing a grin to my lips, I hold the bottle up to her.

"This is the color you chose, no?"

"Um…yes, but you don't have to."

I love the breathless sound of her voice. I run my hand up her calf. Her skin is so smooth beneath my palm.

"I want to. As a thank you. I was surprised by the spa treatment, but it was just what I needed. This is the least I can do to repay you."

I place the nail polish down and start to massage Lizzy's leg and foot. She flinches a way a little and giggles at first.

"Ticklish?"

"Maybe."

"You're full of surprises. You're so good with children. Why aren't you using your degree? If you don't mind me asking."

She bites her lip as if thinking of not answering. My interest is further piqued. I don't realize I'm holding my breath until she does speak.

"When I started school, I had no plan. I sort of fell into the education track." She shrugs. "I met Gio right before I graduated. You know how he can make anything more attractive. He sold me on working for your family."

"In the mail room? Come on, Gio is good, but not that good."

"Well, boss, I'm here now, aren't I?"

"Touché."

"And I was promoted up pretty quickly from the mail room." She laughs.

I nearly swallow my tongue when that laugh becomes a moan as I hit what I believe to be a sweet spot on her foot. I blink away the lust rising within.

Before I drive us both insane, I pick up the nail polish and get started on her toes. With a five going on six-year-old, I'm becoming a pro at this. Lizzy shifts and sits up and plants her foot on my leg.

"Gaming and personal assisting are a hell of a long way from teaching."

She scoffs. "You have no idea how far off the beaten path I've fallen."

I tilt my head as I look into her eyes. Holding her gaze, I lift her foot to my lips and blow on the pink painted toes I just finished. She clears her throat and starts to squirm.

"Why do I feel like you are full of secrets, Liz?"

"Maybe you see yourself when you look at me."

I place her foot back on my lap and start on the next one. No, I don't see myself in Lizzy. She's too sweet and innocent to ever reflect me.

"I overheard Bella earlier. All I ask is that your secrets don't hurt her."

Or me. The thought comes so fast I frown as I paint her big toe.

"Stop looking at my feet like they stink, Dante."

I look up at her and burst into laughter. She joins me as she tries to pull her leg away. I grab her other foot and bring her toes to my lips, kissing them before I lick and nip at her big toe.

"I was thinking, not looking at your toes. You always smell like something I want to devour."

She clears her throat and starts that cute squirming again. I bet her panties are soaked. I think of dipping my fingers in to check but remind myself that all women are dangerous for me.

"I would never hurt Bella. If anything, my secrets will always serve her."

Before I probe into what she means, my phone rings. I bite back a curse. We were just getting comfortable, and I have so much more I want to say to Lizzy. I lean to pick up my phone and see it's Dario. He's been in Italy while I've been away.

"Hello, can I call you back?"

"No, I need to talk to you now," he says tightly.

I know my twin. Something is wrong. He needs me.

"Excuse me," I say to Lizzy as I stand and leave the room.

Lizzy

Thank God, I don't think I would have been able to sit here for one more minute. My phone vibrates, drawing my attention. I look at the text from Jacob and feel a little guilty.

To get my head on straight, I get up and head into the bedroom I'm sharing with Bella. She's still fast asleep.

I move into the bathroom to catch my breath. I look into the mirror and run a hand through my braids. "What's happening?"

My phone goes off, pulling me back into reality. Whatever was going on out there, it can't happen. I need to keep my distance from Dante.

He's going through so much and I can't allow my secret to come out. Gio is trusting me, and I don't want to disappoint him.

"Hey, Jacob," I answer my phone, hoping to be grounded through a conversation with a sweet guy, who I actually have a real chance with, not just a hot night in bed.

Like Dante has asked you into his bed. Get over yourself, Liz.

"Hey, baby. Are you guys still heading back?"

"Yeah, day after tomorrow."

"So we're good for dinner. Did you see my text?"

"Yeah, I thought I replied. Give me a day to get Bella settled back home and I'll get the night off for our date," I reply, knowing I need to make this date happen.

"I'm looking forward to it. Are you gaming tonight? I have some downtime. I can pop in and watch for a while."

"No, I don't think I am. I'm going to get some sleep so I can make sure to pack everything up tomorrow. We have a ton of stuff we purchased during this trip. I may need to ship a few things back."

"Did you get something for your boyfriend?"

"I don't have a boyfriend."

"Ouch, and here I am turning down girls left and right because I miss my girlfriend and can't wait until she gets home."

My cheeks get so hot. We've never talked titles before. Personally, I'm still feeling Jacob out. I've had my heart broken before, so I'm cautious.

"How about we have that first date before we start with labels," I say.

He chuckles. "Okay, babe. I'm going to allow you to get some sleep. I'll see you when you get back."

"See you when I get back."

I hang up and head back into the bedroom. I'm surprised to find Dante in Bella's bed, hugging her close. Not wanting to disturb them, I tiptoe to my bed and climb in.

Exhaustion sets in and I think for once I'm going to get some sleep.

"Change of plans. We leave in the morning," Dante rumbles.

"Is everything okay?"

"My family needs me home."

I leave it at that. The edge in his voice fills in enough gaps for me. Something tells me more change is coming.

CHAPTER TWENTY-FOUR

Fuck you thought?

Dante

We've returned home a day early for a reason. Dario has some shit I need to handle. I thought I made my way out of this life. For five years, I've been a normal husband, father, and business owner.

Leave it to Bethany and her family to drag me back into this shit. For years, I've been playing my part from a distance. If Dario needs something, Gio is there to make it happen. I haven't had to do more than say a word. My guys take care of the rest.

However, this is shit of my creation, so while Dario's in Italy, I need to clean up my own mess. Bethany and Kaling are my problems. Problems that have tried to burrow a hole in my family's business.

So here I am. The real Dante Di Lorenzo. I slip into the back room at one of the restaurants—Dario's to be exact. We keep this place for business like this. I take a seat and cross my ankle over my leg.

"Where is he?" I ask.

Mitch nods toward the freezers. I nod back as I remove my cuff links. "Bring him out."

"Got it, boss."

Mitch and two of my other guys leave the room. I grit my teeth because the last thing I wanted to do after putting my little girl in her own bed for the first time in six weeks is be here. I swear I hope Bella missed out on the thieving, treacherous genes from her mother's side.

As I have the thought, Mitch drags a half-frozen Kaling into the room. He shivers as he's shoved forward. His hands cupped at his mouth. When his gaze lands on me, he tries to turn and run.

I grin and stand. "Put his ass in that chair."

"Dante, no, no, please. Think of Bella. Please don't do this. Please," he pleads.

"You should have thought of Bella before you started to embezzle money from me," I bellow. "By the way, where's your wife? I never thought she'd be so cold as to miss burying her daughter."

"Things are complicated. I sent her away from all of this."

"Now, see, that shows me you knew I would figure this shit out and yet you still chose to fuck with me. So, is it you thinking I'm stupid? Or are you just a huge fucking idiot?"

"You don't understand. Pl...Ple...Please," he chatters out nervously.

"I see you're starting to remember who the fuck I am." I tilt my head. "Did you think I got weak when my daughter was born? Did you think she was going to save you and that cunt?"

"You killed her. I knew it was you."

"I had nothing to do with your lying, thieving daughter's death, but I wish I did."

My guys secure him to the chair and step back. Before I kill this motherfucker, I need a few answers. Lance and Summer found the money trail. It led right to this asshole. However, Summer picked up on something weird. There was money being funneled to a third party.

A third party who has yet to be traced. However, rumors of some bullshit involving this motherfucker and our money have reached Dario in Italy. This makes my brother look bad. We can't have that. Not when Nonno has been talking about the transition happening soon.

Truth is, Nonno Di Lorenzo isn't getting any younger. We all knew this was coming.

"Wha...what are you going to do to me?"

I tilt my head to the side and glare at him. "That depends on you. Tell me who you're working with and what the fuck you've been planning."

"I can't tell you anything."

I punch him in his face like I've wanted to do for years. Every time this fuckup has come to me for money, it has pissed me off. The only reason I tolerated him was because of my wife.

As I glare at him and his now slit cheek, my rage rises. People have been taking advantage of me for far too long. I might not give a fuck if not for the fact it has affected my family.

I'm nothing but loyal and protective of my family. Especially my daughter, brothers, and nonno. Once I feel one of them is threatened, I become a savage you never want to meet. The reason this bastard tried to run.

I throw another punch. An uppercut this time. Kaling's head rocks back with a snap.

"You steal from *me,* and you thought you'd live to enjoy that shit? Fuck, you thought I was some pussy who was going to turn the other cheek?"

His head rolls on his shoulders as he groans. "I only wanted to keep my daughter safe. She got in over her head. I did what I had to do."

I snort. "But you were pulling those strings from the beginning. Did you lose control?"

"She found her way deeper into your world than I wanted her to. I have nothing else to give you."

"You want me to do this the hard way, I see."

His eyes widen with panic as he straightens his head and looks at me. "No, no, please. I can't tell you. If I talk, Bella will be in danger. I'll die first."

I roll my shoulders to contain my rage. "I can make that happen for you. But you're going to tell me one way or the other. Who the fuck is threatening *my* daughter? Talk before I flay your ass, starting with your eyelids."

His eyes harden. This motherfucker looks like he's about to grow a pair. My rage burns through my body like it's going to consume me.

"Your ass is going to grow some balls now? Wrong fucking move. You should never fear anyone more than me. Let me show you why."

The bloodlust that has been dormant for so long bangs at my veins to come out. I crack my knuckles and hold my hand out for my blade. Mitch places it in my palm and it's like coming home.

I move to crouch before Kaling. "Did Bethany ever tell you that after my mother left us, I used to skin birds with this very blade? My father feared I lost my fucking mind. My grandfather was the one to help me channel this shit. I thought your daughter and mine had buried it for good."

I stand and kick him in the chest, toppling him and the chair over. "Pick him up," I bark.

The only other thing that welcomes me back more than the feel of the blade is the screams of my thieving father-in-law as I skin his ass alive. The bastard holds out, to my surprise. My fury gets the best of me and Mitch has to tell me when he's gone as I continue to cut and flay—cloaked in the rage that has consumed me.

"Shit." I lift to my full height and wipe my forearm across my face.

As my rage calms, I clean my blade against the side of my pants leg and pull a handkerchief from my back pocket to wipe my hands. I pull my phone from my pocket.

Giving a nod to my men to take care of this mess, I wait for the call to be answered. Mitch hands me my bag as I pass by him. I nod at him as my call is answered.

"It's done. I got nothing but a threat to Bella's life. I get the feeling someone wants to draw me out," I say.

A grunt comes from the other end. "Not a wise someone. I'll let Dario know. I would have done this for you, you know?"

"It was my problem. I intend to handle my messes. I see where this has gotten out of hand. It's time I remind the world of who the fuck I am. You have your own shit to handle. This is my part. I have it."

"If this is what you want," Gio replies.

"It isn't, but have I ever had a choice?"

"I'm trying to give you one."

I sigh. "I have a date to plan. I'll call you later."

"A date? Oh really?"

"She's five, I'm her father and I'm taking her to a tea party and dinner with a Disney Princess. Calm down."

Gio laughs. "Whatever, brother. You can only ignore what's right in your face for so long."

I hang up. I need to calm and collect myself. I can't think about what Gio is hinting at. I have enough on my plate.

Right as I have that thought, I step into the main dining room. The place should be closed, and no one should be here. So, the dim lighting catches me off guard. The last thing I need is for someone to find what I've done.

It was my intention to head down to the furnace room to strip out of these clothes. I have some sweats in the gym bag Mitch handed me. Not knowing who's here or what they have seen, I pull my gun and follow the sound of their movements.

I move for the kitchen and stop in my tracks when I find Carleen. She has on headphones, so she doesn't hear me. She's cooking something and seems lost in thought.

From here, I can see her gaze is locked on her phone. She sends a text with a smile on her lips. Clearly, she's unaware of the crime I've committed in the restaurant she's co-owner of.

Something in her posture gives me pause. My eyes grow wide. I normally don't get into my brother's business, but I pull my phone as I back up and take a quick photo to send to him.

This life is a thief. Sad part is, while Dario doesn't want it and probably deserves better, it calls me. A part of me loves it. I respect Dario for not dragging Carleen into this. However, I don't know if he deserves to lose his chance at love.

Knowing if this is who I have to become once again, I can't have Lizzy. She's too sweet to be in this world. I've always believed it was the women who have ruined me and my life, but maybe I've been looking at this wrong. It's the life that ruins the women and then they come for me and my heart.

CHAPTER TWENTY-FIVE

Your Valentine

Lizzy

"You look pretty," Bella says while sitting on my bed, watching me get ready for my date with Jacob.

"Thank you. You look pretty too."

She does. She's adorable in the princess dress she's wearing for her daddy-daughter date this evening. The tiara on her head looks like it's worth half a year of my salary. Not to mention the diamond studs in her ears.

"You think so? You think Daddy will like it? I want to make him smile. His real smile is missing today."

She's right, Dante has been brooding all day. I've been steering clear of him. He came in late last night dressed in sweats, not the suit I'd seen him in before he left for the evening. I figured maybe he went for a run, but I noticed something was off with him right away.

"I think your father will think you look precious, and his smile will return the moment he sees you."

Bella tilts her head and looks at me through the mirror. "I thought you would be our valentine. Why are you going out with this Jacob?" she says innocently.

I furrow my brows. I thought Dante was just taking Bella out to spend time with her. Another one of his sweet, fatherly gestures. It didn't dawn on me today is Valentine's Day. Is that what Jacob meant by this date was meant to be special? We talked while I was trying to get through a chapter in this new book.

I had one eye on Bella and the other on my book. Jacob's voice was like white noise. I agreed to the date tonight to get off the phone and back to my book. With all the travel, my brain has been all over the place when it comes to dates.

Thank God for Nyla taking over my old job. She has saved my butt a few times now. I groan as my stomach flips. This date has just pitched my anxiety into overdrive.

I tune back in to answer Bella. "I forgot what day it was, love. I would have loved to be your valentine and join you. Jacob has been so patient for this date, and I don't want to hurt his feelings."

"Okay. I don't want you to hurt his feelings." She climbs off the bed and comes to hold my hand as she looks up at me. "I just want you to be happy. If this Jacob makes you happy, go be his valentine. You can be mine and Daddy's next year," she says.

"Bella, leave Lizzy to get ready. We need to go," Dante says as he appears in my doorway.

I turn to him, a bit startled. His eyes are locked on me. I fidget a little, running my hands down the front of my thighs.

I want to palm my forehead. Now I get why Nyla said to wear red. The only thing I have that's red is this strapless dress. It's a bit snug and stops just above the knee.

I look Dante over. He has on a pair of black jeans and a red polo that stretches nicely over his torso and biceps and a leather jacket is in his hand.

"You should be back in time to help me put Bella to bed," he says tightly. "Take Zek with you. Things are changing and I need to ensure your safety at all times."

His tone is hard. I almost tell him I don't need Zek. However, I bite the words back and nod. I'm sure I can talk Zek into waiting in the car. He has been accompanying Bella and me for the last six weeks.

"I'll be back to help."

Dante

I grunt at her soft-spoken reply as I work my jaw. I want to tell her she can't have the night off. She needs to accompany Bella and me on our date.

It's that fucking dress. That asshole better not touch her. I feel violated all over again. In fact, I feel more rage now than I did last night. I've been trying to shove this part of me back in its box since I returned to the house.

It's the only reason I force myself to let her have her date. Lizzy doesn't deserve the man I am. I don't think she would survive me. As she fidgets and looks all shy, I know she wouldn't.

"I'm only a phone call away," I grumble.

"I've been on dates before. I'm not a child," she says.

"Clearly. Listen…" I shake my head. "Bella, let's go."

Bella walks toward me, looking over her shoulder at Lizzy. It takes everything I am to walk out and not say another word. I pull my phone and text Zek with instructions.

I may not want to personally keep an eye on Lizzy and her date, but I do want to ensure her safety at all times. I work my jaw as I think about all I've dragged her into. I still don't know what Gio was thinking.

CHAPTER TWENTY-SIX

Sweet Date

Lizzy

I'd be lying if I said this hasn't been a really nice date. Jacob has taken me to a friend's restaurant. The ambience is nice and romantic. Jacob has been nothing but polite.

"How's your salmon?" he asks, pointing at my plate with his fork.

I cover my mouth as I chew on the jasmine rice and lemon garlic salmon. The flavor bursts in my mouth. It's delicate, but palette awakening. The lemon garlic sauce works really well with the crispy skin of the fish. It's divine.

"Oh my God, it's delicious. It's not fishy and the lemon garlic sauce is perfect. I love a crispy skin. This is totally it."

"Thanks," he winks at me.

I tilt my head to the side. "You say that like you made this."

He smiles. "I may have had something to do with the prep. I wanted dinner to be perfect. Anthony was once my sous chef. He was able to finish things off for me once we arrived."

I nod. "Okay, I see you, Jacob."

"I'm glad I finally get to see you. So, how's the new job going? Bella? That's her name, right?"

I nod. "It's going well." I don't elaborate as I'm not comfortable talking about Bella to anyone outside of those involved in her life and care.

"The kid is like five or something, right?"

I nod but don't give a verbal answer. "I may not have liked Dante's wife, but that was sort of messed up what happened to her. I think it's sort of cool you're there for the little kid."

"How'd you hear about it?" I say, feeling protective of Dante and Bella. I know for a fact they tried to keep everything out of the press.

"Gossip travels through the restaurants. I thought you were just his nanny, but I've heard that you're actually part of his travel team. You were instrumental in the merger he closed a few weeks ago. Nice work."

I shrug, ready for a change of subject. Even if I didn't sign an NDA, I wouldn't feel comfortable gossiping about my boss's life. Especially not as a part of his live-in staff.

"How's the restaurant going?" I already know the answer, but it's the first thing I can think of to change the topic.

"It's great. We have some critics coming in next week. It's been an awesome transition for my career. You know, with the whole fiasco with Dante's wife and all. I thought I was finished after that shit went viral."

"What exactly happened?"

He rolls his eyes. "I don't want to speak ill of the dead. When you have time, Google the chef surprise. It was really a silly overreaction to what she felt entitled to. I knew who she was, so I made sure the meal was cooked to perfection. Go figure." He shrugs and takes a sip of his beer.

It doesn't sound like it's worth my precious brain cells. I'll pass. I can only imagine what I'll find.

Jacob smiles at me. For the millionth time, I hold my breath to see if that spark will hit me. Nothing. I feel as if I'm on a date with a new friend.

"Tell me, Izzy, what do you do for fun other than game."

I don't tell him how much I hate being called Izzy outside of my channels. I hold that one in because after the other night with Dante painting my toes and his unexpected words, I promised myself I'd really try my best to make this work with Jacob. For my sanity.

"I love to read. Give me a book over people any day." I clamp my mouth shut as I realize what I've said.

I groan and shove a forkful of food into my mouth. Jacob chuckles as he watches me.

"No worries, I'm not offended. I totally get where you're coming from. Sometimes, I wish I could run the kitchen on my own. The noise of it all can be frustrating when you just want to zone out and be in the moment with the masterpiece you're working on," he says.

"I never thought of that. I've been to a few of the restaurants and the kitchen can be a bit noisy. It's also the heart of the place."

"This is true. Tell me, what's your favorite part of working for the Di Lorenzos? You're there from the beginning of the process, no?"

I furrow my brows. There's a slight shift in his speech. It's very small, but it catches my ear. My thoughts start to process it and I tune out for a moment.

"Like, do you like the process of purchasing the restaurants, the building of the locations, the acquisition of the new chefs, or opening day when it all comes together?"

His words draw me back to the conversation. The change is gone and now his questions have my attention. Yes, on occasion I've been a part of all that, but not everyone knows this. Gio has dragged me along from time to time to assist Dante, but even I hadn't realized how often that has been.

"I've been Dante's schedule assistant. I book his dates and travel. I can't say what I enjoy about the process," I reply.

"He seems like such a serious guy. Working for him has to be intense."

"You work for him. You tell me," I say, getting annoyed.

Like, are we on a date, or is he trying to go through me to date Dante himself? Jacob flushes and rubs the back of his neck.

"I'm sorry. I'm a bit nervous and I didn't want to spend dinner fanning out on you. I thought work would be a safe area to talk about," he says quickly.

"No problem. How about this? Tell me about yourself. I'm a good listener when I want to be. Go ahead, you have my attention."

I'll be honest, I'm curious to see if his speech pattern changes again. I can't shake it from a few moments ago.

With a smile, he launches into telling me about himself. I listen to every detail and how he tells them. Unfortunately, or maybe not, he doesn't make the slip again. Maybe I was hearing things.

Charming, that's what I'll call Jacob. As I walk through the door of my new home, that's what plays in my head. Jacob is charming and sweet. Not my type, but I'd hang out with him again.

When he tried to kiss me good night, I turned my face and let him kiss my cheek. I then climbed into my car and took off. I don't kiss on the first date.

I find myself more excited to learn about Bella's date with her father and to give her the little gift I had Denise create for me. I stopped by her place to pick it up before my date.

I stop in my tracks as I find rose petals on the other side of the threshold. They lead from the door up the stairs. I start to feel awkward, wondering if Dante has a date set for after his evening with Bella. Could that be why he wanted me here to help put her to sleep tonight?

I never thought about him bringing a woman home. I hate that I feel jealous. The man is so out of my league—heated stares and words or not. I know I don't have a chance in hell.

I glance up the stairs to find Dante with Bella in his arms. She looks back at me with a sleepy grin, waving me forward.

"You have to follow the petals," she calls down to me.

I tuck my braids behind my ear and start for the stairs. When I get to the top of the stairs, Bella leaps into my arms. Dante places a hand on my back to steady me on my heels. I release a small laugh as my cheeks heat.

"Daddy has a surprise for you," Bella says.

I look up at Dante and lift a brow. He gives a half smile and shrugs. Something has changed again. He doesn't seem as on edge as he did earlier.

I follow the rose petals, trying not to trip over my own feet as Dante keeps his hand on my back. It feels so heavy and warm.

"Bella brought it to my attention that we didn't ask you to be our valentine."

"Right." Bella nods. "You couldn't know we wanted you with us if we didn't ask. We're going to fix that."

Dante chuckles. The flowers lead into Bella's playroom. When we step inside, the lights are off, but Bella's star projector lights up the ceiling and walls with red and white stars. Bella wiggles to get free, so I place her on her feet. She's dressed in a cute red pajama set. Her hair is pulled up in a ponytail on top of her head. She looks like she's fighting to stay awake.

"I called Uncle Gio and asked him what we should play for you." She runs over to the music station and taps at the tablet that's docked in this room.

"Teachme" by Musiq Soulchild starts to play. Dante slips a strong arm around my waist and pulls me into his chest. I look up into his eyes, shocked and unsure. Bella comes back over and takes my purse.

"There's a gift in there for you," I say as I try to calm my racing heart.

Bella gasps before she digs into the bag to search for the little box I have inside for her. I smile down at her as she drops my purse and opens the box.

"Oh, I love it, Lizzy. Thank you," she gushes at the tiny little teddy bear pendant with the blue sapphire eyes resting on the white gold chain.

"I wanted to give you something special."

Dante wraps his hand around the back of my neck and places his forehead to the side of my face before he starts to sway us to the music. My entire body starts to hum. I stop breathing, afraid to ruin the moment. Bella comes and wraps her little body around our legs.

My emotions start to clog my throat. I'm taken aback. The words of the song start to sink in. Gio may have picked it for Bella, but in this moment, it feels as if Dante is the one trying to convey a message.

"How can you know how to make her so happy, and you barely know us?" he breathes against my face.

"Sometimes it's the people who watch from the outside who know us best, even when we don't know they are watching. I've been working for you for years. I've shopped for a few of her birthdays and Christmases."

He pulls back and searches my eyes as I look up at him. His brows dip while he slowly runs his fingertips down my arm, drawing goose bumps. Bella stumbles away and goes to sit in the rug and pillow area. Dante wraps both arms around my waist and pulls me in closer.

I'm caught in a trance as he breathes me in, close enough to kiss me but still seeming out of reach. I allow myself to soak in his presence as well. Although, I do want to kick myself for thinking he's going to kiss me. Instead, he brushes his nose up the bridge of mine. It's actually a more intimate feeling than a kiss.

My breathing hitches. I close my eyes and commit this moment to memory. My body heats and softens from his nearness.

He pushes my braids that have come from behind my ear back in place. It's like a match has been lit against my skin. Just when I believe his arousal starts to poke into me, he speaks, breaking the spell.

"How was your date?"

I blink a few times to remember myself. This is my boss. I have secrets I can never tell him. It's best if I keep my cool and remember my place.

"It was okay. I guess." I lift my shoulder.

He nods and begins to run his hands down my back to my ass. I suck in a breath and stiffen. He groans and shakes his head.

"I'm sorry. I got lost. Um, she's asleep. I should get her into her bed." He nods over to a passed-out Bella.

"I'll help."

"No, I've got it. It's late. You have content to create, don't you?"

I smile. "Yeah, I do. Thanks for the dance."

He reaches into his pocket and pulls a square jewelry box out. "Bella thought I needed to make up for my huge mistake. Happy Valentine's Day, Liz. I hope you like them."

I take the box and pop the lid. A gorgeous pair of diamond studs rest inside. I release a sharp intake of air.

"Thank you," I whisper.

"They're not as beautiful as you are, but maybe they can show you a fraction of my gratitude."

I look up at him, searching his eyes. He looks away quickly and runs a hand through his hair. I cup the side of his face and lift on my toes to kiss his cheek. "It's my pleasure," I say softly.

"Good night, Liz," he says before moving to pick up a snoring Bella.

Dante

I want to strangle Gio. He couldn't have picked a better song to sum up the crazy feelings I have swirling on the inside for Lizzy. It's like I looked up one day and there she was. The perfect fit in almost every way.

Lizzy would be perfect for clean-cut Dante. That Dante wants nothing more than to bury himself in all those thick curves. I would have fucked the shit out of her right there in that playroom if Bella wasn't there.

I stare into space as I sit on my bed, trying to piece together my fucked-up life in my head. Nothing is black and white anymore. I feel like the other shoe is hanging over my head, waiting to drop.

"Fuck me. She bought her a teddy bear."

Bella loves teddy bears. I'm sure she'll wear that bear for the rest of her life. My own wife, Bella's mother, hadn't cared to take the time to learn teddy bears were Bella's favorite.

I don't even realize I've picked up my phone and dialed until my brother's tired voice comes through the line. I clear my throat and speak the words ringing in my head.

"Gio, what am I missing?" I say as my brother answers the phone.

"What do you mean?"

"Lizzy. What is it about her?" I sigh and run a hand through my hair. "You know what? Never mind."

"You're calling in the middle of the night. It's something."

"No, it's been a long week."

"She's addictive, isn't she?"

White-hot jealousy runs through me. I know the two have said they're only friends but just the thought of Gio having Lizzy as a part of his world makes me see red. *Not my Lizzy.*

"Fuck," I mutter.

"You want her. What's holding you back, little brother?"

"You know who I am. It wouldn't be right."

"Maybe you should take a deeper look. You're making an assumption. Get to know her. See who she really is. It's in her eyes. If you read them, you will see."

"Gio, what aren't you telling me?"

He laughs in my ear and hangs up the phone. I bite back a curse and toss my phone on the nightstand. I flop back onto the bed and look up at the ceiling. My mind turns to Lizzy. She felt so good in my arms.

There's so much chemistry there, I know she had to feel it. I didn't mean to caress her ass, it just felt right. I started to grow hard as I held her close. I had to ask her about her date, so I didn't embarrass myself. She always smells so good.

Frustrated, I pinch my eyes closed and pray for strength. When I admit to myself sleep isn't going to come to me. I grab my tablet and pull up Twitch.

She's already live. I smile when the first thing I notice after the commercial is Lizzy, with the earrings I gifted her shining back at me. Bella was so upset with me for not inviting Liz on our date. In her words, I let Jacob steal our valentine.

He can't make her happy like we can, Daddy. You have to fix it.

Her words echo and rattle around in my head. I purse my lips. Can I trust Lizzy? Can I try one more time? I want her so bad.

Fuck.

CHAPTER TWENTY-SEVEN

Little Tears

Lizzy

Two months later...

"Bella," I call out from the bottom of the stairs. "Sweetie, we have to go."

"What is she looking for?" Dante asks from the door behind me.

I turn to look at him. "I don't know. She said she needed to find something before we could leave."

He purses his lips as he looks down at his watch and runs a hand through his hair. I know he needs to get to the office. However, he's not going to leave Bella.

For the last two weeks, he's refused to let us out of his sight. I haven't driven to the office on my own since he started to insist we ride in with him.

He has put in an entire classroom for her at the office. He even insists on leading her instruction a few times a week. He makes time for his daughter.

God have mercy on anyone who has a problem with her presence in the office. She loves going to work with her father and offers to help whenever she isn't going through her lessons. She's become Nyla's little buddy as my sister now handles keeping Dante up to speed with his schedule.

Dante's phone rings and he pulls it from his pocket. He murmurs a few words, and a dark cloud falls over his face. His gaze flickers to me.

"I'll go up and see if I can help," I say and hurry up the stairs.

"Bella," I call as I rush up the steps in my heels.

I get to the top of the stairs and hurry down the hall. I pop my head into her bedroom first, but she's not in there. However, I furrow my brow as I find a mess. Things are tossed about as if she had been in here searching for something. Next, I double back for her playroom. When I step inside, I find her searching frantically as she runs her forearm under her nose.

Her body jerks with her small sobs and sniffles. As if giving up, she flops on her butt and covers her face with her palms.

"Bella? Sweetie, what's going on?"

She turns to me with big fat tears in her eyes. Her lips tremble and her shoulders sag as if defeat has set in. My heart tugs from the sight.

"I can't find it," she sobs.

I kick off my heels and pad over to her. Taking a seat beside her, I open my arms for her. She launches her body at me. I have no choice but to hold on tight to keep us from tumbling to the floor.

"What can't you find?" I say soothingly.

"My necklace. The one you gave me. I'm so sorry. I didn't mean to lose it."

"It's okay, we can look for it later."

"It's not okay. I should have taken better care of it." She's crying uncontrollably at this point. I feel terrible. I never thought she'd be so upset about misplacing the necklace. I'm sure I can get another. Actually, I know I can find it.

"Shh, Bella. I promise I'll find it."

"You shouldn't have to. Mommy said I needed to take better care of my things or I wouldn't get any more nice stuff. I'm sorry. I'll find it. Please don't stop getting me things. You always give me the best stuff."

"Oh, honey. Calm down, please. I know I can find it and you don't have to worry about me not getting you things. How about we do some shopping during our lunch break? I'll get you anything you want," I say softly.

She pulls away and wipes at her tears. "Really?"

"Yes, of course. Are you ready to wash your face so we can leave? Your father is waiting."

"Okay." She wraps her arms around my neck and gives me a tight hug. "Thank you."

"Actually, Liz, I want you two to stay here today," Dante says, startling me.

I turn to find him in the doorway, that look still on his face. His attention is on his phone as his fingers fly over the screen.

"Is everything okay?"

"Something has come up and you guys will be safer here. Jace is on his way to spend the day with you. Don't leave this house."

His tone makes me furrow my brows and snap my head back. He frowns and looks up at me. His face softens and he moves over to us and squats to place a hand on my back as he leans to kiss Bella on her forehead.

"It's better if you two remain home, safe. Please don't go out until I come home. It will give me peace of mind. That means both of you," he says the last part pointedly.

I nod my understanding as I look up into his eyes. I had plans this evening after work, but I guess I'll have to change those. I haven't gone skating with my team or to practice in a while, but I think they will understand.

He looks as if he wants to say more, but he shakes his head and stands to leave.

"Well, kiddo, I guess it's you and me for the day. Let's change," I say to Bella.

"Can we look for my necklace? Oh, and will we still go shopping at lunch?"

"I'll work on finding the necklace while you change. We can totally go shopping at lunch."

Dante

I see I'm going to have to reveal who the fuck I am again. Jace noticed someone following Lizzy and Bella a few weeks back. I had been leaving for the office without them to allow Bella and Lizzy to sleep in.

I was livid when Jace and Gio first informed me. I had Mitch look into it. He had the understanding that I had no patience and whoever had been following them needed to be found ASAP, or someone else would lose their life for failing to do their fucking job.

The call that came in as we waited for Bella was Mitch with the location of the piece of shit following my assistant and my baby girl. I won't be heading into the office today.

I'm on my way to get answers. I want to know who the fuck has lost their mind and why they are trying to make me kill them and everyone they know and care about.

"This is it, boss."

I look out the window at the colonial-style home. We're in a quaint little neighborhood. I now have a million questions. The back passenger door opens and Mitch climbs into the back of the SUV.

"This is just some nerdy guy. A nobody. I think he's a fan of her channel," Mitch grumbles, then sighs.

I shrug my suit jacket off my shoulders and tug it off, then toss it on the seat beside me. "Not a chance I'm willing to take, and if he is, and he's following her, that's a problem too."

Mitch grunts. "How do you want me to handle this?"

"You're not. Who's in the house with him?"

"He has two roommates. Neither are here. They both left for work. They usually don't return until late in the evening."

I nod.

"Boss, you're not going to do this in broad daylight?"

"The fuck I'm not."

Lizzy lives under my roof so she's mine to protect. I step from the car and head to the front door of the house. Mitch is hot on my heels. Once on the porch, I look around quickly before I ring the bell.

It takes a second ring before I hear someone moving around inside. A figure appears behind the barrier. I pull my Glock from the holster at my back.

As soon as he opens the door, I push my way inside. Swiftly, I grab this motherfucker by the face and shove my gun into his mouth. I look him over and snort. Some lanky motherfucker with shaggy brown hair and glasses.

"Why the fuck have you been following my assistant and my daughter?" I shout into his face.

My rage pulses through me as I look into his eyes. My nostrils flare and my chest heaves. He tries to speak around the gun. I pull it back and shove it against his temple.

"I...I...I'm a huge fan. I just wanted to get a look at Izzy in person. Someone doxed her on the boards. It was taken down, but not before I took a screenshot. I meant no harm, I wanted to see where she works. I don't know anything about the little girl. I thought Izzy had a kid or something. I took a few pics to dig up more information. They would go crazy for that shit on the boards."

"You took pictures. Where are they?"

"On my phone."

"Where's your phone?"

He pulls the phone out with trembling hands. I'm tempted to put a bullet in his head.

"Unlock it," I snarl. I snatch the phone and find the pictures. "Have you uploaded these anywhere?"

"No, not yet."

"If you're lying to me. I'll come back and blow your brains out all over this place. Stay the fuck away from them."

To drive my point home, I crack him in the head with the butt of the gun. He falls to the floor, knocked out cold. I delete the photos and toss his phone on top of him.

"I want guys on Lizzy, no matter what. Even if she's not with Bella. That channel is a fucking problem."

I've seen the threats and the crazy way they talk to her in the chat. I've wanted to hunt them down and put a bullet in all their heads. However, it dawned on me some of her fans are a bunch of silly kids.

Although, doxing her is an issue. That puts Bella in danger. I don't like it.

Who the fuck would do some shit like that?

CHAPTER TWENTY-EIGHT
We Need to Talk

Lizzy

I found the necklace without an issue. While Bella changed, I went to my room and activated the tracker that was placed inside the bear. I'll have to have the chain fixed. It looks like the clasp was caught on something and broke.

After her lessons, we spent the rest of the day in my gaming room. Bella was so excited to get a look around. We did some online shopping. She's probably the only kid in the world who could have anything but decides to ask for books.

I purchased her a ton of books, happy to see a smile on her little face. However, I haven't been able to shake the feeling that something very wrong happened today.

I called the office to see if I could assist Dante remotely, only to be told he never came into the office. I've been a bit concerned all day.

"We need to talk."

I look up from the book I'm reading as I sit in the kitchen. Dante looks tired and there's something in his eyes as he looks at me. I shrug it off and stand.

"Have you eaten? The chef left a plate for you. I can heat it up," I offer.

He waves me off. "I can take care of that. Is Bella sleeping?"

"Yes, she tried to stay up and wait for you."

"Did she find her necklace?"

"I found it."

"Good. Listen, it's come to my attention that someone was following you a few weeks back. It seems he was a fan or something."

"Are you serious?" I bite out.

He nods. "Someone doxed you on some boards or something."

Rage fills me. A lot of crazy shit happens in the gaming industry, especially to female gamers. However, doxing is the worst thing you can do. You're placing the person in danger by revealing their true identity and personal information.

"Dante, I'm so sorry. I had no idea. I would never want to place Bella in danger. I'll resign if you want."

He holds up his hand. "Hold on. Slow down. I knew you had a public thing going on with your channel before promoting you. I'm telling you this, so you know why I'm increasing your personal security."

"Personal security?" I almost scoff. "I don't need personal security. Technically, I'm only your assistant."

He closes the distance between us and swivels the barstool I'm seated on to face him. Dante steps between my legs and places one hand on the back of the stool and the other on the countertop as he looks down at me.

His gaze is so intense as he looks into my eyes with his hazel ones. I fidget from the waves of energy coming off him as he searches my face.

"A man was following you and took pictures of you and my daughter. You will have personal security. You have quite the following, one point five million is a lot. That's a whole lot of opportunity for crazy. I think this is something you should have had in place over half a million followers ago."

My mouth pops open. I didn't know he knew so much about my channel and followers. However, his words hit their mark. There are a lot of crazies out there—If only he knew, neither Bella nor I are ever in any real danger. I don't need security.

However, I do plan to have Aunt Denise look into the forums to see if she can figure out what the hell is going on. How has someone gotten enough information on me to share? I don't have a good feeling about this.

"If you think it's best," I reply, knowing when to pick my battles.

He cups my face and runs his thumb across my bottom lip. "Your safety is as important to me as Bella's. There's more to who I am, Liz. My wife's death could have been because of me. I won't have anything happen to you or Bella."

I tilt my head and grin as I look up at him through my lashes. He doesn't know it, but the same can be said for me. However, I keep that to myself. "You don't have to worry about me," I reply.

He stares at me for a while before he nods at his own thoughts. He rubs his fingers over his bottom lip before blowing out a breath.

"I think I'm going to place Bella in a school. I'm not going to be traveling as much. She can acclimate to being back in school and make some friends her own age."

"So, you want me to move out?" I'm surprised by how hurt I feel from the thought.

"No," he says firmly. "I'm not going to change her life that much. You have been good for her. I don't want any of that to change, but Zek can handle dropping her off and picking her up. I want you to come with me to look at the school I'm considering this week."

"Okay, but what will I do during the day?"

"Liz, you're my PA. You'll come to the office with me and assist me like you've been doing for the last six months. You've been balancing everything well. I'm actually impressed. How are your sales and sponsorships? Have you experienced any declines?"

"No, we're doing great. The fans like that my content has become more scheduled to accommodate my work schedule. It's not as random as it used to be," I reply.

"Good."

He pulls back and shrugs from his suit jacket, placing it on the stool beside mine before crossing his arms over his chest, still standing comfortably between my thighs. His face pinches a bit before he speaks again.

"How are things with Jacob? Are you still dating?"

I start to chew on my lip until his gaze drops to my mouth. His eyes darken with desire, knocking the wind from my lungs. Since Valentine's Day, Dante has been nothing but professional. I'm taken aback by the look in his eyes.

"I'm always busy, so we haven't gone on another date. We still text."

"Are you in a relationship?"

I laugh nervously. "I'm in a relationship with my jobs these days. He wants more, but I don't know if it's what I want. He's sweet enough." I bite my lip. "But I don't think he's for me."

Dante lifts a brow. He allows his gaze to roam over me. I tug at my thigh-high socks and squirm in my seat. Dante licks his lips. I go to pull my shorts down as my soaked panties make me aware of the fact that they have been riding into my crotch. His nostrils flare.

"You're not into nice guys?" He snorts with the question.

"Not my preference. They don't know what to do with me."

I don't know where the words come from, but it's the truth. I'm a bit much for most guys when they get to know the real me.

Slowly, as if he's thinking of his actions, he leans into my ear and pauses for a few beats. Then places his palms on the seat beneath me.

Goose bumps rise on my neck as his breath tickles my skin. His cologne fills my head and I almost moan. "Have you ever fucked a killer?" he breathes in my ear. Then shakes his head.

"Never mind, don't answer that." He sighs and backs away. "Get some sleep. You're with me tomorrow. My father is coming for Bella in the morning."

With that, he turns and leaves me hot, bothered, and confused. What just happened?

Dante

I need to figure my shit out before I do something stupid. The woman has a very strong sexual harassment case against me as it is. I either need to keep this professional or grow the balls to claim what I know is mine.

I've fought my feelings for months. However, this woman isn't anything I thought she was. Gio is right, there's something in Lizzy's eyes that shouldn't be there.

How? Why? Who is she?

I don't need personal security.

She said the words with so much confidence. Like she's me. Ha! Lizzy is no me. I remind myself of this as I step in the shower to wash the day away. The things I've done today alone would make her run from me. My gun is still smoking from the last visit of my day.

"Forget her hurting you. You'll ruin her life," I remind myself out loud.

CHAPTER TWENTY-NINE

Fishy Deals

Lizzy
A month later…

"These look great," Dante says as I stand beside him, looking over a few new menu mock-ups on my tablet that's on his desk.

My chest swells with pride. I worked hard with the graphic team to come up with a few choices Dante would like. I love that he's trusting me with so many new tasks.

I'd do anything to lighten his load. He always looks so stressed. Now that Bella no longer comes to the office, things have changed. He's not in as great a mood every day. He's not putting on a brave face for his little girl. He's all business.

I suck in a breath as he places his hand on my back as he swipes to the next mock-up with the other. "What do you think of this one?" he asks and points to my tablet.

"I don't think it fits the restaurant. Maybe the City Island location, but not this one," I reply.

"Knock, knock," Gio croons from the door, grabbing both our attention.

Like only Gio can do, he saunters in and takes a seat in front of Dante's desk. Jace is right behind him, but he moves to the seating area across the office.

I expect Dante to remove his hand, but he starts to run it up and down my back absently. "I agree. Send the other one to print. I want this one to go to the City Island location. Have them change the text and you can approve the final for print when it's done."

I stand up straight and his hand falls away. I take a calming breath and wiggle a bit as my panties start sticking to my lips. I tug at my blue silk blouse, trying not to sweat all over the place.

"What's up?" he says to Gio.

Gio looks to me, then back to Dante. A grin tugs at his lips before he steeples his fingers in front of his mouth.

"I came to talk a little business."

Dante holds up a finger.

"Liz, how's the Easter egg hunt planning going?"

I tap my tablet that's now in my hand. "Check your email. Everything is set up. If you want any changes, let me know."

"Thanks."

"No problem. Oh, you might want to look over yesterday's point-of-sale spreadsheets. The numbers look off. Dario called. He wanted you to know he'll be away a little longer."

He nods. "I'm heading over to the restaurant today to check on things."

"I'll come with you," Gio says.

"Good, we can talk in the car…" He pauses as he narrows his eyes at the screen before him. "What the fuck? These numbers are more than off. Tell Nyla to clear the rest of my day."

Without a word, I leave to do just that. The look on his face says a million words.

Dante

"Have you seen these?" I seethe.

"No, but what I came to talk about might be the reason for whatever you're looking at."

I look up at my brother to give him my full attention. I get a sinking feeling as I take in his expression. It's like I'm Alice being sucked into another world. Things have been quiet. Other than the fact that my mother-in-law hasn't surfaced, I haven't had to be that guy in weeks.

I honestly started to feel like a normal guy. I thought I could do this. Be the CEO and the Capo my family needs. Acceptance had started to set in. I've even considered taking Lizzy out on a date.

I roll my eyes. "What now?"

"Gustloff's fat, greasy ass delivered a bunch of bad fish to the restaurants. None of it was salvageable. They couldn't serve seafood at any of the locations last night. Today's shipment was worse."

I clench my fist. "Has he lost his fucking mind? Does he know what this means?"

"He knows. I'm just curious as to why he has the balls to do this, knowing the cost."

"Jace, have Zek come for Lizzy."

"Take her with you," Gio says.

I look at him as if he's lost his fucking mind. He knows what I'm about to do. Why the fuck would I take Lizzy? This isn't some routine check-in.

"She's going home, where she'll be safe."

"Don't you sound like an overprotective boyfriend," he taunts.

"She's not my girlfriend, she's my employee. Thanks to you, she's still texting Jacob."

It's an excuse. I know it is. Lizzy doesn't seem to be interested in Jacob, but I want Gio to back off, I have enough on my plate.

"Thanks to me?"

"Yeah, you. You're the one who introduced them."

Gio rolls his eyes. "Fine, I'll get rid of him."

"Are you crazy? Do you see the numbers he's bringing in?"

He shrugs. "There are always several ways to handle a situation. If a man wants something that's already his, he should go after it."

Jace scoffs so hard I have to look to make sure it was him. The look he gives Gio could kill. Without turning, Gio says, "When did I ask you anything? We leave in five. Go handle the chef."

Jace grunts but gets up to leave. I shake my head and turn my attention back to the screen. There's more to this. For Gustloff to call death down on himself, there had to be some reward.

I send a text to Mitch to have him meet me for this visit. Kaling comes to mind. I expected his wife to inquire about his whereabouts by now. *Crickets.*

I step inside the warehouse with Gio and Jace and frown. With each step I take into this funky ass place, I grow angrier. This shithole smells horrible. It smells worse than a whorehouse with no running water.

I'm already aggravated because I don't know when we'll be able to get our seafood deliveries back on track. Each day we're without a supplier, we're losing money. Dario's restaurant is known specifically for its seafood menu. This move was intended to hurt.

"What the hell? Did someone kill this fuck before me? He's never been this careless with this place," I mumble as I cover my face with my handkerchief.

"That's probably the next shipment his ass thinks he's going to dump on us," Gio says.

"The scent will cover the stench of death when you're done," Jace offers.

I grunt. "Who are you kidding? This funky ass motherfucker already smells like death. That's probably his ass," I snort.

"Fuck outta here. The way this place smells. That would mean someone gave him some pussy. Rancid, yes, but pussy nonetheless. The bastard couldn't pay for it, believe me." Gio chuckles.

We reach the back of the warehouse and Gio moves aside the plastic flaps. I walk through first and move to tap on the steel door to Gustloff's fake freezer. His office, as he calls it. Someone opens the door, allowing us to enter. At least the stench doesn't reach back here.

This slob sits playing cards like he's a king at the round table in the center of the room. There are five others seated with him. I pull both my guns before Gustloff's guy can come to search me. I tap the one in my right hand against the cheek of the guy seated directly in front of me.

"Get up, you're in my seat," I demand.

The asshole looks over his shoulder at me, then back at Gustloff, who nods as he laughs to himself. Yeah, someone has put a battery in this asshole's back. He has the confidence of a man who runs shit, and this motherfucker can't run his mouth properly.

The asshole in front of me grunts before he stands. He looks me over and I glare at him to let him know it's nothing to put a bullet in his head. He runs a hand through his hair and keeps it moving like a wise man.

I place both my guns on the table and smooth my tie down as I take a seat. Little does Gustloff know, I'm about to wipe that smug ass look off his fucking face.

"Tell me, Gustloff. What do you think has changed about me since we made this arrangement between us because the terms of service are still the same, yet you have breached the contract?" I tilt my head and study him closely.

"I remember you were a snot-nosed, arrogant little shit back then." He snorts and lifts his glass to his lips. "The Di Lorenzo name means nothing to me anymore." I pull in a calming breath through my nose and clench my fists on my thighs. "Rumor has it your family is about to fall. As you can see, I made a business decision to secure my future."

"Arrogant I may have been, but you were desperate. That's why you didn't take the time to read the contracts. You see, it was never about the money for me, although you're going to cough up what you owe. Let me tell you why the Di Lorenzo family will outlive you and whoever your new business partner is.

"My grandfather taught us all, know what a man's weakness is. What he fears to lose most. Then find out how to control it. I owned you from the day I first sat at this table.

"You fear losing your money. Your real money is in the drug business. You needed to move weight, and I had the ships and aircraft to help you do so. All you had to do was use this front to deliver my seafood. I provided the boats and the space. You provided the workers. Workers who I've been treating ten times better than you have for over ten years."

I tilt my head to the other side. "You see how I don't need you?"

I lift my gun and shoot the guy to my left, blowing his brains out. He slumps against the table. I pick up the other gun and aim to my right side.

"Move and you're next," I say as Gio and Jace hold their guns to the heads of the others in the room.

"Gustloff, my funky friend. Do you know what those contracts said?"

"Fuck you."

"No, you fucked yourself. You signed everything over to me that night. The contract stated it would all belong to my family and me in the event of your untimely demise. I own everything.

"With you gone, the guys can sleep at night, not having to worry about getting pinched by the Coast Guard and my pilots can relax knowing that they don't have to smuggle for your foul ass anymore either. So, fuck you."

With my arms crossed in front of me, I pull the trigger on the guy to my left and my right before uncrossing my arms and taking out the other two. Two shots go off behind me and I know Jace and Gio have taken care of the other two, leaving Gustloff panting and knowing it's his turn next.

"I was told to give you a message," Gustloff growls.

"So, you were set up for slaughter."

He shrugs and grunts. "At least you're getting what's coming to you and your family."

"Go on, give your message."

"You're all going to die—"

I put a bullet in his head and two in his chest before he can complete his final word. I stand and holster my guns and button my suit jacket.

Jace opens the door and Mitch enters. I move past Mitch and nod.

"Clean this shit up. Then shut this shit down for a deep clean. I want it up and running within a week, not a day longer. Keep the guys working on the boats. We'll use McGee's warehouse to process and handle deliveries for now. I'll cut a deal with him for the favor," I say.

"And the drugs?" Mitch asks.

"Bury them with the slob. Find my money. It's in this room," I say and leave the way we came.

Gio clasps me on the shoulder. "Take nothing he said to heart. I've got this handled."

I grunt. "I figured."

CHAPTER THIRTY

Total Jerk

Lizzy

"Lizzy?"

I look up from my tablet and smile. "What's up, ladybug?"

Bella gives me a sleepy smile and scoots closer to me on the couch. I lift my arm so she can snuggle under it. I've been working on emails and invoices that Dante noted for me to handle. There are also a ton of supply orders I need to push through for him.

I've been busy all evening. Not that I'm complaining. I'm actually loving my new assignment. Bella always has stories to share about her new friends at school when she gets home, and I've fallen in step with Dante's busy days.

I don't sleep much, so I've been getting content in on those sleepless nights and during my scheduled downtime. I smile as I realize how well it has all fallen into place.

"Do you miss me during the day?" Bella asks.

I look down at her and smile. "Of course, I do. It's hard having to work so hard without my best friend."

"I'll have to tell Daddy not to work you so hard. We need you around here. I don't want you to quit or leave."

I wrinkle my brows and sniff at my armpits. "Do I smell bad? Why are you always trying to get me to leave?"

She giggles and wraps her arms around me. "I'm not trying to get you to leave. I want you to always stay."

"I don't know. I mean, I like it here, I don't plan to leave, but you keep saying things that make me think you want me to go."

She giggles some more. "Lizzy, stop it. I want you to stay. I love you."

My heart swells. I love this kid too. I move my tablet to the coffee table and wrap her in my embrace. "I love you too, ladybug."

"I like it when you call me that. Can we go skating again this weekend?"

"I'll have to check with your dad first. If he's okay with it, we can go. You're getting so much better. You'll be trading your wheels out for roller blades in no time."

Her eyes brighten. "I can't wait to get big, so I can skate like you. I told all my friends at school about you. They think you're so cool. I do too."

"Not as cool as you." I tap the tip of her nose.

Bella yawns and places her head on my chest. I know she's been holding on for Dante, but it's getting late. I run a hand over her silky hair.

"Hey, I think it's time to head upstairs. I'll read you your bedtime story and make sure your dad comes in to kiss you good night."

"Okay," she yawns.

I stand and lift her to carry her upstairs. She's out before we hit the steps. I chuckle and kiss her forehead.

"Hey, guys. Thanks for joining me tonight. It's been a busy day, so I'm looking to blow off a little steam," I say to my fans as I get my Twitch session started.

Ny says she'll come join me in a bit, she's looking into something. I know how my sister gets when she's trying to figure something out.

I would have been on sooner, but Jacob had been texting me. He's been a bit weird lately. Almost insisting we go on another date. I'm not really interested in another date. Friends, yes, but not a date. I already figured out things wouldn't work between us.

While Dante may be totally out of my league, I know I wouldn't be satisfied with Jacob. Then there's the confusion I'm still dealing with from a month ago.

Dante has been a gentleman since that night he whispered in my ear. Not that I don't shiver every time I think about his words. We're in the friend zone and I like that. It makes working together flow smoothly.

I talked to my sister earlier about my conflict with Jacob. I told her how Jacob seems to be under the impression we're a couple. I don't want to hurt his feelings, but I want to take a step back from the relationship. That's when she rushed off the phone, saying she had something she needed to handle.

"*Aww*, Shield, thank you. I need to go get them done again," I say, running a hand over my knotless braids. It's definitely time for a refresh.

Shield_44: You're always beautiful.

Jacob_eats: She is.

The_Dane_2: You guys make me sick. You always suck up and tell her she's beautiful on here. Why not tell her all the shit you guys say in the forum? @Shield_44 and @Jacob_eats, I see you. I've seen your comments.

I blink as I read The Dane's comment. I chose to ignore it. I know they can be vicious in the forums. That's why I stay away from them. I have pretty thick skin, but even I spent days crying after one visit. It was the first and last time I went over there.

I start my gameplay as if nothing has happened. I learned a long time ago if you let the fans see something bothers you, the trolls lock in on it and attack. I'm here to play and be peaceful tonight.

This is my getaway. I'm not going to let anyone ruin that. Not tonight.

I'm in the zone and win the first battle royal with ease. Sometimes playing singles can be fun. Although I do love playing with my sister more.

One of my screens grabs my attention as I wait to join a new lobby for another round. Thinking it's Nyla telling me she's ready, I turn my attention to the screen with Discord up to read her message.

I furrow my brows as I read the first message. My heart sinks as the images start to pop up. I know when my sister is determined, she can find anything, but I almost want to call her and scream stop. I know she means well, but this hurts more than I ever thought it could.

"I need to go, guys," I say as best I can and cut the live.

I pick up my phone and call my sister. "Hello, do you see this?"

"Please stop," I sob.

"Liz?" she says with sadness in her voice. "Are you crying? You said you didn't really like him. I only wanted you to see the shit he's been spewing behind your back, so you'd stop wasting your time thinking he's some nice guy."

I close my eyes, not wanting to see the harsh words Jacob has said about me on the forums. Yeah, I didn't like him as a boyfriend, but I thought of him as a friend. This hurts so bad.

I think back to all the teasing and hurtful things said to me in high school, the reason I hate being around people. If it weren't for my big sister dressing me up like a superhero and telling me I was special, I probably wouldn't have made it out of junior high school and high school, forget about college.

"Don't cry, Liz. You're beautiful and amazing. I'm so sorry." Now she sounds like she wants to sob.

"Thanks, Ny. I need a minute. I'll call you back."

"I love you, Liz. Everything I do is for you."

"I know. I love you too. Later."

I hang up and pull up my playlist. I scroll for the song I'm looking for and crank the music up. Jessie Reyez's "Figures" comes through the speakers. I won't lie. I'm hurt. Old wounds have opened and surfaced.

Dante

I climb out of the back of the car as we pull up in front of the house. Bella is probably in bed by now. I'll take a shower, go to kiss her good night and then I can have a drink to settle my demons.

There's a fine line between knowing who I have to be and being who I am. I'm starting to crave this shit again. That dark place is taking over. I could have handled tonight differently, but I wouldn't have been satisfied.

My mind turns to Lizzy. I want to bury myself in her light. These last few months have allowed me to get to know her. She's smart and resourceful. Gio is right, there's something in her eyes, but I'm having a hard time believing it's what I think it is.

I push into the house and music blares from the direction of Lizzy's gaming room. It's a bit loud. I've never heard her play music so loud before. Not to mention, it's a melancholy tune. My hackles go up.

I jog up to my room and grab my tablet to check in on her channel to see if I can find out what's going on. It's not live. I clench my teeth and toss the device down on the bed.

I need to get out of these clothes and shower. However, the need to go check on her is so strong. I strip out of my clothes quickly and head for my bathroom. I make quick work of a thorough shower.

When I step out of the shower, I look into the mirror. My hair has grown a bit and my face is covered in stubble. I have a few meetings this week. I'll shave and go for a cut in the morning.

I head for my closet for a pair of sweats and a T-shirt. I only stop to check my tablet one more time.

Finding Liz still isn't on, but hearing the music still floating through the house, I toss the tablet back down and head to check on Bella. She's sound asleep. God, I love this little girl. It's because of her I can't allow myself to be consumed by this dark world we've inherited with our last name.

"I love you," I whisper against her little forehead.

Rage fills me as I think of the fact that someone's threatening my family, my daughter. For her and her safety, I'll become that guy all over again. Bella stirs a little and tightens her hold on her teddy bear.

A smile comes to my face. It's the same bear she built with Liz. I turn and head to find out what's going on with our angel. Her face may be enough to pull me from this funk.

"What's wrong, *mio Angelo?*"

The same song is still playing. My thoughts turn to Jacob. Gio works fast. I know this is his work. I feel it.

However, I don't like that it may have hurt Lizzy. Honestly, I was only using Jacob as an excuse. I hope like hell I haven't caused her pain.

I get to the door to her game room and place my palm against it as I listen to the words of the song that's still on repeat. I know I've fucked up as the words sink in. I ball my fist that's pressed to the door. After another few beats, I knock.

There's no answer at first, so I turn the knob. The music is pretty loud, she may not have heard my knock. The door cracks open as I turn and push in. I stick my head in and find her sitting on the floor, curled into a ball. Her knees pulled into her chest and her arms held tightly around them as she rocks herself back and forth.

She tries to wipe away her tears on her sleeve but not before I see her face covered in them. I step fully into the room and close the door, so the music doesn't reach upstairs. I clear my throat and shove my hands into my pockets.

"Everything okay?"

Her full lips tremble as she purses them, and more tears fall. She shakes her head, apparently not able to speak. I move closer and squat before her, placing a hand on one of her knees.

"It's been a shit day for me too. You want to come have a drink with me and tell me about it?"

She wipes at her tears with her hoodie sleeve again, then stares at me as if she's undecided. I reach to run my fingers along her temple. I nod toward the door.

"Come on. I want to show you something. It's my favorite part of the house. It's my secret place. If you promise not to tell, I'll share a bottle of grappa with you."

I hold out my hand and stand. She places her hand in mine and I pull her up. Reaching for her face, I wipe the rest of her tears away. All her innocence shows in this moment. I've never seen her more vulnerable.

I keep her hand clasped in mine as I lead her out of the room. She pulls her phone from her hoodie and the music stops. I realize in the silence that my heart is beating like a teenager with his first girlfriend.

"We're going to the roof," I say to distract my thoughts. "I wanted a man cave. I was a bit over the top when I had this place built. It was what I needed at the time though. A place to think."

I unlock the door with my fingerprint and lead her up the stairs behind the door on the second level. She follows me up silently. However, as soon as we step out on the rooftop, she gasps.

"The lock is print recognition because of Bella. When she was born, I had the system put in."

"This is breathtaking," she whispers.

I look around and smile, this is my sanctuary. This place takes me places. Bethany couldn't follow me up here and I could get lost in my own world.

"Come with me," I say and tug her forward.

CHAPTER THIRTY-ONE

Secret Place

Lizzy

The place is breathtaking. It's like a rooftop bachelor pad with a pool included. It's like I've been transported far away from my problems. I follow as he tugs me into the rooftop apartment.

He releases my hand as we step inside, and I turn in a circle to take it all in. The place has floor-to-ceiling windows and modern furnishings. The night sky is gorgeous tonight. I wrap my arms around my middle and take in the sight.

Dante returns with a bottle of liquor and two tumblers in his hands. He bumps my hip with his and nods for the pool outside. I follow as he moves to what looks like a platform that sits right at the lip of the roof. I take a seat on my butt next to him as he sits with his knees bent into his chest.

"I never would have noticed this from down there," I say, nodding down at the backyard.

"I had it built on the back end of the house and designed to be positioned just right to be out of view. Believe it or not, it all started with this spot right here."

"Really?" I say as I take the tumbler he's just filled and hands to me.

"Yeah." He inhales deeply. "After my mother left us, I used to sit on the roof of our house for hours, watching and waiting for her to pull into the driveway. My uncle was the one to figure it out. He'd sit with me and talk to me for hours. Up here is a place of comfort for me," he says and shrugs.

My heart tugs for him as a little boy. That must have been so hard. I go to take a sip from the tumbler and frown. Dante bursts into laughter. It transforms his face. I like seeing him like this.

"Grappa will burn through life, sweetheart. Whatever is troubling you will be a distant memory tomorrow. I promise you that," he says and throws his glass back.

I take a sip and look down in my glass. Tears burn the backs of my eyes. I try to force them down. I close my eyes tight as my insecurities start to claw through my brain.

"Jacob turned out to be a total jerk," I murmur.

"Did you guys break up?"

"We were never together. My sister did some digging and found a thread on one of the forums with Jacob's handle. He was shit-talking about me," I reply.

"Shit-talking? Like what?"

"From what I read in the screenshots. He thinks I'm an attention seeker. I could stand to go on a diet. I'm a nerd," I choke out the last part, unable to finish.

"What the fuck?" Dante seethes, causing me to drain the rest of my glass. I hold it out toward him, and he fills it again. I tap my fingers against the glass and think about the next thing pushing to come out of my lips.

I drain my glass. *What the hell? Here goes nothing.* I take in a deep breath as my chest burns from the liquor.

"It's not so much that I care about Jacob, you know. There was no spark there, I'll get over it. It's the things he said." My lips tremble as I fall back into my past.

"My sister is twelve years older than me. I kind of grew up like an only child. School was horrible for me. I was teased and bullied. I suffered in silence for years.

"In high school, it became unbearable. When Nyla found out, she lost it. She came up to the school and made me stop them. I beat one girl so bad I was arrested. Dad was so upset.

"He wasn't mad at me for standing up for myself. It was the excessive force I used that made him angry...I wasn't supposed to—" I cut off, knowing I'm saying too much. "—My sister, on the other hand, was proud of me. She took time to put me back together and helped me find my confidence and backbone."

"It sounds like your sister loves you."

"Yeah, she does." I smile. "But that's just the thing. I felt like I failed her. I've wanted to be like Nyla all my life. She's the popular one, the pretty one, the skinnier one, the badass boss. She seems so happy with her life. She travels the world and leaves her mark.

"Reading those comments Jacob wrote brought home how much I feel like that loser from high school. I'm twenty-nine and single, I haven't moved out of my dad's, I'm still not as confident in myself as I'd like to be."

Dante throws back another drink and looks at me thoughtfully. I hold my glass out for another drink and he fills the glass. I toss it back this time and peer at him.

"I've seen your sister. Is she gorgeous? Yes, but so are you. Liz, you are one of the most stunning women I've laid eyes on. Who cares about being skinny when you have curves like yours? There are women paying to get what you have and killing themselves to get it."

I look down into my now empty glass. Dante moves closer and lifts my face with his fingertips. He searches my face and continues with his words.

"You have to know how beautiful you are. My little girl looks up to you and tries to imitate that beauty all the time." His gaze drops to my lips.

Something shifts in the atmosphere and his eyes take on a heated look. Desire and lust fill his hazel eyes and the heat I see is undeniable. His voice becomes husky as he starts again.

"If you were mine, I'd kiss, lick, and fuck every single inch of your body until you thought I was the creator of life itself. I'd put a hurting on that body so good you'd have love for it just because of the pleasure I bring it. However, it's not your body that makes me want to strip you bare and fuck you senseless. It's your heart and your mind. You're brilliant. You've been impressing me in the office every day. And the business you have built, I'm in awe of you."

I lower my lashes. "Thanks. That means so much coming from you," I breathe, trying to ignore his heated words.

He gives a dark chuckle. "You can relax. I'm not in the mood to seduce you tonight. I have too much shit going on in my head."

He reaches into his pocket and pulls his phone out. A few taps and Rema's "Calm Down" fills the air as Dante stands.

He winks at me. "Come dance with me."

I look up at him curiously. Dante is so tall and built I can't see him dancing. Especially not to something like this. He smiles and chuckles.

"You'd be surprised by the music I enjoy."

I hiccup and stand, pulling my shorts out of my butt. I'm glad I have my hoodie on, there's a slight chill up here. I stumble a little, but Dante wraps my waist and pulls me into his chest. I wiggle my toes in my socks. I don't have on shoes.

That thought is forgotten as Dante places a hand on the small of my back and starts to move our hips to the song. My mouth falls open as he begins to move me around the rooftop. His moves are sexy.

I laugh when he spins me out and pulls me back into him, placing his hands on my hips. "Come on, Lizzy. Show me what you got."

I throw my head back as the liquor begins to course through my veins and gives me new courage. I rock my hips in his hold. He gives me a huge smile and pulls me back to his chest and slips a leg between mine as he rocks and sways our bodies.

I lift my palms up and he places his against mine. Then he pushes his forehead to mine. His breath is warm and smells of alcohol. This is so different from the Dante I know in the office.

I love the happiness in his eyes. It makes me forget my problems and smile. The song ends and I'm left breathing heavily.

I lift a questioning brow at him. "Have you ever wondered why we don't just have a bunch of Italian restaurants?" he breathes as he looks down into my eyes.

"Sort of."

"It was Nonno's one request before I married. He wanted me to spend two years traveling the world with Dario. We immersed ourselves in so many different cultures. The food, the spices, the music. All of it. If Dario cooks you a curry, believe me, it will be authentic to whatever region it's from.

"The food stuck with him. The music and vibes stuck with me."

"That's cool," I say goofily.

The song changes to one with a similar vibe. I think it's Rema too. He spins me and turns my back to his front. Banding his arms around me, he rocks our bodies to the beat of the music some more. My cheeks heat and my body hums. His warm breath fans my ear and my nipples tighten.

I look over my shoulder and smile up at him. This is fun—a whole new side of Dante I never thought existed, let alone that I'd get to see.

"I guess you're single, single now," Dante says as he stares down at my lips.

I shrug. "Do you think you'll get back out there?"

I don't know what makes me ask. Blame it on the alcohol. A spark fills his eyes, and he pulls my arms up around his neck.

"I'm considering it."

I feel a pang in my heart and turn away from him. He spins me back to face him, but I keep my eyes on his chest. He clicks his tongue, bringing my attention back to his face.

"You really don't get it," he says with a grin.

"Get what?" I say as I look up at him in confusion.

"Nothing, Liz."

Dante

Her laugh is like music. I'm glad she's having a good time after the way I found her earlier. If I weren't contemplating murder, I would have fucked her on this roof tonight.

Jacob may make me money, but I can find a ton of chefs to replace him. However, as my mind sobers, I know I need to find out how Gio's hand played in this before I fly off the handle.

"This has been fun, thank you," she says.

"It's the least I can do. I've been having fun too. You helped me get my mind off the bullshit."

She has. In the last three hours, we have danced, talked, and finished two bottles of grappa. Lizzy is definitely drunk. She is an adorable drunk.

She narrows her eyes as she gives me a drunken smile. "You know, if I didn't know better, I'd think you were as dangerous as your brother," she says in a teasing tone.

I wink at her. "You have no idea, gorgeous."

"Me gorgeous, nope, that would be you," she says and taps my nose.

I catch her hand and bring her fingers to my lips. I kiss them and she bites her lip as she watches the action. I smile at her as her mouth falls open. God, she's so cute. I'm tempted to pull her into me to taste her plump lips.

"Okay, sweetheart. I think I should get you downstairs."

I stand from the outdoor sofa on the rooftop and hold out my hand. She places her palm in mine. When she stands, she's unsteady.

I wrap an arm around her waist and guide her to the stairs. We get halfway down when she groans and looks up at me.

"Oh God, Dante, I think I'm going to be sick."

"Hold on a sec, baby. I'll get you to your room." I lift her in my arms and clear the rest of the stairs before I push through the exit and let the door close behind me. She has her arms wrapped tightly around my neck.

When we make it into her room, she leaps from my arms and races for the bathroom. I follow behind her and reach for her braids as she retches into the toilet. I hold her hair with one hand and rub her back with the other.

I feel bad. Grappa would put me on my ass if I drank enough of it. Lizzy consumed almost as much as I did. I'm a lot bigger than she is.

She's sniffling for an entirely different reason this time. I don't know how long we're in here, but I know her stomach has to be empty when I get up and wet a towel for her to clean her face. Releasing a deep breath, she turns to look over her shoulder at me.

She has a little smile on her lips and tears in her eyes. I can't help wondering what's going on in her head.

"Good thing you're not thinking about dating me. I think I just royally Lizzyed this night," she says with that smile.

I look at her, I mean, really look at her and I think I start to sober up. Images of the time we've spent together—like the night I painted her toes and all the moments we spent in my office. Flashes of all the moments she's been with Bella—like the time she gave Bella the necklace and how Lizzy was the one Bella ran to when her own mother made her cry.

Then all the moments when she doesn't know I'm watching her, like the time Bella told her she just wanted to see her happy. Then there's the way my nonno smiled at her and all our moments in the office and…tonight. It all flashes through my thoughts. I remember her words and Gio's.

It was the excessive force I used that made him angry.

You're making an assumption. Get to know her. See who she really is. It's in her eyes. If you read them, you will see.

"Well, shit," I murmur.

I've fallen in love with her. I want more than to fuck Lizzy. I want her and that look in her eyes tells me she just might be able to handle the real me. God, I hope I'm not making a mistake. I don't need to hurt my daughter.

You mean, you don't want to be hurt. Man up, Dante.

She blinks and her smile falls a bit. I smile at her and kiss her forehead. "If that means you've made it one of the most interesting nights I've had in a long time. Yeah, you did," I say, trying to bring her smile back and cover up the feelings that surface.

She returns the smile, but it turns shy or maybe embarrassed as if she's just realized what has happened while we've been in here. I rub my hand up and down her back. Searching her face, I move the braids that have fallen into her face out of the way.

"Get some sleep. I'll check on you later."

"Thank you, Dante," she calls after me.

I nod as I leave to process my feelings. This was not supposed to happen.

CHAPTER THIRTY-TWO

Cheer Up Lizzy

Dante

"I did what you wanted. I got the chef out of the way," Gio says nonchalantly.

I blow out a breath. I'm more frustrated with myself than him. Gio gets things done and I should have known better. I still can't get Liz's face from last night out of my head.

How can a woman be so gorgeous even after watching her puke in the toilet while holding her hair back? I'm still trying to make sense of it.

"Well, now she's been in her room all day. She lets Bella in to sit with her, but she hasn't come out. That shit hurt her feelings," I grumble into the phone.

"Yeah, I get that. You're not the only one pissed off about it. I'm sending reinforcements. I'll fix it. You can stop whining."

"Whatever."

"Have you talked to Dario?"

"No, I'm giving him space to figure shit out."

"I think I may take a trip to check in on him."

"That's not a bad idea. Maybe I'll take Bella for a trip. With everything happening here, it might be good to go home. No one would dare try the family back home," I muse.

"This is a fact."

"That could be why Dario is choosing not to come back. I don't blame him. He's doing what is right for him," I say.

"Never said he wasn't. Listen, I need to go. Help is on the way. I love you, little brother. Everything I do is for you and Dario. You don't have to worry. This will blow over and you will have what you want."

"The question is…what do I want?"

He scoffs. "I thought you figured that out."

I scratch my chin as my thoughts race. "No, I don't think I have."

"That's the problem. Please stop thinking."

He's right, but I don't tell him he is. I stayed up all night thinking about how I feel about Lizzy and what my life has become. On the one hand, I want the peace she brings to my world. On the other, I want someone who can understand and handle my secrets and I'm not sure yet if that's Lizzy.

"I should have some flowers delivered or some shit."

Gio roars with laughter. "I forget you've never dated as a grown adult. Flowers are good, bro. Go with it. See you later."

I hang up and run a hand through my hair. We had a good time last night. I thought she was over that fuck. It's kind of pissing me off that she's locked in her room over him. She deserves better and he doesn't deserve her tears. I don't care how much Gio had to do with this.

Maybe I should take this as a sign that I'll only fuck things up. Bella is attached. If Lizzy can't handle my world, Bella will lose her. I can't afford to take that chance.

Lizzy

"Lizzy?" I look up from my kindle and find Bella looking at me expectantly.

She's been keeping me company while I read. Technically, it's Saturday and my day off. However, I don't mind the company.

I woke with a pounding headache. I haven't been able to show my face after last night. I only remember half the things Dante said to me. What I do remember is throwing up in front of him. I'm so embarrassed. Only me.

"What's up?" I say to Bella as I try not to think about last night.

"I think I've read all my new books. Can we get some more?"

"Sure, why not?" I smile at her snuggled under my blankets. We're both still in our pj's. Taking a shower is the most I've done today. I dread having to get us both lunch. If I could hide out in here for the rest of my life, I would.

My heart starts to race when a knock sounds on the door. The last thing I want is to face Dante. My face burns as I think of him holding my hair for me.

I know I'm shit at holding my liquor. I don't know what I was thinking. Time stops as Bella jumps up and runs to answer the door. I only breathe easier when my sister comes into view.

I've never been happier to see her. I toss the covers back and get up as she enters the room. She looks around. "Wow, this place is nice."

"Nyla," Bella sings and wraps around my sister's legs.

"Hey, pretty girl. How's it going?"

Bella giggles. "I'm spending time with Lizzy. We're reading and hanging out."

"Sounds like fun. Do you know she used to sit and read with me when she was around your age?"

"Really?"

"Yup."

"Bella," Dante calls as he appears in the doorway.

"Yes, Daddy?"

"Come with me. I'll get you something to eat. Let's let Lizzy have some time to herself to hang with her sister."

"Okay," Bella says sadly.

"Hey, we'll hang some more later. It's time to change our nail polish."

"Yes," Bella cheers and pumps her little fist.

Dante smiles and places a hand on top of Bella's head to lead her out of the room. I can't even look up at him. I keep my gaze down and pull into myself. I release the breath I don't realize I'm holding once the door is closed again.

"Okay, what was that about?"

I groan and fall back on my bed. "Kill me now," I mutter.

"Why haven't you been answering my calls this morning?"

I sit up and look for my phone. Swiping my hand under my pillow, I find the device filled with missed calls. I groan again.

"I'm sorry. I woke with the worse hangover. I just needed the room to stop spinning. I didn't think to check my phone."

"So, you're not still mad at me?"

"For what?" I ask and look at her in confusion.

"For showing you who that creep really is."

"Who, Jacob? Oh God, no. I'm so over that. I'm too busy dying of embarrassment to think about him."

"Explain?" Nyla says and places down the bags she entered with. I look at the bags curiously but shrug and begin to tell her about what I remember from last night.

"I'm such a goofball. Like, why am I so awkward? You got all the cool genes. My boss is totally hot and held my hair while I puked my guts out. Why is this my life?"

"Girl, please. The fact that he stayed to hold your hair speaks volumes. You have to stop being so hard on yourself," she replies. "If you ask me, you should get dressed and go see if you can pick up where you guys left off."

"You're kidding, right? I'm sure it was only the alcohol talking. He's not interested in me. He can have anyone he wants."

Nyla snorts and makes a face of disgust. I frown and start to fidget. I know that look. She gives it to me every time she's about to ream me for not having confidence in myself.

"And why wouldn't he want you?"

"Come on, Ny."

"No, you come on. I'm so glad I went shopping first. I thought you were in here beating yourself up over that asshat, but you're sitting in here talking nonsense in that brain of yours. Get up," she commands.

I stand and shift from foot to foot, playing with the hem of my T-shirt. Nyla shoves the bags at me and shoos me into the bathroom.

"You go put that on. I'm going to help you remember who you are. I've been gone too long, and someone needs to help you see the amazing vixen who's my living, breathing, badass sister," she says as I head into the bathroom.

I place the bags on the counter and peek inside the first two. Those have shoe boxes in them. The last bag, I have to sift through the tissue paper to find the little lacy bra and panty sets, one red the other black with matching garters. At the bottom of the bag rests two silk robes to match each set.

I can't help the laugh that comes to my lips. Ny used to do this all the time. Have me dress up and look in the mirror as she pointed out all the things she thought were great about me.

It looks like I'm going to get the adult version of that today. Since I showered already, I change into the red sexy outfit and open the shoeboxes to find matching patent leather heels for each outfit.

I slip them on and head out into the bedroom with the robe tugged tightly around me. Ny sits on the foot of the bed with her head bent over her phone. I move into the room and stop in front of her.

She looks up and smiles. "There's my sister. Go look at yourself." She points to the full-length mirror inside the walk-in closet in my room.

I move into the closet and stand before the mirror. Slowly, I open the robe and have to admit, this set looks cute on me. I've always been the bottom-heavy sister. You can see my hips and ass coming a mile away. I once hated my curves. Kids made fun of me in school for being tall and curvy. It took forever for my breasts to come in, but my behind popped like someone inflated me.

After learning what my body is capable of, I appreciate it. Looking now, I can't say I see the flaws I used to. What I see is a sexy woman. I know that's Nyla's point.

"I get it," I say. "But he will forever have the image of me barfing etched in his brain."

"Nah, you're going to get over that, sis. I have an idea. I think it will be a confidence booster for you."

"Oh, no, what are you about to get me into?"

"You'll thank me later." She winks at me through the mirror. It's then I notice her small camera bag on her shoulder. I groan and tell myself I can trust Nyla.

"Okay. I want you to pick a song that makes you feel sexy. And another you would use to tell your man how you feel."

Two songs pop in my head right away. I give a small smile and nod my head. Nyla pulls out her Bluetooth speaker and sets it up. She then brings out her camera with its own lighting attached.

"Remember, you're only as confident as you feel. You're never the opinion of others. It's not like you don't know how gorgeous you are. You're just shy. Don't let that put you in a box.

"I want you to have fun. Like those silly TikTok videos you make. Look at the camera and be the real you. Be fierce, like when you dress up for those cons. Show me the superhero I know you are. Be Izzy Gunz. She fears nothing," Nyla encourages.

I nod as I take her phone and find the first song. I pull up "Pressure" by Ari Lennox and hand the phone back.

"Okay," Ny sings out. "Give me one of those walks."

I take in a deep breath and move to the back of the closet. I get into character and start to do a slow model walk.

"Oww, that's my girl. Give me all that face."

I reach and release my braids from their bun. I flip them forward, then whip them back. I lose myself to the song. I think about Jacob's harsh words and they're like fire in my veins. I'm not a goofy slob.

"Make it sexy, Liz. You got this."

Suddenly Dante's words from last night come to me. *If you were mine, I'd kiss, lick, and fuck every single inch of your body until you thought I was the creator of life itself. I'd put a hurting on that body so good you'd have love for it just because of the pleasure I bring it. However, it's not your body that makes me want to strip you bare and fuck you senseless.*

It's like a switch is turned on. Confidence fills me and I get into performing for the camera. I let the robe slip off my shoulder and throw myself all in.

I love my sister. Everyone should have a Ny in their life. Jacob forgotten and my confidence restored after the embarrassment of a lifetime. I enjoy an afternoon of acting silly with my big sister. It's just what I need to pull me out of my funk.

However, I do make sure she deletes all the footage before she leaves. I may feel more confident, but I wouldn't want anyone to see those videos.

Dante

After Nyla left, Lizzy came to join us for dinner, and she had a huge smile on her face. I was happy to see it there. I don't know what her sister did, but Lizzy seemed to have a new confidence. It looks good on her.

"You want to watch a movie with me?" I ask as we walk out of Bella's bedroom.

We've just put her down for the night. It was a challenge to keep her out of Lizzy and Nyla's hair earlier. We could hear the music coming from Lizzy's room. Bella danced around while looking in the direction of the music longingly.

I know she wanted to hang with the girls, but my gut told me Lizzy and her sister needed the time together. Eventually, I had to get Bella out of the house and took her out for ice cream. We returned to laughter and two beautiful women in my kitchen eating pizza.

Lizzy looks up at me shyly. "I would love to, but tonight is actually one of my scheduled content nights. After jumping off on them last night, I should probably stick to the schedule," she says softly.

I nod. "Sure, no problem. Maybe another time."

I look her over and take in her outfit. It's not her usual gaming uniform of shorts, socks, and a tank top. I like this better. She has on an oversized long-sleeve T-shirt with the Izzy Gunz logo on the front. Her sweatpants with Izzy Gunz printed down the leg are a bit baggy as well. Her braids are loose and hanging over one shoulder.

I clear my throat and look into her eyes. "New merch?" I point to the outfit.

She looks down and smiles. "Yeah, some of the female fans have complained about the little shorts and asked for something with more coverage. I guess I get it. It took a long time for Nyla to talk me into wearing our merch on cam. Actually, I almost didn't cam up at first. Viewership sucked." She clamps her mouth shut.

"I'm sorry, I ramble when I'm nervous."

"Why are you nervous? I'm fascinated by your business. I'm fascinated by all things Lizzy, if I'm honest."

She looks up at me through her lashes. I can see her trying to see if I'm bullshitting her. I move in to crowd her space.

"I mean everything I say, Liz—"

Her phone rings, cutting me off. I bare my teeth as she rushes to answer it. Another sign I need to back off. I pull a hand down my face and take a step back.

"Good night," I call over my shoulder and walk away as I toss a wave.

I need a drink. It's been about seven months since burying Bethany, maybe it's time I find someone to keep me company in my bed.

Fuck that.

The idea doesn't get to take root as images of Lizzy writhing beneath me fill my head. She's the only one I want in my bed.

I head for the rooftop to have a drink and clear my mind. It's not lost on me that I stop at my bedroom to grab my laptop. I plan to watch Lizzy's channel while I sip. Fuck, who am I kidding? I'm at the point where I might rub one out while I watch. I crave her that much.

What the fuck is she doing to you, Dante?

I sit with a tumbler in my hand, watching Lizzy game. My eyes are tired, and I should probably call it a night. Bella and I have a brunch date tomorrow. Lizzy has plans to go to her father's.

My phone buzzes, grabbing my attention. I pick it up and grind my teeth. I'll be ending another business relationship. It doesn't escape me that all my illegal connections are being targeted.

This is the second relationship that had a second source of income coming from it. These are the deals I established when I was old enough to become Capo. The deals Nonno trusted me to make.

I frown and toss the phone back on the desk. Blood money is a waste of my time. I've made billions without it. It's the power that's the real hit. Someone is hell-bent on making it look like I'm losing control.

"Fuck around and find out," I murmur, all my Jersey coming out.

I'm going to have to prove a point, but first, I need answers. Kaling and Gustloff had reasons for their actions. I know neither acted alone. I'd like to know where my former mother-in-law is. I get the feeling I can get some answers from her.

As the thought crosses my brain, I pick the phone back up and shoot a text to Mitch. It's time I focus on the whole picture. Bethany's death was when all of this started, so what am I missing?

I empty my glass and fill it again. Lizzy's sweet laugh draws my attention as I drop my phone on the desk again. She enjoys herself so much when she does this.

However, in the blink of an eye, the atmosphere changes. I know it's that fucking chat. I hate these fucking trolls. I zero in on the chat and start to read. As I thought, they're in there talking shit.

"Ignore them, baby," I murmur to the screen.

My blood boils as I watch her face transform, even though she's not responding. The threats start and that's when I start to feel murderous. However, it's when a sad look comes to her eyes that I find myself wanting to shut this shit down and forbid her from gaming live anymore.

"I'm sorry you feel that way, Squid Kid," Lizzy says.

I look through the fast-moving chat to find what Squid Kid has said.

Squid_Kid: You're a hack. Like how old are you anyway?

"You know what, Squid Kid? I beat you fair and square. I've been playing for years. I don't have to cheat," Lizzy says.

Squid_Kid: You think you're hot shit for beating a sixteen-year-old?

She snorts but doesn't reply again. She doesn't have to. I can see the frustration written all over her face. The kid keeps going anyway.

Squid_Kid: How does it feel to live in your daddy's basement while you bullshit the world into thinking you're really good at this?

Squid_Kid: I bet your fat ass is single. That's why you come on here all the time.

Squid_Kid: Look at you. Who would want you? You couldn't pay for a date. Go get a life you old hag.

That's it. I've had enough. I stand and slam the top of my laptop shut. Before I can think about what I'm about to do, I'm moving. I jog down the stairs from the rooftop and push through the door to the second level. I don't even take a pause.

Determined, I jog down to the first floor, where Lizzy's gaming room is. I don't knock. Instead, I enter and walk right in. I don't think about the fact that I'm shirtless and only in a pair of sweatpants.

I pad barefoot up behind her and make sure I'm in the view of the camera. I reach beneath her braids and cup the back of her neck to tilt her face up toward me. I wrap my other hand around her neck and dip my head to take her lips.

I kiss the shit out of her. I mean, I own her mouth. However, I'm not expecting the punch to the gut. I deepen the kiss as I'm drawn into her essence. She tastes so fucking good. I groan and move my hand on the back of her neck into her hair.

She whimpers in my mouth, and I remember what I came in here to do. I pull away slowly and kiss the tip of her nose than her forehead. Looking into her eyes, I'm sure the fire I see there matches my own.

"I'll be waiting when you're done, baby. Don't keep me waiting." I peck her lips once more because I can't help myself.

She stares after me as I back away. I turn because I'm sure everyone can see how hard I am. I exit the room, hoping she knows I mean it when I say I'll be waiting. While I did only intend to prove she's desired and not single...*fuck*.

Gio is right. I've known what I've wanted all along. Lizzy is mine. She has been since I moved her into my home. After that kiss, there's no way I'm not going to claim my woman.

I can't even remember why I've been telling myself not to. Nothing makes sense without her as mine. Damn, I need to sober up.

CHAPTER THIRTY-THREE

Just for You

Lizzy

"Hey, Lizzy. No Bella today?" Peter says awkwardly as he passes by my desk.

I try not to frown at him. I don't like this guy. However, he's never done anything wrong to me, so I try to be nice.

"No, not today," I reply.

"Cool, cool, you planning on creating some new content this week? I have my notifications set for when you go live."

"Well, then if I do decide to, you'll get a notification, won't you?"

I plaster on a fake smile. This guy is totally ruining my daydreaming. I turn to my computer and act like I've found something to do. I've been finished with my work tasks for hours now. Other than getting the conference room set up. I look at the clock, I still have some time.

"Okay, um. I just wanted to stop by and say hi. It's so cool that I work at the same place as such a huge influencer. You're so dope." I turn back to him, and he looks like a scared rabbit.

"Listen, I don't bring my gaming into my work life. I get it. I think I'd be the same way if, like my favorite author, worked here, but for me, they're two different worlds. This is my work."

He blanches, then swallows hard. "Um, okay. Um, well, let me know if you need anything or, like, ever want to hang out. We can talk about normal shit. No gossip and no gaming, right?"

I give him a more genuine smile. "Maybe."

He scurries away, looking back over his shoulder at me as he goes. Now I get why Ny won't cam up. I can't blame her.

Peter forgotten, I get lost in my thoughts. I sit at my desk with my fingers touching my lips. It's two days later and that kiss still has my lips tingling. My face heats as I think of how my fans reacted in the chat.

They had so many questions I didn't have answers to myself. I sat confused and so turned on my clit ached. I ended the night once Nyla called with her own million and one questions.

"I see that kiss still has your nose wide open," Nyla teases as she walks up to my desk.

I sigh and shake my head. I warred with myself all night Saturday. I know Dante said he would be waiting for me, but I didn't want to embarrass myself again by going to his room. Instead, I spent the night tossing and turning.

I didn't see him all Sunday. He and Bella spent the day out. All that confidence building I did with Ny wasn't enough to get me to go talk to him once they came home for the night. This morning the ride into work was intense.

Dante seemed to be in a mood, and I felt foolish about bringing the other night up. However, I can't stop smiling.

"I don't know what you're talking about," I say and start to fix the papers on my desk.

"Sure, whatever, did you at least put on the lingerie like I told you?"

I roll my eyes. I did listen to her. Although I don't know why.

She gives me a knowing look when I don't answer. I squirm in my seat under her gaze. Sometimes my sister knows me too well. I drop my eyes to my desk, and she laughs at me. I mean, a deep belly laugh. I pick up a paper clip and throw it at her.

"Don't you have some work to do?"

"Nope, I don't know how you did this boring job for so long," she mutters.

"Gio made it fun," I say and watch for her reaction. This time, she's the one to start squirming as a frown comes to her face.

"That puppet master is the last person I want to spend all my time with. I try to keep the schedule in order, so I don't have to get involved with him."

"You sure about that?" I say as Dante and Gio come off the elevator, Jace following behind them.

Nyla stiffens before she even turns to see them. I snicker, but my laughter is cut off when Dante looks in my direction and locks gazes with me. There's so much heat in his eyes my panties flood and a shiver runs through me.

Dante and Gio head for the conference room, where Dante's next meeting awaits. I stand and gather the box of presentation folders.

"Do you have to sit through this one?" Nyla asks.

"No, I just need to get these in there. I should have done it by now instead of daydreaming."

"Have lunch with me."

"Okay, give me a sec."

"Let me get that for you," Jace comes over and says, plucking the box from my arms.

"Where are you taking this to?"

"The conference room."

I don't miss that his gaze is locked on Nyla. She turns back for her desk area, placing a hand on Jace's waist as she passes by him. It's such a subtle gesture but brings a huge smile to Jace's face.

As he moves forward, holding the box he took from me, I watch my sister. I wonder if she realizes what she just did. I turn my attention to Jace and note how handsome he is.

His long blond hair is pulled up in a topknot today. Jace has pretty but masculine features. His eyes seem to change colors. I've seen them green, gray and a very light brown. I've rarely seen him smile, but it's gorgeous when he does.

Yet, there's no mistaking this man is dangerous. I've seen Gio lose his temper. Somehow that triggers Jace and Lord, that's something I'll forever avoid. I've seen both men transform before my eyes.

I open the conference room door for Jace to pass me by. His cologne leaves a trail. Yes, Jace is an attractive man. However, my attention is stolen the moment I enter the room. Dante looks up as I turn my eyes to him. He still has that intense pissed-off look from this morning on his face. He nods me over and I move to the head of the table where he sits.

He stands and dips his head to lean into my ear. "I've been dealing with bullshit all morning. I haven't eaten. Can you order lunch for us and join me in my office? We'll be working late tonight. Gio is going to spend time with Bella. Plan to have dinner here as well."

"No problem. Is there anything you have a taste for?"

He drops his eyes to my mouth and licks his lips. Suddenly his expression changes as if he's annoyed.

"No, you decide. I'll eat whatever you choose."

"Got it."

He nods and I turn to rush out. Gio stops me before I can exit. He holds my arm and looks over my face. I don't know what he sees, but he looks over my head and grunts. I look over my shoulder to see Dante watching us with a frown.

Gio releases me and goes to take a seat at the table. I shrug it off and head to tell Nyla plans have changed. I find her at her desk, smiling at two vases full of roses.

"Hey, Dante wants me to have lunch with him. Can we do a rain check?"

She gives me a knowing smile. "Sure, we can. Don't forget anything I taught you. You know how to bring them to their knees. Make me proud, baby sis. Make me proud."

I suck my teeth at her and roll my eyes. I'm not going to throw myself at my boss. Besides, he's having a bad day. I can ask him about that kiss another time. I'm sure it meant nothing. I've been reading too many romance novels.

Making my way to my desk, I pull out the menus and decide what we should have for lunch and dinner while I'm at it.

Dante

My phone buzzes right as I get ready to call this meeting into session. With all that's going on, I check it before I get started. I frown when I see it's Gio. He's been a pain in my ass all morning.

It's not like I haven't tried to seal the deal with Lizzy. I waited up for her. She never came. I didn't want to turn into a creep and hover around her bedroom or something.

I'm not about to chase anyone either. I have too much shit going on for that. I told her what I wanted. The ball is now in her court.

Gio: *You're fucking this up.*
Me: *Whatever.*

I look across the table at him and frown. He purses his lips and shakes his head. Ignoring him, I sit back in my seat and get this meeting started.

We're moving into producing our own wine. It will be a huge move for the restaurants and hopefully in the mass market. I already have a firm handle on a distributor and both Dario and I think we can snag a few ribbons before the first pitch for sales.

That's where it's at. Having the awards to back the brand. We're ready.

Justin, my lead spirits manager, begins the pitch as I sit with my fingers steepled in front of me. I can't wait for this meeting to be over. I'm starving. That breakfast Lizzy made me this morning was burned through as I beat the shit out of Angelo for fucking over my West Coast dairy deliveries.

Another asshole who thought he was more important to me than he was. We own the trucks. The farms belong to me. He only supplied the truckers. Truckers I've been treating like kings for years. They're loyal to the Di Lorenzo name. Just like Nonno wanted.

I've done my part. Therefore, Angelo was expendable. However, I'm going to need to get my dick wet soon. All this rage and violence with no balance is the shit that causes me to snap.

My phone goes off as Justin goes over projected profit margins. I know all this already. I pick my phone up and see it's from Gio again. Some video link. I roll my eyes and put my phone back down, face down.

I look at Gio and he's staring down at his phone with a smug ass grin on his lips. My phone goes off a few more times. I flip it over.

Gio: *You might want to look at this.*

Then there's another video link. I lift a brow and swipe to unlock my phone. I pick it up as the still frames of the videos come into view.

I mute the sound on my phone and hit play on the first video. My eyes hood as I watch and nearly salivate on my phone. I clear my throat and shift in my seat.

I roll my tongue in my mouth, remembering her sweet mouth. Lizzy looks fucking fantastic. My head nearly explodes as I realize Gio has seen this.

I look to him and narrow my eyes. He has a brow lifted at me as he smiles. I shove my phone into my suit jacket and stand.

"Gentlemen, my apologies. Something has come up. I need to excuse myself, but my brother and the rest of my team are more than capable of handling things."

I rush from the conference room, heading for my office to watch this video in private. I don't even bother to look at Lizzy at her desk. I close my office door and pull my phone back out.

Sitting at my desk, I turn the volume back up and press play. A woman sings of pressure as Lizzy does this sexy slow walk and looks into the camera. I remember this song playing while she and

Nyla were in her room. Her red robe slips from her shoulder and she stops walking. The camera pans out as she rolls her body, looking like she has the confidence of a goddess.

I bite my lip and wipe at my forehead. She lets the robe fall to the floor and starts to run her hands over her body as she rocks and circles her hips. I get so hard I have to squeeze to relieve some of the pressure.

"Fuck, baby," I mutter.

She looks so fucking good. It's not just the sexy garter. It's the confident way she moves her body. I can't help but to think of her riding me like that. If she wants me to apply the pressure to that fat pussy, I'd be more than glad to.

"Damn."

She turns her ass to the camera and squats as she rocks her hips. However, it's when she moves into a handstand and winds her ass in the air that I have to put my fist in my mouth and bite down.

I stop the video and move to the next one. This one is a bit different. She lies back on the bed in black lingerie. This time she's singing at the camera. I listen to the words and let them sink in.

I think I know this song. It's from the *Suicide Squad* soundtrack. "Gangsta." I know it too from overhearing the music playing Saturday. This time I listen to every word as if she's singing them to me. The sensual way she's moving on the bed has my attention too, but not as much as the words and the look in her eyes.

Could she have as many secrets as I do? Am I what she needs? Because I know she's what I want. I damn sure know I can love her better than anyone else.

Our conversation from a few months ago comes back to me.

He's sweet enough. But I don't think he's for me… You're not into nice guys?… Not my preference. They don't know what to do with me.

"Fuck, baby, do I know what to do with you," I breathe as the video ends.

The frame freezes and that's when I see it. The look in her eyes. Lizzy is hiding her own secrets. Secrets I think are as dark as mine. I stop warring with myself and text Gio.

Me: *Yeah, I get it. Don't let Bella wait up tonight.*

I'm suddenly grateful my brother offered to babysit. Lizzy and I need to talk.

CHAPTER THIRTY-FOUR

Not if You're Mine

Lizzy

I'm not sure what's going on with Dante today. He's been staring at me all day. The entire time through lunch, my stomach churned, and I wasn't able to eat. It was the same as we had dinner. He's making me nervous.

I've been dropping things and rambling. I almost asked to leave early with Nyla. It's bad enough I've sweated through my blouse. My pits are drenched.

His eyes are on me again. I uncross and recross my legs as I sit in one of the seats in front of his desk. He watches the movement and licks his lips. I pinch the top of my blouse and tug at it, trying to cool off.

His lips turn up into a smile and he sits back in his seat. It's as if he's come to some decision at that very second. The plans we're going over are forgotten. I hold my breath as I wait for what he'll say next. Something in his expression tells me it's not going to be about this grand opening.

"Why didn't you come to me the other night?"

I gasp, then bite my lip. "I didn't know you were serious."

He stands and rounds the desk until he's in front of me. He leans his butt against the desk and crosses his legs at the ankles. His gaze runs over me.

"Why wouldn't I have been serious?"

I shrug, looking anywhere but at him. He pushes off the desk and moves closer. I blink rapidly as he crowds my space.

The next thing I know, he plants his palms on the arms of the chair I'm in and leans in to capture my lips. I gasp into his mouth, and he groans, grasping my throat as he devours my mouth. My toes curl in my heels. My scalp tingles.

I don't realize I've tangled my fingers in his hair until he pulls back a little to nip at my bottom lip before diving into my mouth again. I almost jump out of my skin when he reaches for my breast and palms it, brushing his thumb across my hardened nipple. I whimper and suck his tongue into my mouth.

He breaks the kiss and puts his forehead to mine. "Do you still question me?"

I shake my head because I can't find words at the moment. Damn, the man kisses like he's trying to find my soul. My panties are soaked. Now that's what I call claiming what you want.

Guys have to be forward with me, or I'm going to miss the entire clue. However, that doesn't mean I'll be interested if they are. In this moment, there is no question that I want this man.

He pushes off the chair and backs away, returning to his perch up against his desk. My heart is racing. I reach to touch my scorched lips.

"Come here, baby," he croons smoothly.

I stand awkwardly and turn to place my tablet on the chair. Dante groans behind me. I turn and stumble forward. He catches me before I fall, tugging me to his chest.

I feel like such a goof. That's until he captures my lips in another kiss. He kisses me senseless. I cling to his suit jacket and open for him as he consumes my mouth. I love the way he kisses. Its promises of dirty, nasty things I'm so here for. All the shit I'd only do for my man, I want to do them with Dante.

"Lizzy, I don't have room in my life for games. I want you. When I say that, it means you're mine. I come with a daughter and a lot of other shit. If you can't accept all of that, tell me now. I'll back off."

Oh my God. Am I dreaming? Is he serious? Hell yeah, I'll take him and Bella and I damn sure will be his.

I grab him by the back of the neck and pull him to me. Not having to think twice, I plant a kiss on his lips, letting him know I'm all in. He grasps my face in one hand and takes over the kiss.

Our tongues dance together as he slides his other hand to my ass. He squeezes as he deepens the kiss. I allow my fingers to find purchase in the top of his hair.

"Fuck," I breathe when he moves his lips to make open-mouthed kisses along my face and down my neck.

Maybe I'm not ready for this. I'm on fire and all he's doing is kissing me.

Dante

I'm showing restraint I didn't know I had. She smells so good, and images of those videos keep playing in my head. I spin to turn her toward the desk, pushing her against it. She shivers as I swirl my tongue against her neck.

I need her clothes off. She moans and pushes her breasts toward me when I reach for the buttons of her shirt and start to release them. When her bra begins to come into view, I groan. It looks like the black one from the video.

Wanting to know if she has on the garter as well, I abandon the last few buttons and reach to pull her black skirt up. My erection pounds against my zipper as the garter belt and sexy lacy panties come into view. I push so she props her ass on the desk and shove my hand into her panties.

Finding her nub, I rub it and return to kissing her sexy mouth. I can't get enough of kissing her. Her moans are making me so hard I can't see straight.

Repositioning my hand, I allow my fingers to rub her wet pussy as my palm massages her clit. The sound makes my mouth water. I get ready to lower to my knees for a taste, but she reaches to run her hand over my length and squeezes me over my pants.

I lose my train of thought and push two long, thick fingers into her core as she starts to suck on my tongue like it's my cock in her mouth. She moans loudly around my tongue and tries to back away.

"Don't run now, baby. Not if you're really mine. Take all I give you."

"Shit," she whimpers.

Biting her lip, she looks me in the eyes. I love the look on her face. I suck my own lip between my teeth when she trails her hands over the seams of her bra cups before tugging them down to allow her gorgeous breasts to fall free.

Still working her pussy, I cup one breast and lean in to wrap my lips around her puckered chocolate-tipped nipple. Her head falls back and my name floats from her lips. I look up at her exposed throat and release her peak.

I lunge for her throat, kissing and biting at the flesh. Her legs begin to shake as her tight walls begin to squeeze my fingers. I milk her for another orgasm, knowing I can pull another before she comes down from the first. I place my knuckles against her mound and start to rub.

Her eyes grow wide and she starts to keen. I attack her mouth again. I'll never get tired of kissing her. Her mouth is intoxicating.

Seeming to catch her second wind, she reaches for my belt and releases it. I pull back and shrug from my jacket, tossing it back over the chair she was seated in earlier. Lizzy tugs my belt free, then reaches to pull my shirt from my pants.

She lifts from the desk and shifts us, so my back is now to the desk as she lowers to her knees. I grin at her and start to unbutton my shirt.

Her gaze flicks up to mine as she unzips my pants. I spring free and a surprised expression fills her face. Yeah, my length and the bend in it have that effect. It's been years since I've been with anyone other than my ex-wife, but as a teen, I used to get a kick out of first impressions.

A smile comes to her lips as she reaches for me. Pushing it up against my stomach, she leans in and licks up my shaft. She spits on it and takes the crown in her mouth, still smiling. It's so hot as she looks me in the eyes while doing it.

Lizzy starts to stroke me and bites her lip as she watches her hand move over me. I lean forward, cupping the back of her head and take her lips as she continues to stroke me.

When she sucks my tongue into her mouth, I don't know if I want to kiss her or have her suck on my dick like that more. I release her mouth and straighten. I widen my stance and reach into my pants to scoop my balls out.

"Oh yeah, good girl," I croon when she tilts her head, pushes my shaft against my belly, and dives in to suck my balls.

I relax as she goes back to bobbing up and down my length. Placing both hands behind her head, I guide her and hold her in place until she starts to cough and choke. I release her and she pulls back, smiling and sucking in a breath through her teeth.

I work my cuff links off and shrug out of my shirt. I need inside her soon. As if reading my thoughts, she deep throats me one last time before she stands, still stroking as she uses my thigh to steady herself as she rises.

She looks so sexy with her skirt bunched around her waist, those perky tits pushing at her bra and that smile on her face. I reach to palm her ass and tug her into me. I take her lips and slip my fingers into her from behind while kneading one of her breasts.

Swiftly, I spin and push her over the desk. Her ass is in the air in front of me, giving me a full view of her soaked pussy lips. I lower and lick her from front to back. I suck in a breath as her taste fills all my senses, causing my mouth to water. She cries out as I dive in and really eat her delicious offering.

"Dante, baby, please," she sings.

My heart swells. Her pleas soothe wounds I hadn't noticed were open. I reward her by pushing in even more, bringing her essence down as I push two fingers in and tap at her G-spot. With my other hand, I massage her mound.

In no time, I have her screaming and coming all over my face. I palm her fat ass and knead her cheeks. Kissing one globe and then the other. I suck in the flesh on the cheek I just pressed my lips to. She squeals and circles her hips. I slap her ass and watch it jiggle.

"Yeah, I've had enough of this."

I stand and lift her left leg onto the desk. Shoving my pants down, I step up behind her and pass my cock through her wetness, teasing her. She whimpers and presses her forehead to the desk. I stroke myself a few times as I run my thumb through her folds up to her puckered hole.

She circles her hips, then pops her ass for me. I'm done for. I thrust into her tight pussy and nearly lose my shit. I grab her hips and hold on tight as I still and grind my teeth.

"You're mine now," I grunt through clenched teeth.

"Yes, yes, oh God, Dante. You're so deep and so big."

I pound the shit out of her tight pussy. The sound of my pelvis clapping her cheeks fills the room. I throw my head back and pant as my spine tingles.

It's been so long since I've been in some pussy, but I don't think this feeling has anything to do with that. Lizzy is perfect. The way she's taking me, the joy I see in her face as she looks back over her shoulder. The genuine pleasure of it all.

"Shit, baby, come for me."

"I can't, it's too much," she whimpers.

I reach for her clit and circle it as I shift to thrust down into her. I love that she's tall and a full-bodied woman, but I'm still able to dominate her body.

"Oh shit," she screams.

I pull out and release my cum across her ass as I pin her in place with my palm on the center of her back. I have never come that hard in my life.

"Don't move."

I stumble around my desk and get some baby wipes from my desk. I'm in the habit of keeping them in there for Bella. I clean off and fix my pants before rounding the desk to clean Lizzy.

I fix her clothes and stand her up, turning her in my embrace. I take her lips and kiss her passionately. She looks away from me shyly and tugs her bra up. I pinch her chin and bring her face back to me.

"What's the matter?"

"I work for you. What will people—"

"I'm a grown-ass man and I own this place. I plan to have you all over this office. No one will question if you're mine, Liz. They will know. And once they know, they will know to keep their opinions to themselves."

CHAPTER THIRTY-FIVE

Lizzy

"Do you and Daddy have to work late again?" Bella asks from her perch at the kitchen island.

I flip the pancake in the pan, then take Bella the bacon and pancakes that are done so she can eat and be ready for school. She gives me a happy smile.

"I don't know yet," I reply. "I have to log on to his schedule for the day, but he could always change his mind."

At that moment, Dante strolls into the kitchen with a smile on his face, looking sexy as sin. He walks over and kisses the top of Bella's head and snatches a piece of bacon from her plate.

"Hey, Daddy," she pouts and frowns. "Ask Lizzy to make you your own bacon."

Dante smiles as he chews. He narrows his eyes and points the unchewed piece of bacon at Bella. "I thought we shared around here. You had your spoon in my bowl of ice cream the other night and I didn't complain."

"Bacon is different, there are no friends in bacon," she says with a serious look on her face.

I laugh and place two more slices on her plate. Dante laughs and walks up behind me, splaying his hand on my belly. I turn my face up to look at him and he pecks my lips.

"And I thought I told you to let the chef do his job. Why are you making breakfast?" he says, looking into my eyes.

I turn away and look down. "I don't mind. I wanted to."

He kisses the top of my head and then leans into my ear to whisper. "I'm having your things moved into my room. I'd like for you to find us a new bedroom set and have them deliver it ASAP."

He then kisses my neck before nuzzling behind my ear. Bella's little gasp grabs my attention. I look up and find her watching us. Her eyes are shining with joy. She pumps her little arm and whispers to herself, "Yes."

Dante chuckles. I look to him and smile. He's in such a good mood this morning. Honestly, I haven't stopped smiling myself. Especially since I was awakened in the middle of the night by his warm mouth as he slipped into my room and bed. I was surprised to wake in his arms this morning. I thought he would return to his room so Bella wouldn't find out about us.

"Is Lizzy going to be my new mommy?"

I suck in a breath and pull my lip between my teeth. Dante inhales as he runs his hands up and down my arms. I stiffen, not sure what to say.

"*Shh.* Don't scare her off, Bella. I'm working on it."

I whip my head around to look up at him. He winks down at me and pecks my lips. My heart soars. I don't know if he's teasing or not, but I can't help thinking of them as my little family. I wonder if Dante wants more children. It didn't escape me that while he didn't use condoms, he did pull out every time.

"Yay," Bella squeals and hops down from her stool to round the island and wrap herself around my leg.

Dante

I sit staring at Bella and Lizzy as they read and sit on the couch. This is the life I want. To come home to my girls and see them safe and happy.

The fact that it takes so little to make these two happy tightens my chest. Bella has been consuming books so fast, on the way home, I stopped so Lizzy and I could pick her up an e-reader. I smile as I think about how I watched Liz in the bookstore.

She was entranced by the books, reading the backs and stacking them in her hands. Then she switched to taking pics of books—I assume to purchase them later. I waved someone over to take her books to the counter and she only filled her arms with more.

They've been sitting like this since dinner. Tearing through their treasures. For the millionth time, I think of how much I've fallen for this woman.

I take a sip of my brandy and my thoughts turn to tonight. I can't wait to climb into bed with my new obsession. I'll be sleeping in her bed tonight. She wasn't able to get our new furniture delivered until the end of the week. I decided to have the bedroom painted while we wait.

You're damn right I want to erase Bethany and her toxic aura from my life. I've never been this content in my life.

Bella's e-reader falls from her hands as she nods off again.

"Hey, ladybug, that book will be here tomorrow," Lizzy says softly as she looks down at Bella tucked into her side.

"But I like sitting here with you. I'm not ready to go to bed."

My heart swells. I know the feeling. Lizzy has this thing about her. She makes you want to be close to her.

"I'll tell you what. We have skating tomorrow, but we can sit together and read when we get home."

"Okay."

I stand and place my glass down. "Come on, baby. I'll read you one more for bedtime," I croon as I pick Bella up into my arms.

"Are you coming, Lizzy? You and Daddy can tuck me in as a family."

I look to Lizzy, and she has that shocked, bewildered look on her face again. I wonder what she thought I meant when I said she's mine. I would never dangle a relationship I didn't intend to keep in front of my daughter.

I didn't think twice this morning about showing Liz affection in front of Bella because, in my mind, she's ours. I'll do anything I have to, to make sure she's happy and never leaves our lives.

I smile at Liz and hold my hand out for hers. She shakes her head as if to clear it and takes my hand. When our palms touch. I know this is right. Everything else in my life will kneel to my command because I've found my other half. This is the life I want. I won't allow the other to take that from me.

CHAPTER THIRTY-SIX

My Calm

Lizzy

Two months later…

"You look so pretty," Bella says as she sits in my lap while I finish my makeup.

Dante had offered to bring someone in to do my hair and makeup. While I did accept the help with my hair, I refused the offer to have my makeup done, feeling it was overkill. When it comes to my hair, my natural curls can be a lot of work.

I could use all the help I could get. Knowing Dante has a few events he wants me to accompany him to, I took my braids out and decided to wait a bit before getting them done again.

"Thank you."

"I wish I were big enough to go to the party too."

"Someday, you will be, and you won't want to go." I laugh. "I would love to stay home with a book in my hands."

"But you're going because you love Daddy, right?"

Butterflies take off in my belly. God, do I love that man. I have to fight every day not to tell him how much I've fallen in love with him. Waking up in his arms every morning still feels so surreal.

"I care for your father a lot," I reply.

"Baby, we need to go."

I look up in the mirror, startled. Dante stands dressed in his tux. His legs are spread wide as his hands are shoved in his pockets. I don't miss the heat in his eyes as he looks at me.

Gah, the man is putting a hurting on that tux. Dante is simply gorgeous in every sense of the word. The hard-muscled body beneath his suit is a testament to how much God loves him and his entire existence.

Bella jumps from my lap and runs to hug her father's leg. She's tall for her age, but she looks so small next to her father. He places a hand on top of her head and smiles down at her.

"Daddy, will you see Grandpa at the party?"

A look I can't explain crosses Dante's face quickly. Bella has been asking after her maternal grandfather lately and Dante gets that same look every time.

"No," he says. "I'm not sure where your grandpa and grandma are. You know they take off whenever it suits them."

"Oh, okay. Is Nonno coming back soon?"

"Actually, I'm going to take you and Lizzy to see Nonno and Uncle Dario soon."

"Yay," Bella squeals. Dante lifts her and kisses her cheek. Her face is lit with excitement.

I furrow my brows. This is news to me. I've always wanted to go to Italy. Nyla has been a few times. My chest fills with excitement.

Dante lifts his hand for mine. I grab my clutch and move to place my hand in his. He tugs me close and pecks my lips.

"You look stunning," he says against my mouth.

I smile. I wasn't sure about this dress when Nyla helped me pick it out. The slits on both sides feel so inappropriate to me. You're not supposed to wear underwear because of how high up the waist they go, but I found a high-waisted thong, which makes me feel a little more comfortable.

"It's not too much?"

He slips a hand into one slit and palms my ass. "You'll keep close to me all night, but it's perfect," he says as he squeezes.

Bella's nanny appears to retrieve her. Dante leads me down to the waiting car. When we climb into the car, he places his hand on my thigh and gives it a squeeze.

Dante

I want to say fuck this fundraiser and spend the night teaching Lizzy a lesson in tempting me. She looks so fucking gorgeous. I want her to ride my face while I slap her ass and make her drip down all over me.

It's going to be a long night. My mind turns to overhearing Bella ask if Lizzy loves me. I want to hear those words from her lips. I've been in love with her. However, I can see in her eyes that she's holding back from me.

Liz sighs in relief beside me, drawing my attention. I look at her as she's replying to a text.

"The wine finally arrived at the venue," she says.

I nod. We're having shipment issues again. A few of our trucks have been ambushed. They have covered their tracks better this time.

I can't just take someone's head off and defuse the situation. I think this is all by design. Whoever has been coming for me isn't confident enough to come at me head-on any longer.

I still haven't found whoever Kaling was working with. Bella kills me every time she asks after that bastard. I don't know what to tell her. I can't tell her I tortured the son of a bitch to death.

Lizzy moves closer and cups my face, turning it to her. She kisses my lips then places her forehead against my cheek.

"I didn't mean to make you upset. I thought you would want to know. Tell me how I can make you feel better."

I take her lips and kiss her deeply. I note quickly that the partition is up and tug her thigh over mine. Moving my hand into the slit of her dress, I find her core and run my fingers against her folds, finding the fabric of her thong drenched and stuck to her flesh.

"You're always so wet for me," I say against her lips. "You're all I ever need to calm me and make things better."

"Dante," she whimpers as I move her thong aside and pump my fingers inside her.

I move my lips to her temple. "Come for me. We don't have much time."

"My dress," she pants.

Shit, she's a squirter. Still, I wonder if the black fabric will hide the wetness if she comes. Thinking better of it, I back off and rub her pearl, gently bringing her to a less intense orgasm.

A smile comes to my lips as the knowledge that she'll be aching for me all night sets in. I kiss her hard before bringing my hand to my lips. I lock eyes with her as I suck my fingers clean.

There's that look in her eyes again. I plan to pull the words from her sooner than later. I haven't come inside her yet because a part of me is still reluctant.

I want to hear her say she loves me before I spill my seed into her. I need to hear the sincerity of her words. Never again will I have a child with a woman who doesn't love me the way I love her.

I fix her dress and give her thigh a gentle squeeze. "We're here."

CHAPTER THIRTY-SEVEN

Dating a Di Lorenzo

Dante

I stand about a yard away from Lizzy, but I can't take my eyes off her. She fits right into my world effortlessly. Not like Bethany. I used to watch as people would practically run from her, and I'd have to smooth things over after.

Not Liz, they're surrounding her and eating out of her palm. It's that light that comes from her. I'm not the only one drawn to it. I lift my glass to my lips and take a sip of my champagne.

"It's good to see you with a genuine smile," Gio says as he appears at my side.

"Good evening, brother."

"How are things going with you and my dear friend?"

I shake my head. Turning, I look my brother in his hazel eyes. They sparkle with mischief.

"You knew what you were doing bringing her into my life. How do you think things are going? She's almost everything I told you I wanted when we were younger."

"How do you know she's not everything?" He has a small smile in the corner of his lips. "I'm always thorough, Dante."

I narrow my eyes at him. I think his words over. I know I haven't learned all of Lizzy's secrets, but it's hard to see her as anything but the sweet woman I've fallen in love with.

Her sweet laugh fills the air, drawing my attention to her. I start to list all the things I once told my brother I wanted so long ago.

Lizzy is gorgeous. Tonight, her curly hair has been straightened and has a silky look to it as it rests over her shoulder in deep waves. Her brown skin is glowing. Liz isn't rail thin like most of the women here. Her body packs a punch in that figure-hugging black dress. I've watched as the men here have salivated watching her.

"You checked off beauty. She has her own kind of grace," I muse aloud.

Gio grunts.

"She's undeniably smart. I love her humor."

"She'll make the perfect mother. She's perfect to give you that son you want."

I look to Gio and study him. All other thoughts freeze. My brother knows me a little too well. Every time I make love to Liz, I think of her swelling with my seed and giving me a son, my own heir to the Di Lorenzo throne.

When I hear those three words spill from her lips for the first time, I know I won't have the restraint to pull from her body any longer. The thought takes root and I'm tempted to coax them from her tonight.

I grunt in reply to my brother's words and walk off to close the distance between myself and the woman who stays on my mind. I place my glass on a passing tray and walk up right behind her. I splay a hand on her belly and pull her snug to my front and kiss her bare shoulder before leaning into her ear.

Lizzy

"Dance with me," Dante breathes in my ear.

I look over my shoulder and smile at him. I felt him watching me this entire time. I was wondering how long it would take before he would come to rescue me. These people are nice enough, but I think they're more nosy than anything.

I turn and allow him to lead me to the dance floor. This music isn't fun and flirty like our dance on the rooftop and it's not sensual like our first dance. However, once Dante clasps one of my hands to his shoulder and the other around my waist, I'm transported to another world.

He glides us around the floor to the orchestra music. He's so smooth. I smile up at him and my heart swells. I've loved every side of Dante I've come to know so far. He's supportive, protective, and loving.

"What are you thinking?"

I shake my head. "I never thought this would be my life. Look at me. I'm all dressed up at a ball with my boyfriend."

He frowns as I say the last word and I pause, dropping my head. He reaches for my face and turns it to him. I look into his eyes and chide myself for being so awkward and goofy.

"I don't like the title boyfriend. I'm a grown man and you're my very grown woman. I haven't been a boy in years and I'm much more than your friend."

My smile returns. "Well, what should I call you?"

He captures my lips for a searing kiss. "If I have it my way, you'll be my fiancée soon enough."

My lips part and I duck my head. Guilt seizes me because he still doesn't truly know who I am. I don't know how he will take it once he finds out—that is, if he finds out. Which I have this deep fear he will.

He kisses the side of my neck. "Don't look so shocked," he says against my skin, sending a shiver through me.

"I think I'm waiting to wake up. Like, did I slip and hit my head that night on the rooftop?"

He laughs and tightens his hold on me. "No, this is all very real."

"Okay," I say and lift my hands to play in the nape of his hair. "Tell me something about you I still don't know. If you're going to be my fiancé, I should know more about you."

He lifts a brow and searches my face. There's a momentary war that crosses his features, I fear he's not going to respond. Something lights his eyes and causes me to relax.

"My father and Riccardo wanted to have me committed when I was younger. Not so much my father, but my grandfather pushed it. Nonno started to come to the States then, and he stepped in."

I gasp and look into his eyes. "Seriously?"

He nods. "I had so much anger after my mother left us. I blamed myself and that began to fester. I was already surrounded by..." He pauses, searching my eyes again for a moment. After seeming to come to a conclusion, he continues.

"I was surrounded by violence, and I started to do weird shit. I had no place to put all the anger and the outlets I created for myself scared the shit out of them." He snorts.

"Is that why you two seem to have so much tension?"

"You got it, baby." He winks.

"You know, Gio always told me dating a Di Lorenzo came with its own baggage."

Dante smiles and spins me, then dips me low. He kisses my collarbone. "Only you would have a smile and gentle words for a killer," he murmurs against my skin, then lifts me upright.

I'm tempted to tell him I know a mirror when I see one, but I keep the thought to myself. Loss makes you a different person, some snap under pressure, others thrive on it.

It's been a beautiful night. I didn't think I'd enjoy myself so much. My feet ache and I can't wait to get home and get into bed.

Dante has to stick around a little longer. He's been shaking hands with donors as they leave the event.

I adore how he's focused and determined. The charity fell short a few thousand from the goal. Dante has charmed a few more donations from those who have stopped to ask for favors.

So, I suck it up and allow him to do his thing no matter how tired I am. This charity means a lot to him. Some lucky young men are going to get to travel and learn to cook, all expenses paid. Dante turns to me and pulls me into his side to kiss my temple.

"We'll only be a little longer," he murmurs.

I yawn and place my head on his shoulder as he wraps his arm around my waist. I absorb some of his strength and try to hold my eyes open. It's at that moment something catches my eye.

Suddenly, it's like the atmosphere shifts. Tires squeal somewhere nearby just before gunfire rings out. From the moment I notice something is off, my instincts kick in and I go to reach into my clutch, but Dante throws his body against mine, covering me like a human shield.

I scream and clench his tux jacket as his back bows. His face is tight with pain. I fall backward, tumbling to the stairs we've been standing on. Dante's big body lands on top of mine.

Zek and Mitch appear out of nowhere and start to fire back at the speeding car. Our car races up and Mitch helps Dante up as he rushes us both into the car. We're sped away as panic seizes me.

My heart is racing. I feel like it's going to pound out of my chest. Dante groans and reaches for me.

"Babe, are you okay?" I say frantically.

He slumps down in his seat and tugs me against his chest as he starts to unbutton his dress shirt. I cup his face with a shaky hand. Tears run down my cheeks as I look him over for signs of an exit wound.

"I'm fine, were you hit? Are you okay?"

"I'm fine. Why would you throw yourself in front of a bullet for me?"

He looks at me like I've lost my mind. I drop my eyes to his chest and see the bulletproof vest. It's one of Denise's designs. I know it well. It's superthin, but effective as fuck.

"Please promise me you won't ever do that again," I whisper against his lips.

He crushes his lips to mine in a searing kiss. All tongue and passion. I'm breathless when he pulls away.

"That's a promise I will never make. Because I will break it every time."

More tears fill my eyes and this time, it's because it hits me how much I love this man. I never would have forgiven myself if something happened to him.

He pulls me to straddle his lap and I go willingly, needing to be closer to him. He's back devouring my mouth. I grasp his face and return the kiss. He slips his hands into the slits of my dress and palms my ass.

Groaning into my mouth, he squeezes my ass and brings my hips into his growing erection. I reach to push his tux jacket and shirt from his shoulders. He winces a bit as he helps to get them off.

"Sorry," I murmur.

"You're fine. I'll be sore tomorrow, but it's fine."

"Maybe we shouldn't."

He growls and slips his fingers inside me from behind. "I need to be inside you. Someone tried to take you from me. I have to have you now," he breathes into my mouth.

I comb my fingers through his hair and lock them in the top as I grind into his lap. The sound of my panties tearing fills the SUV. We break the kiss and I reach to release the Velcro strips of his vest. He eases it over his head and tosses it aside. I lean in to kiss his chest.

As if with impatience, he reaches to grab a handful of my hair and tugs my head back. We lock eyes and I see he's not in the mood for slow and easy.

Reaching for his belt, I work on releasing him as I take in the darkness in his eyes. This isn't my Dante. This is the look he has when he comes in late from business that doesn't hit his schedule or my emails.

The man who crawls into bed and fucks me so hard I have to soak the next morning to walk straight. I nod my understanding as I wrap my hand around him and move my dress out of the way with the other.

He brings my hips to him and pulls me down onto his hard, pulsing shaft. I bite my lip and groan. He feels so good and superhard. It's almost too much. The sound of my sex creaming all over him fills the car. I try to back off, leaning back on his thighs to keep from sinking too far down on his thick length, that hook in his dick already driving me crazy.

He grunts and grasps my ass tighter, pulling me back into an upright ride. "Don't run from me," he breathes into my mouth as he continues with those drugging kisses of his.

I whimper and roll my head back. He leans in to kiss my throat. I reach up to place my palms against the roof of the car as I ride him. Closing my eyes, I just feel.

If I questioned my love for him before, I know as it flows through me now, I can't deny him. I'd give everything I am to this man. The words are right on the tip of my tongue.

Dante peels the front of my dress down and he pulls my nipple into his mouth. My thighs start to tremble and the force of my orgasm rocks through my entire being. It's as if I can feel his heartbeat within my own.

Dante

I thrust up into her, ignoring the burning in my back. The vest did its job, but the bullets still stunned the fuck out of me. All I could think was to cover Lizzy, I couldn't lose her.

I release her breast from my mouth and bury my face between her mounds. Clawing my fingers down her back, I breathe her in.

"Fuck," I growl to keep from calling out how much I love her.

I'm going to fucking kill someone. I pull back to look into her face and the ecstasy I see there pushes me into a rage. I finally have the perfect woman in my life, and someone tried to take that from me.

Placing my hand over her heart, I drill up into her, trying with my body to show her how much I love her. She bites her lips and I want to be the one tasting the soft pillows.

I slide my hand up her chest, around her neck, and tug her head down to me. I'll be the first to say when I kiss her, it's desperate. If my kisses were flames, we'd both go up in smoke.

"I love you," she whimpers into my mouth.

I freeze. Although I've been waiting to hear those words, they're like a punch to the gut because I was just thinking the same thing. The last of the bands around my heart clatter to the ground and it pumps freely for this woman. I don't know how I do it in this small space, but I flip her onto her back and hover over her as I slow my thrusts and start to make love to her.

She wraps her long, thick legs around my back, and I cradle her head as I push into her warm body. I break the kiss to look into her eyes. She darts her eyes away from me, but not before I see the tears.

I lean into her ear. "I love you too. God, baby, I love you so much."

This time when I feel her about to come, my balls tingle. I know without a doubt I'm going to come inside her for the first time. I capture her lips and groan into her mouth as my release brings with it all my emotions and an explosion within my body and mind.

CHAPTER THIRTY-EIGHT

Never Fear

Lizzy

I can still feel the rage rolling off him. It's been hours since we arrived home, but Dante is still pissed off. He glides his fingers across my thigh as he looks down at me.

I reach to cup his jaw and run my thumb across his cheek. He lowers his eyes to my lips, causing his long lashes to fan his cheekbones.

"You and Bella should go stay with Dario until I get this all taken care of," he says.

I had a feeling something like this was coming. He drags his fingers up to my belly and splays his hand against my stomach. I drag my hand down to hold over his heart.

"I thought we were all going. Can't you come with us?"

He pecks my lips. "I always want to be where you are, but I need to silence this problem. Baby, for months, someone's been trying to get my attention. I don't want you to see the man I'm about to become. You're safer with my brother and Nonno."

"Dante?"

The words are right there. I want to tell him the truth. I think back to Jace's warning and clamp my lips shut. I close my eyes and shake my head.

"Never mind. I'll do whatever you feel is needed."

He rolls me flat onto my back and hovers over me before pushing inside me. I throw my head back into the pillow and cry out.

"I love you, Liz. I'll always keep you safe. You don't have to be afraid. I'll make this right."

I'm not afraid. Fear is the last emotion I feel. At least not for whoever is out there. I need to talk to Gio. I have to tell Dante the truth.

Dante takes my lips and pours so much passion into the kiss all my thoughts are forgotten. I allow myself to stay in the moment.

When I feel his hot seed spill into me what seems like hours later, I know in my heart something has changed between us and I'm determined to come clean.

I wake with a smile on my face. Dante has his arm wrapped tightly around me as he breathes evenly, telling me he's fast asleep. My phone lights up on the bedside table.

I reach for it and see it's Gio. I slip from under Dante's arm and sit up.

Gio: *Izzy.*

Me: *Yes?*

Gio: *I'm here. Come to your game room.*

I get up and grab a robe to pull on. I know if Gio is calling me Izzy, this is business. My heart pounds. If he wants to reassign me now, it will break my heart.

My phone goes off in my hand again. I go to answer the text but freeze when I see it's Jacob. After his initial calls that I ignored the first week, he had stopped calling and texting.

I ignore the text and keep moving downstairs. I slip into my game room to find Gio pacing like an angry bear. I dart my gaze around the room and find the person I'm looking for in the shadows.

I have no idea why Gio looks so pissed at me. I rub my forehead and steel myself for whatever he's here for. I clench my fist at my side and toss my phone down on the little desk in the room, then fold my arms across my chest.

"What happened? Did you freeze or something? Why are they still alive, Izzy?"

"I don't walk with guns at the ready, Gio. My gun was in my clutch. Dante covered me and knocked me to the ground before I could pull."

He grunts and his nostrils flare. I burst into tears. "I can't do this, Gio. He needs to know who I am. He put his life in danger to cover me," I choke out. I pause and take a calming breath.

"I…I love him. I can't allow that to happen again."

Gio walks over to me with a smile. He looks into my eyes and nods.

"Good. You shouldn't hide it from him anymore. You're both ready." He lifts his hand and waves Jace over. "He has the address. Kill them all."

I lick my lips and nod. "Gladly." I smirk as I allow that door to open and the real Izzy to step out. Jace hands me a piece of paper and my case that holds my guns and skates.

"Izzy, be careful. He'll kill me if something happens to you, and I'll never forgive myself."

I snort. "As if you don't know who I am."

Gio gives me a knowing grin and nods at me. My phone lights up on the desk, grabbing his attention. He turns to pick it up with a frown.

"Block him," he says firmly, handing me the phone.

I look down at another text from Jacob. Unlocking the phone, I do as Gio says without a second thought. The only man I want is upstairs, sleeping in our bed.

"Have fun," Gio says as I put the phone in my robe pocket.

Jace opens the door to the room and they both slip out silently. I head to my old room to shower and change before I head to take care of this little problem. I won't have to leave without my man for Italy.

Once dressed and wearing my contacts, I head out to the garage where my car has been since Dante stopped allowing me to travel without Zek to guard me. Case in hand, I climb into my car and start the engine. I pull out of the garage with a smile on my face. It's been a while since I've let Izzy out to play.

CHAPTER THIRTY-NINE

Catching Bodies

Dante

I wake with a sharp inhale. It's clear something feels off right away. Lizzy's warm, soft body is gone. I flex my fingers against the cool sheets. With another inhale, I roll onto my back.

Before I can think twice, I pull the gun from behind my headboard and aim. My eyes clear and I put the safety back on and release a breath. "Damn it, Gio. Jace, what the fuck are you two doing in here? Where's Liz?"

"Get up and throw on some pants. I have something I want you to see."

I narrow my eyes at Gio. Curiosity piqued, I get up, tugging the top sheet around my waist. I find a pair of sweats in my closet and tug them on.

"Where's Liz?" I ask as I come out of the closet. My patience is wearing thin as the shooting from earlier comes to mind.

"Come with me," Gio says and starts out of the room.

We go downstairs and enter Lizzy's game room. Jace moves to turn on the screens. Gio waves for me to sit in the gaming chair. I move to take a seat and feel my blood pressure rising.

"Gio, you need to start talking. Where is my woman? What are you two doing here?"

"Do you love her?"

"What?"

"You heard me. Do you love her?"

I run a hand through my hair. A million thoughts run through my mind. I lift my gaze to Gio's. I know he would never bring someone into my life who I couldn't trust.

"Yes, I love her. Now where the fuck is she?" I snarl, losing my patience.

"She's there," Jace murmurs.

I look at the screens and Lizzy's car comes into view. She steps from the car dressed in all black. I watch the screen as she moves to the back seat and sits with her legs hanging out of the car.

"What is this?"

"Keep watching," Gio croons.

She opens a case and pulls out a pair of gold rollerblades. I watch as she changes her heavy black boots for the skates, then lifts from her seat and pulls two gold Glocks from the same case. My mouth falls open when she screws pearl-looking silencers on each gun. They seem to be etched with gold designs in the pearl. She places the guns in the thigh holsters on each of her legs.

Smoothly, she rolls to the back of the car and pops the trunk. Reaching in, she pulls out a rifle and fastens it to her back before pulling out a matte-black bat. I lift a brow when she closes the trunk and looks up with a grin on her lips, as if looking right into the camera, knowing it's there.

I look at Gio. He smiles and tilts his head toward the monitors. I have a million questions for him.

"You wanted to know what you were missing about her. I'm going to show you. The drones will catch it all."

Lizzy

I park about a half mile away from the address Jace handed to me and get out to change into my skates and suit up. Once I'm ready, I allow the weight of the guns and the bat in my palms to wash over me. I become that other person. The one I keep hidden away.

I turn my head up and grin. I'm ready. Pushing forward, I take off on my blades. In my palms, my bat is held out in front of me as I pump my legs, then glide forward. I eat up the half a mile in no time.

"Okay, Auntie Denise. I'm coming up on the targets. You there?"

"Always, hon. You have two out front. They're not armed, just muscle."

"Got it."

I roll up to the front gate where the two are and drop my bat to my side.

The biggest of the two looks me over. "You need to keep moving," he warns.

I smirk and twirl my bat at my side. The other one pulls a knife.

"He said keep it moving."

I stop rotating my wrist and swing at the first guy's nuts. The howl that comes from him is like music to my ears. The other guy lunges at me with his knife.

I block him with the bat. I turn my feet to second position and bend my knees to spin around him. Then I swing at his head with the bat so hard he spins as he falls to the ground fast asleep. The snap his neck makes, causes me to nod at myself in approval.

I turn to the other guys still holding his balls groaning and spin on my skates before hitting him just as hard upside his head.

"Nice, baby girl," Aunt Denise croons in my ear. "Lose the bat. Time for the lead. You're going to head toward the back. You have about four waiting for you. Be careful, they're moving back and forth, you could have more company at any time."

"Got it," I say and prop my bat against the gate. I'll get that later.

I pull my pistols and push forward. I round the corner and see the guys standing at the back door. One has just lit a cigarette and blows out a ring of smoke. I aim and put a bullet in his head first.

That gets the attention of the other three. They pull their guns and start to fire. I drop low and glide on one leg as if my other leg is to help me aim straight, I fire at their knees.

I take their legs out and roll over them to place a bullet in each of their heads as I roll by their writhing bodies. I reholster my guns and pull my rifle from my back.

"Nice," Denise purrs. "Okay. The last ten are aware you're there. The place has little cover. You're going to have to move and quick."

I lick my lips. "Got it."

I roll in and black out. It's like I'm in the game. I listen, breathe, and fire.

Dante

I sit on the edge of my seat, holding my breath. I can't believe what I'm watching. Lizzy is fucking amazing. I thought I was going to lose my mind when that guy charged at her with that knife.

She handled it without blinking. The force she hit those guys with made me cringe. My heart nearly came out of my chest when she rounded the building and took out those guys. This is not my sweet personal assistant and woman. This is even next level from the woman I watch playing video games.

However, as I look at the screen and watch her clear out this warehouse, I can see the skilled shooter who has built a brand executing virtual missions like this. Lizzy is no small woman, but she moves on those blades so gracefully. She's so fluid and nimble. When she drops, bending backward to roll beneath a chain in her way and comes up on the other side shooting, I'm in awe and ready to come out of my skin.

"She's fucking amazing," Gio breathes with pride beside me.

I can't speak. I don't know how to feel.

"Look out," I scream as if she can hear me.

As if she does, she spins on those damn skates and fills the guy who was rushing toward her with bullets. The drone seems to pan out to give a view of the entire room from above. She's cleared the place all by herself.

I'm speechless once again. With a smile on her lips, she rolls out of the building. I fall back in my chair and run a hand through my hair.

"Job complete," Jace says and holds his phone up to Gio.

Gio looks at me and nods. "The problem from earlier has been addressed. That's who she is. She's everything you wanted. I checked all the boxes."

I growl at my brother. All this time, I should've known. "Have you lost your fucking mind?"

Lizzy

I roll out the way I came and head toward the gate I entered through. Once I have my bat. I blow the place with the trigger I have to the second drone Denise is flying—the rifle and trigger are a part of some of the gifts hidden in my car, thanks to her.

I grin and push forward. Taking my phone out, I take a picture of the blaze behind me and send it to Jace.

"Thanks, Auntie."

"You're welcome, baby. See you later."

I roll back to my car and return everything to its place and put my boots back on.

"Nice work, Izzy. Now go home to your man," I say as I start the car and take off.

Fury

Lizzy

I step from my car as I park in the garage to find Jace and Gio waiting for me. Gio has a grim look on his face. I did the job and made sure everyone was taken care of. What's wrong with him?

"He knows," Gio says. "And he's not happy about it."

I groan.

"He's more pissed at me than about who you are. He'll get over it. Go take care of my family, Liz."

With that, the two leave. I run my hands down the front of my leggings. All the confidence I had just an hour ago is gone. It's back to real life.

I move into the house and debate going to hide in my game room like a chicken. Instead, I kick my boots off and peel off my socks in the mudroom and head through the kitchen. I pad softly to the foyer, headed for the stairs.

A hand lands on my shoulder, startling me. On instinct, I grab the hand and spin around under the person's arm and twist the limb behind them. Before I can get a tight lock to break their arm or register who it is, they twist out of my hold and I'm airborne.

My back hits the wall behind me and a hard body is pressed against me. Dante hisses and nips my bottom lip as he squeezes my throat. I try to calm my racing heart.

"I don't know if I want to strangle you or fuck you," he says tightly.

I drag my foot up the back of his thigh and used my toes to pull him into me by his ass. Instantly his hard dick presses into me. He looks down into my face with heat in his eyes. I can tell he's equally pissed and turned on.

I bite his lower lip and pull. His eyes filled with so much desire my skin heats. I feel like his gaze comes with its own pressure. I flick my tongue against his lip.

"Good thing I'll let you do both," I purr as I keep my eyes locked on his.

He growls and crushes my lips with his. I lock my fingers in his hair and grind my core into him. He nips and sucks at my lips, making me whimper into his mouth. I can taste that he's been drinking.

He breaks the kiss and searches my face with those gorgeous hazel eyes. There's a war happening within his gaze. I stay silent as he processes whatever is going on in his head.

"I don't think you understand how much I love you. Gio was wrong for sending you there. I would have handled it." He shakes his head. "But I can't deny how amazing you are."

He runs his nose up the bridge of mine. I start to pant with anticipation. He kisses my nose then stares at me as if in awe.

"You're everything I ever wanted. If I knew you were out there, I would have waited for you," he breathes against my lips.

"We're right where we should be."

He releases my throat and allows me to slide down the front of his body. Silently, he laces his fingers with mine and starts upstairs. He's taking this a lot better than I thought.

It's as if I can finally breathe. After months of worrying about how he would feel about me being an assassin hired by his brother to become a part of his life, I can finally relax. Although, I know Gio does nothing without a purpose and a plan. I can't help wondering what his endgame is here.

We make it to the bedroom and Dante silences all my thoughts as he drops his sweats and reaches for my hoodie to unzip it. He lets it fall to the floor and reaches for my tank top.

I reach to unclasp my bra as he works my panties and leggings down my legs. Once I'm standing before him completely naked, he lifts me onto his waist as if I weigh nothing. He grasps the back of my neck and brings my lips to his.

This kiss is different. It's filled with passion and something else. His tight hold on me says so much in itself. If I didn't know before this man loves me, I have no doubts in this moment.

He carries us into the bathroom and steps into the shower where I had plans to go when I tried to sneak back in. I sip from his lips as he devours mine.

He slams my back against the shower wall and tugs at my ponytail, tilting my head back. He dives in to kiss my throat as he turns the shower on without turning away from me. I moan as he sucks at my flesh and places a trail of open-mouthed kisses along my neck down to my breasts.

"You're mine to protect. Mine to keep safe. I never want you to place yourself in danger like that again."

With that, he thrusts inside me, causing me to cry out as I bow my back away from the shower wall. His thrusts are rough, almost frantic. I cling to his shoulders as he bounces me on his hard length. He feels so hard.

"I love you, Liz. I can't lose you. You're everything I wanted and a ton of shit I didn't know I needed."

He squeezes one breast as he continues to fuck me hard into the shower wall. I reach for the wall behind me as if I can find purchase. My hands slide against the wet wall. Needing something to anchor me, I reach to lace my fingers in his hair.

He groans and takes my mouth. I lock my legs high on his back, but they fall apart as he shifts, causing my lower half to pull away from the wall. He places a hand on my stomach, and I swear he's massaging his dick inside me.

"Dante," I scream.

"Yes, baby. Call my name. Let me know you know who you belong to. This is my pussy. You answer to no man but me."

His words reach through my sex-fogged brain. Suddenly, I understand some of his anger. I don't think it's so much what I do. It's that I do it for Gio.

I cup his face and look into his eyes. However, my orgasm hits hard and all thoughts are lost. I try to note to come back to this later, but my head fills with the fact that I can't stop coming while he continues to thrust until he fills me with his cum as he roars his release.

I'm spent as he pulls out and washes me before carrying me to bed.

Dante

I run my hand over her damp ponytail. It's already started to curl and frizz. I kiss her forehead and close my eyes. She's safe and in my arms. I can breathe again.

"Go ahead and ask. It's killing you," she says sleepily.

"How did you end up one of his—"

"I'm not one of his. I'm more of an independent contractor. When I met your brother, he was looking for something." She shrugs. "I think I fit the bill. We got to talking, and we became friends. A few months later, he hired me. I came to work in your company in the mail room and moved up as he told me to. It's something we do sometimes."

"We?" I murmur.

"My aunt and my mom started a security firm for female clients. You know, women in power who need protection but don't want some big dude following them around. You'd be surprised how many times that situation can go wrong."

I snort. "So Gio thinks I'm a woman?"

She laughs and slaps my chest. "No. We've had clients who wanted female bodyguards. Well, that was before. At some point, the business changed. There's more money in what we do now."

"I bet."

"We never take jobs that aren't worthy. There are a lot of sick fucks out there who deserve to see the barrel of one of my guns." She looks up at me. "Besides, tonight was the first time Gio has asked for my services. I had thought for a moment he wanted me for Bella. You know, to protect her."

I inhale through my nose. "Is that the last of your secrets?"

"No, remember the girl from high school?"

I nod.

"I beat her to within an inch of her life. I have a really bad temper. It's why I took being bullied. I knew what releasing that rage would do. Wh...what Nyla found was my suicide note when it all became too much.

"Dad, he was so hurt that he missed it, but he and Aunt Denise allowed me to work for the company and I channeled all that rage into what we do. Our third family business."

I stare at her. She is everything I've ever wanted. The perfect, unexpected mirror of my soul.

I palm her face and run my thumb across her lips. "Is that it?"

She lifts her head from my chest and smiles sadly at me. "My parents were murdered in front of me. I was three but I remember a little. They were protecting someone. I remember the pretty lady with the dark hair. She held me while we were in the panic room. She tried to turn me away from the monitors.

"But I saw. My parents didn't have a chance. They killed them both. It all happened so fast. They were gone by the time Auntie Denise and Elijah got there."

She slides her hand up my chest as her eyes take on a distant look. I run my fingers across her cheek.

She looks into my eyes with tears gathering in hers. "I'm sorry. I don't know why I told you that."

I kiss her trembling lips and pull back to look into her eyes. "You can feel free to tell me anything. I'm sorry about what happened."

"I was fucked up for so long after. Auntie Denise started to teach me how to fight and shoot as early as five. My skills grew from there. I always felt like she was preparing us for those people to come back and try to finish the job.

"They were the monsters waiting in the dark. Then one day I stopped fearing someone coming for me because I was the monster now."

"Baby, you couldn't be a monster if you tried. Although, I'm sure no monster wants to fuck with you." I laugh.

She nuzzles her forehead to my chin. "I love you."

"I love you more."

"Where's Gio?"

"I don't know," Dario shrugged. "His friends are over."

I get excited. I want to be cool, like Gio and his friends. At least, I think they're cool.

Bored out of my mind, I turned and ran into the house to find Gio and his friends. I got to Gio's room and reached for the door. Mom rushed in from the side doors.

"Dante," she barked.

I turn to find my mother looking as if she'd seen a ghost. She shook her head at me. Her cheeks turned red with anger.

"What have I told you about going into Gio's room uninvited? You have to respect others' privacy. Get your hand off that door. Where's Dario?"

"I…I only wanted to hang with Gio," I whispered.

She ran a hand through her hair. I didn't understand why she was so upset with me.

"You can't go in there. You need to listen when I tell you something, Dante. Go to your room. You boys are out to make me crazy."

I pop up out of my sleep with a gasp and those words ringing in my ears. I look down at Lizzy sleeping next to me. She's here. She's safe. She would never leave Bella and me without a word. Not like my mother.

I, to this day, wonder what made her so upset. Did she leave because of what freaked her out before she came through the door and found me, or did she leave because I didn't listen and drove her crazy?

I exhale and run a hand through my hair. Something about Liz's story brought those days back. The last day I saw my mother. I wish I could forget it.

"It doesn't matter anymore," I breathe to myself and settle back into the sheets.

Italy and Family

Dante

Three weeks later...

"You've been working nonstop for the last three weeks. I think you need to take some time to relax. I've had you blocked from the remote system," I say as I run my hand down Lizzy's back and over her ass.

She looks up at me with a small smile. I continue my thoughts as I try to stay on topic. "All you do is work and take care of Bella. Do something for you today," I say and kiss her shoulder.

She turns onto her back under the sheet and lifts her hand in the air. I lace my fingers with hers while keeping them in the air and lean in to peck her lips.

"Isn't that my job, though, to take care of you and Bella?" she says with a smile.

I pull a face. "You know what I mean, smart-ass."

She giggles as I reach beneath the sheet and grasp her thick thigh, tugging it toward me. I'm fully dressed to attend a meeting with my brothers and Nonno. I wish I had the time to bury myself in her. I love our lazy morning sex and the talks we have after. I feel complete on those mornings. Like I can take on the world.

"I wanted to go into the village and explore anyway. I'll take your offering."

"You do know this was meant to be a vacation for you? I thought maybe you would create content, but I hadn't planned for you to work on office things."

"Meanwhile, you're on your phone all times of the day and night." She frowns. "Nope, if my boss is working, I'm working. I already think Michelle hates me now."

I snort. "Michelle doesn't do half the work you do. I've been thinking of letting her go for a while. You've always gone above and beyond in your job, and Michelle has been hiding behind that," I muse aloud.

Lizzy pushes me on my back and straddles my lap. I reach for the globes of her full ass and knead her cheeks. I'm tempted to say fuck this meeting and get lost in her for the rest of the day.

"I'll relax for the day if you promise me dinner. Just the two of us. Someplace romantic and as Italy as it gets," she purrs.

"I know the perfect place. Be ready by six."

"I love you," she says and leans in to brush a kiss against my lips.

I hold the back of her neck and deepen the kiss. A single moan from her lips and my plans change, I'll get there when I get there. I flip her onto her back and make love to her like I've wanted to all morning. What has this woman done to me?

"I think that all went well," Nonno says as he looks around the table at my brothers and me. We're back at the house, sitting in the backyard beneath the pergola. "It's good to have you all here. I think it's time we display our strength as a family. You three are stronger together."

"It's good to be here, Nonno," I say.

It is, Italy is like a second home for me. I spent a lot of time with my grandfather here after things got really bad. He gave me what I needed. Uncle Lucas tried to help my father with me as much as he could, but it was Nonno who got through to me.

These last three weeks have been exactly what I've needed. As we sit here and have a drink with my grandfather, I can't help thinking about my mother. He lost a daughter when she left us.

Lately, I've found it harder to believe my mother did leave us. Something else had to have happened. Nonno spoils us. As his only daughter, I can't see him treating her any differently.

She walked away from us, but why never contact her father again? The bitterness in my heart loosens. I've been willing to take a second look at a lot of things now that I have Lizzy in my life.

Which has led me to wanting answers. Being here in Italy, I feel like they surround me, I just don't know where to look first.

"You three have made me so proud," Nonno says, drawing me back into the conversation. "Dante, my father's father, started our first restaurant right here in Italy. It wasn't much, but he cooked for the people and they loved him. His brother joined him in the business and the people learned to respect them both.

"We gained power and the Di Lorenzo name was established as one of the strongest. What you have done in America with the family business reminds me of them. You've done well with all I've taught you."

"Thanks, Nonno. That means a lot."

"Dario, it's been good to have you here. It shows the other families there's still strength in the Di Lorenzo blood. We don't plan to go anywhere anytime soon. They needed to see your fresh face here."

He takes a sip of his drink and fixes his eyes on Dario. I get the feeling I know what he's about to say. From the look on Dario's face, so does he.

"You have secured things here, but you're needed in the States. Our problems lurk there. You boys have been keeping order, but this thing has festered for years far beyond you three. It's time you show them who you are," he says the last part with his eyes trained on Gio.

This shocks me a bit. My grandfather is nothing if not intentional. I read right through the message he's sending.

"Nonno, you know why I'm still here. I have to think about their safety. I don't know if now is the time to go back."

"We hide from no one. You will return and face this life you have created for yourself," Nonno says firmly, his eyes hard. "You are not alone. They will be safe. Trust your brothers. I've raised you all to be who you needed to be. It will all fall into place.

"Di Lorenzo men are never defined by the wants of others. We are the tides, the waters move to our will. *Capisci?*" he finishes.

"I hear you. We'll return with Dante and Gio."

"Good. I will miss you."

"You're not coming with us this time?" I say and look more closely at my grandfather. He looks tired. His youthful looks are starting to fade a bit.

"I have done my part. I am needed here for this final act." He looks to Gio. "It's my hope you all learn to know the true power of a father's love. You will outlive your time to do for your *bambini*. *La mia famiglia* is everything to me. That's what's important. Never forget that."

"We won't," my brothers and I say in unison.

"Now, Dante. When are you going to make me a *nipote?*"

I chuckle. "Soon, Nonno, soon."

I've been praying every time I release my seed inside Lizzy that she gives me a son. I thought I'd never want another child after Bethany, but Lizzy is so different. She's loving, patient, and she loves Bella like she's her own.

Yes, I hope to announce the birth of my son soon. Within the year, if I have anything to say about it.

CHAPTER FORTY-ONE

Excuse Me

Lizzy

"Can we get Daddy something?" Bella looks up at me to ask as we stroll the street with the little shops and vendors.

"I don't see why not."

I look into the reflection of the shop window before us. The same redhead comes into view. I noticed her two stores ago. She puts her head down and moves to one of the street vendors to act like she's picking something up.

"Lizzy, I can't thank you enough for this," Carleen says, drawing my attention. "I've been trapped in that house for months. I don't know what you said to get me out but thank you so much."

I give her a smile. "Don't worry about it. I'm glad you could join us."

"Oh, look at that. It's so cute. Do you mind if we go into this one?"

"Sure, listen, why don't you and Bella go inside? I'll be right behind you," I say.

Carleen and Bella head into the store and the bell over the door rings out through the air. I keep moving and dip into the little alley. I pull my gun and peek around the corner to see what the woman who's been following us does.

Just like I thought, she moves toward the shop. She stares inside the window, watching Bella and Carleen. Smooth as a cat, I ease out of the alley and come up behind her, placing my gun to the back of her head.

"Why are you following us?" I snarl.

"You don't want to do that," she says calmly. She holds her hand up in a gesture as if to stay someone. "My men have orders to protect me at all costs."

She nods at our reflection in the storefront window. My lips part when I see the red dot. I shove my gun at her head.

"I'll drop you before they can pull the trigger. I die, you die with me." I shrug.

"Relax, Elizabeth."

I gasp as my name comes out of her mouth. "Excuse me?"

She turns to me, and I feel like I've been sucker punched. Suddenly, I'm three all over again. Only her hair is different. She isn't a redhead in my memories.

I drop my gun and holster it at my back. I'm so confused as I look into her hazel eyes. My brain glitches as images of my parents falling play on repeat.

She moves forward and cups my face. "You're so beautiful. You look just like your mother. They would be so proud of you."

While there are tears in her eyes, she has this air about her. This woman is fierce and holds a sense of power.

"Who are you?"

"A friend."

I snort. "Really?" I say bitterly.

"I never meant for what happened to your parents. I will forever regret that."

"What do you want?"

"I just wanted to see. Everyone is so grown up now. I only wanted to see."

I go to ask more questions, but as if the woman on the verge of tears were never here, her face hardens, and she turns and disappears. I look in the glass and the red dot is gone. My gaze turns to Bella and Carleen.

Why did she want to see them? Who is that woman? My parents died protecting her, so she must have been a friend.

"Hello, Lizzy."

A chill runs through me as the words are spoken. I turn to find Riccardo, Gio's parental grandfather. For some reason, I don't think this man likes me.

I didn't know he was even here in Italy. Last I heard he was back home in Jersey. This trip is a Di Lorenzo thing. Not even the guys' dad came along for this trip. Although, Dante did tell me Riccardo Esposito and Giuseppe Di Lorenzo were once best friends, I get the feeling that has all changed.

"Hello, Mr. Esposito," I reply.

He waves me off. "Oh please. You are dating my grandson quite seriously, aren't you?"

I'm taken aback by the way he says the word grandson. I look him in his blue eyes, feeling a little defensive. I don't want to answer his question.

"It seems Dante is quite taken with you," he says when I don't answer. "You should call me Riccardo or Papa Riccardo. After all, if I know my grandson well, we will be family soon."

I breathe a breath of relief when I look over Riccardo's shoulder to see Gio hovering over him. Jace is next to appear.

"Riccardo," Gio rumbles, grabbing the man's attention away from me.

I tap on the window and gesture for Bella and Carleen to come out. I'm ready to head back to the house. This has been way more than my brain can handle. I need to sit and process these events.

"Gio, I wasn't expecting you here."

"That seems to be a theme. Why are you here in Italy?"

"Can't I visit home?"

Gio tilts his head to the side. "If it were home to you, I'd expect nothing less, but this hasn't been your home in years. Are you even welcome here anymore?" He narrows his eyes on the man before him as if he's a stranger and not his grandfather.

Riccardo looks to Jace and frowns. "Some things will never change. Have a good day, Lizzy. I'm sure I'll see you again."

He goes to walk away but stops and turns to me as Bella and Carleen step out of the store. He looks me over and then looks over Carleen. "May the best grandson win," he mutters and walks off.

"What the heck was that about?" Carleen asks.

I shrug my shoulders. "I have no idea."

"Ignore him. I'll handle him when the time is right." Gio turns on his megawatt smile, letting the deep frown fall from his face. "Ladies, there are shops all around. Uncle Gio is here to spend money. Shall we?"

Carleen laughs. "I thought you were here to take me back to my cage. Spend away, as long as it's not online shopping, I'm down."

Gio wraps an arm around her shoulders. He kisses her forehead and smiles down at her. "You will be free soon."

CHAPTER FORTY-TWO

Family Legacy

Lizzy

We get back to the house and I get this feeling Jace and Gio are up to something. Gio holds Bella back as he whispers something to her. Jace has that secret smile on his lips. Dante hasn't answered my last few texts.

I chalked it up as the poor reception we've been getting here at times. I want to talk to him about the strange woman in town and his grandfather. Something about both encounters has been nagging at me.

"Ugh, we're back just in time," Carleen says as she pulls her soaked shirt front from her chest.

I step through the front door right behind her and we both freeze. There are roses all over the foyer. Vases upon vases of red roses. Dante sits at the foot of the stairs, looking as handsome as ever, with a red rose clenched between his fingers. He's dressed in a black suit with a white shirt that's open at the top.

His dark hair is combed neatly into place. I can't wait to mess it up later. As if hearing my thoughts, he bites his lip and crooks his finger at me.

I move forward to him and take the rose he hands me. I'm not ready for the kiss he plants on my lips. It speaks so many words, my breath is taken away as I try to decipher them.

"Our date awaits. Go get dressed."

"Okay," I breathe as I look at him dreamily, all thoughts of the events of the day are forgotten. I don't want to ruin this date.

I rush up to the room we've been sharing and pull up short in the closet. I don't know what I was thinking when I asked him to take me out on a date, I don't have a thing to wear. I enter the closet and gasp when I find a garment bag and shoebox. There's a note pinned to the garment bag.

Called in a favor from your sister. She says this will be perfect. Dante will love it. Enjoy the night.

-G

I can't help the smile that comes to my lips. Gio has become such a good friend over the years. I'm glad to have him in my life.

I open the garment bag to find a matching black-and-powder blue panty set and a powder blue pantsuit. This has my sister written all over it.

I rush into the bathroom to freshen up. In my rush, I forget to tie my hair up before my shower. When I step out and look into the mirror, I groan. There's no way I have enough time to make this look like something. I grab a brush and create the best top bun I can.

I rush to apply my makeup, keeping it simple. I use extra setting spray, so my makeup doesn't come off on the suit. Once I lotion up, I put on the undergarments and smile into the mirror. They're sexy and give me a bit of a confidence boost before I dress in the pantsuit.

I look in the mirror after placing on the shoes and even I don't recognize the woman looking back at me. There's a glow on my cheeks and my smile is brighter than I've ever seen it.

All at once, it hits me. I'm dating and I've fallen in love with Dante Di Lorenzo, and he loves me back. I never thought this would be my life, but as I look in the mirror, I have a thought.

If not me, then who? I deserve this love. The gorgeous woman in the mirror deserves to be happy.

With that thought, I throw my shoulders back and lift my head. With a confidence I don't normally have, I go to get my man.

Dante

"Watch your step," I murmur as we step onto the old walkway.

I've tortured men for hours without breaking a sweat or having a second thought about it. However, as I guide Lizzy into this restaurant with my hand on her back, I'm the most nervous I've ever been in my life. My grandfather's question about having a son caused me to think about some things.

I made a last-minute decision and Dario offered to fly with me in the helicopter, while Gio and Jace went to keep Lizzy from returning back to the house too soon.

I was able to fly to my jeweler and back before they returned. By the time Lizzy arrived at the house, the foyer of my family home was filled with roses. I sat on the steps with a single rose in my hand, dressed for dinner.

The smile on her face was priceless. I almost dropped to one knee there. It killed me to have to wait for her to get ready, but when she appeared at the top of the stairs, I was speechless.

I never thought a pantsuit could look so sexy. The light blue suit accents all her assets. The flared-leg pants called attention to her long legs. The suit jacket hugged her breasts, revealing that she didn't have a blouse beneath. I could kiss the tailor who made it. The black heels made the entire outfit go from classy to sexy.

"This place is adorable and totally romantic, Dante," Lizzy gasps, pulling me from my thoughts.

"Welcome to *Amore Domestico*," I breathe in her ear.

"Wait, this is your family's first restaurant, right? It's on the list. I've talked to the chef here before."

"One and the very same. This is where my great-great-grandfather started it all."

"That must be so great to be a part of so much culture. Your grandfather always sounds so proud as he tells his stories. Have you ever thought about writing his stories down and making like a memoir cookbook or something to sell in all the restaurants?"

I kiss her lips. "I love the way your mind works. I'll suggest that to the marketing team for a mock-up and present it to the board. I think Nonno would like that."

I lead her to our table and pull her seat. I love that while everything, including her makeup, is perfect, her hair is in a soft bun that has curls trying to pop free. It reminds me of her personality.

I take my seat and sample the wine before giving the nod for our glasses to be filled. I lift my glass for a toast.

"To finding your other half," I croon.

Liz blushes and ducks her head as she takes a small sip. I don't think I will ever get tired of this shy side of her. This woman has so many facets. It's like I've been peeling back layers and I love what I find with each depth I reveal.

"This is really more than what I was expecting. The roses blew me away. Thanks, Dante."

"You haven't seen anything yet," I say and think of the ring in my pocket. This is the perfect place to propose. It's where my family's legacy started.

Tonight will be a new beginning.

Lizzy

I pat my full stomach, I've been to several of the Di Lorenzo restaurants, but this is by far the best meal I've had from one.

"That was amazing," I sigh as I sit back in my seat. "You have a great chef here."

Dante smiles. "Actually, Dario and Carleen did me a favor. They cooked for us tonight."

"Oh wow, I feel so special."

"You are. I wanted tonight to be special for you, for us."

I tilt my head and study him. Dante does everything with purpose. I'm not going to ignore all he has done today.

I grin at him. "What are you up to, Mr. Di Lorenzo?"

"First, I know you wanted this to be just us tonight, but someone found out what I was up to and wanted to be here, so I hope you can forgive me," he says.

Bella appears with a huge smile on her face. She's dressed up in her Book Princess outfit I made her. I push my chair back and open my arms for her to sit in my lap. She wraps her arms around my neck and gives me a squeeze.

"Hey, you," I say and kiss her little nose. I look to Dante. "You are more than forgiven. Now all my favorite people are here, but what's going on?"

"We want to ask you a question."

He stands and reaches into his inside suit jacket pocket. My mouth falls open when he drops to his knee. I can't hold back the tears.

"Stop crying, Mommy. We only want to ask you to marry us," Bella says innocently.

I start to cry harder when Bella calls me Mommy. I love this little girl so much. It's an honor to have her call me Mommy.

Dante snorts a laugh and shakes his head. "That was my part, Bella."

"Oh, sorry."

Dante moves closer and kisses the top of her head. "It's fine. Lizzy, I think you already know how crazy we are about you." Bella nods her head. "I remember the exact moment I knew I was in love with you. You looked over your shoulder after emptying your stomach and gave me this smile I'll never forget. Right in that moment, I knew I was in love. I could name a million things about you I love.

"With each day I spend with you, I lose another piece of my heart. I swear, I never saw you coming, but now that you're here, I don't want to let you go. Liz, baby, will you marry me?"

"Us," Bella says in exasperation.

"I'm sorry, sweetheart. Will you marry us? We are a bit of a package deal." He gives a little shrug and pulls a playful face at Bella.

She takes the ring box from his hands and holds it up at me as she turns to look expectantly at me. When I don't answer right away, she gives me the best puppy eyes I've ever seen. I laugh and squeeze her little face.

"Yes, I'll marry you, and you," I say, looking at Dante with my last word.

"*Yes*, it was my dress. I told you."

Dante palms her forehead and leans in to kiss me before pecking her cheek. "You were so right. I couldn't have done this without you. I love you too, munchkin."

"I love you too, Daddy."

I hold a shaky hand out as Dante plucks the ring from the box. It's stunning. The center diamond is surrounded by a halo of diamonds and the three-row band is covered by diamonds. It's definitely a showstopper.

"Wow," I exhale as Dante settles it into place.

"You did it. You got me a new mommy, who loves me," Bella sings.

Dante looks to me and swallows hard. His eyes get suspiciously misty. More tears fall from my eyes when Dante pulls me to him to kiss me deeply. He breaks the kiss to whisper in my ear. "Thank you."

"You don't have to thank me. I love you both."
He places his forehead to mine. "I know."

CHAPTER FORTY-THREE

Is This Love

Lizzy

I'm still floating on cloud nine. After the proposal, we had dessert as a family. Bella passed out from all the excitement before we made it back to the house.

With a face-splitting smile, I move to Dante's Bluetooth speaker in the bedroom we share and hook up my phone. Corinne Bailey Rae starts to croon "Is This Love," and I wrap my arms around my middle and start to sway to the music as the lyrics touch my bones.

I'm engaged. Dante asked me to marry him. I guess fairy tales do happen for me. My heart is so full.

"You know, she never would have forgiven me if I proposed without her. She was upset when she found out I intended to," Dante says as he walks into the room while removing his cuff links.

I move to the foot of the bed and pull my shoes from my feet, unable to remove the goofy smile from my face. Dante comes and tugs me into his arms. I drop my shoes, straighten, and wrap my arms around his neck.

"I thought it was perfect. I wouldn't have changed a thing," I purr.

He drags his hands down to my ass and squeezes. I lift on my toes as he tugs me into his body. The look in his eyes heats me all over.

He runs his nose up the bridge of mine. I love when he does that. I sigh and sink into his body.

"The only thing I would change is getting to make love to my fiancée to end the night," he says against my lips.

"Is that right?" I nip at his lip, then do the same to his chin.

"Yes, it is. Maybe we can work on making our next baby."

I gasp and burst into tears like a big baby. Dante palms my face, searching it frantically.

"What? What did I say wrong?"

"You want a baby with me?" I sob like a dork.

Dante tries his best not to laugh at me but fails. Wiping my tears away with his thumbs, he then kisses me. I glide my hands to hold his face as he does.

"Yes, I want more than one baby with you."

He reaches to unbutton my jacket and pushes it from my shoulders. Dipping his head, he kisses one shoulder, then the top of my breast before moving to do the same to the other side.

I drop my head back as this time he dips his tongue into my bra cup and finds my nipple to tease with his wet mouth. I lock my hands in his hair to hold him there as I curl my toes into the carpet.

Swiftly, without my notice, he unclasps my bra. It falls to the floor and he grasps my waist, tugging me closer to wrap his mouth around my other nipple.

I wrap my leg around his waist and hold him to me tightly. Dante makes quick work of unfastening my pants. He shoves a hand inside my panties and finds my nub to massage like only he can.

"Dante," I whisper.

He lifts me onto his waist and closes the distance to the bed. My back hits the mattress. He travels down my body with open-mouthed kisses. Hooking his fingers into my pants and panties, he peels them down my body.

Standing from the bed, he gives me a sexy grin as he works to get his clothes off. I return the grin and reach to play with my pussy for him.

"Liz," he says as if in warning.

Instead of pulling my hand back, I reach for my nipple with my free hand and pinch and roll it as I bite down on my lip. The sound of my juices fills the room.

Before he can get fully naked, I scoot up the bed to reach for the vibrator in the nightstand drawer. I turn it on and use it to help me put on a show for my man.

Dante licks his lips as he gets his socks off. Reaching for my ankles, he tugs me down the bed some and then wraps his arms around my thighs, to bring me down to the edge of the bed. I don't stop my show for him. His eyes are filled with desire.

While I bring myself to climax, he pulls my toes into his mouth. I start to keen and convulse when he pushes two fingers into me as I hold the wand to my clit.

He begins to stroke himself. It's a beautiful sight to see. His muscles work with the restraint he's trying to keep. I lick my fingers and go back to rubbing my hardened peak, alternating between kneading my breast and rolling my nipple. I think that's the last straw.

He knocks my hand from between my legs, the wand falling to the floor. Ignoring it, he guides his fat head into me, then pulls out. I whimper, looking down to see his tip glistening.

"You don't like me teasing you, do you?" he says and pushes only the tip in once more.

"Please, Dante, please."

He chuckles darkly and shoves into me to the hilt. My body takes him in like it's his home. I fit around him like a glove. I'm out of my mind with want for him, even as he's thrusting inside me.

Dante

I watch her breasts bounce as I pound into her sweetness. I love everything about this woman. Her large dark areolas, how her nipples pucker to tiny peaks.

I could get lost in this pussy for hours. She clamps around me as if confirming my thoughts. I slow and palm the backs of her thighs, tilting her body so she lifts to a new angle.

Planting a foot on the bed, I start to thrust downward. She loses it and starts to cry out. I move one hand to her belly and push down as my cock massages her insides.

Thoughts of her belly swollen with our son fill my mind. I want it so bad I can taste it. As deep as I am, it's not enough. I pull out and flip her onto all fours, guide her to the center of the bed and climb on behind her.

I now have a view of her full figure in all its glory. Her fat pussy is the prettiest I've ever seen. My mouth waters and I have to answer the call of her dripping lips.

"Whose pussy is this, Liz?" I growl before I dive in for a taste.

"Oh my God. It's yours. It will always be yours."

I hum into her, reaching to rub her clit. I get what I'm looking for as she squirts into my mouth. I palm her cheeks, pulling them apart, needing to get closer, deeper, more.

I lift to my knees and run my length through her wet folds. She moans and wiggles her ass.

"You want me inside this tight pussy?"

"Yes, please, yes."

I slap her ass and watch it jiggle. I'll never get tired of that. Grasping her hips, I shove into her heat. My hold on her is bruising, but I can't help myself. Knowing she said yes and that she's going to be my wife does something to me.

The way her pussy ripples around me tells me I'm bringing her pleasure. I start to chase my demons within this pussy.

I lift to my feet and hover over her while holding her in place as I pump my hips. All my insecurities and anger are fought with each wet thrust.

"You're never going to let anyone touch what's mine, Liz. I'm the only man who will have this pussy ever again."

Even as I hear myself say the words, I know she doesn't deserve them, she's not Bethany. I pound harder because of my anger with myself. All while she calls my name and takes it.

"I love you so much," I pant.

I'm getting close. I pull out and lie on my back. Running a hand through my hair and wiping sweat from my face, I catch my breath for a beat.

"Come here, baby," I say.

She comes to me so willingly. The love I see in her eyes takes something from me. It's my hurt, my anger, all the rage. I feel it lift from my body.

As Lizzy straddles my hips and sinks down on me, I feel like I receive a new life. I palm her ass and accept the slow grind she starts with her sexy hips. I don't want her to change a thing.

I hated all the work my late wife started to have done. Maybe that was my fault. I didn't tell her she was beautiful enough. I internally snort at the thought. It's bullshit, but I won't fail Lizzy in that way.

"You're gorgeous," I groan. "I love every part of you."

I lift to capture her lips. "These are my favorite."

I duck my head to take one of her nipples into my mouth. I suck one and then move to the other. "Perfection. The perfect size and I love your fucking nipples. You have no idea how much your tits turn me on."

I splay my palms on her fleshy belly. "I can't wait to place a baby here."

I grind my hips into her from below. "This pussy. From the first time I was inside you, I knew I'd never want another."

"Dante," she gasps and throws her head back.

"Yes, baby? How can I serve you?" I drag my hands to her thighs and squeeze. "So fucking perfect," I croon.

I don't get a reply as she cries out while convulsing and raining all over me. I tug her into my arms and pump up into her a few last times before I spill inside her with a smile on my lips.

"Sleep well, *Amore mio.*"

CHAPTER FORTY-FOUR

Crossing the Line

Lizzy

I'm frustrated and wish we could go back to Italy. A month wasn't enough. These fans are sucking the fun out of gaming for me.

I'm trying to focus on the game and allow Denise to handle the chat. We have a real asshole in here tonight. I'm trying not to lose my temper.

"I don't know how the hell he's doing this," Denise growls in frustration. "It's like he's jumping IP addresses as fast as I'm shutting him down. I've blocked him like thirteen times already, but I know it's the same asshole."

"Don't worry about it. We'll ignore it."

"I don't like it. He's threatened you repeatedly," she hisses in my ear.

"I know."

"They're all losing their minds over you getting engaged. Did they all think they could date you someday? This is insane."

I laugh because my mic isn't on and they can't hear Denise in my ear, but she's right. The moment I cammed up and my hand came up on-screen holding the controller with my engagement ring on, they lost it with questions, and some had mean comments to type.

Izzy, what the fuck is that? Izzy, you can't be serious? You're engaged? I thought we were in this together.

Those were just a few they began with. If I hadn't missed out on so much content while away, I would have logged off. Not that there aren't some who seem genuinely happy for me.

It's the crazy's threatening to find me and rape me who are making this awful. They'd die trying, but it's still disheartening to know this is what happens to female gamers. I've seen it, but it's never been this bad for me.

I end a battle royal and decide to take a peek in the chat. My face burns with anger as I see Jacob pop up.

Jacob_eats: Why did you block my calls?

Jacob_eats: Wait is that an engagement ring? What the fuck, Izzy?

"You see that, Denise? Can you block him?"

"On it. Um, Iz. You have company."

I look at my screen to find my fiancé standing behind me with his arms folded over his chest and gun holsters strapped to his shoulders. The look on Dante's face reads murder.

My face burns with embarrassment. I know he watches the channel sometimes, so I have an idea why he's here. Knowing he's seen the comments causes a shiver to run through me. I'm not naive to who Dante is and what he's capable of.

He moves to me and wraps his hand around my throat as he keeps his glare on the camera. He kisses the side of my face. Then stands and folds his arms over his chest again.

Black Cloud: I told y'all to stop fucking with her. That man looks like he will find you. Just be happy for her and back off.

Unicorn_31: Oh my God. Did anyone else cream their panties? That was so fucking hot.

Unicorn_31: Damn that dude is huge. Y'all don't want them problems.

KoolKid: Fuck this game. I want to see those two go at it.

KoolKid: BTW. Congrats, Izzy. You're my fave and you deserve all the happiness.

"Well, that's a way to get rid of assholes. It looks like that jerk is gone," Denise says in my ear.

"Hey, I think I'm done for the night, guys. Y'all have a good one," I say as I turn my mic back on.

I shut down and stand, turning to Dante. He looks at me with the same anger playing across his face. Yeah, he need not watch my channel anymore.

"You shouldn't have done that. Content is forever. What if the authorities see that?"

"These are my licensed pieces. They're both clean. I have a right to protect what's mine. They can come knocking. They would find nothing."

I shake my head. "Thanks for the save, babe. That was getting ridiculous."

He pulls me into a passionate kiss by the back of my neck. "I hate your channel. That shit is going to have me murder someone."

I place my head against his chest. "I hope not. Bella and I need you."

He snorts. "As if I'd get caught. Listen, baby. I know you built all of this before me, but…it's just getting out of hand. Maybe we need to look at it and see how you can step back without losing your revenue."

"It's not about the money, but yeah, I hear you. It's not fun anymore. Maybe I will take a break or something. I do have a wedding to plan."

All the tension leaves his body. He tightens his arms around me and kisses the top of my head. I feel so safe and secure in his embrace.

"Come on, let's get some ice cream and watch a movie."

"Okay."

CHAPTER FORTY-FIVE

You're Fired

Dante

I have my head down, looking over some emails on my tablet. Lizzy and Nyla are out of the office wedding planning today. I had to insist Liz take the day off to begin the planning. I want her to have the wedding of her dreams, but I don't want to wait forever to get married.

I frown and flip back to the screen that has me out of my office. I narrow my eyes at the reports. Something isn't right. I scroll to see who prepared this. It's not Liz's work. Things are missing and jumbled. My reports haven't looked like this in months.

I tap a few buttons to reveal a part of the system my employees don't know about. I bare my teeth as I find the time stamp and signature of the one who filed the report. As I near the bend that will lead me to the reception desk, I pause.

"Have you seen that ring?" I overhear Michelle say.

"Oh my God, I was watching her channel and saw. So much for not dating coworkers."

"Well, I saw it in person yesterday. Man, I wish I would have thought to sleep my way through this place. She gets to go on trips and now she's engaged to all that fine, money, and power. Ugh, I totally fucked up."

"But she doesn't need the money. Some dude posted her net worth on one of the forums. She's worth like fifty-seven million all by herself."

"See, she doesn't even need the come up. I should totally sabotage her and seduce the boss." Michelle snickers. "I mean, she's always got her head stuck in a book. How the fuck does she manage to get so much work done? It drives me crazy. I sit here slaving and by ten I look up and she's done."

"Good luck with that one. I tried to apply for her old position, but her sister was hired instead. Now that I think about it, something fishy is going on around here. I wouldn't have wanted that job anyway. Did you notice how no one even talks about the fact that his wife was murdered? Why not?"

I grind my teeth. I'm still trying to place the other voice. I pull up all the applicants for Lizzy's old job. I scan the list. I'm firing these two today. As soon as I find out from HR if there's anything stopping me, they're both gone, no matter the cost.

"Old fat nerdy cow," Michelle says bitterly. "She probably ate his wife and ran the car off the road after."

The guy chuckles, but it sounds off. Almost forced. "To be fair. I don't think she's fat. She's curvy."

"Whatever. Did you need something?"

I step from behind the wall and glare at the two. This little fuck is the intern who used to lurk around Lizzy. He can go now without question. As I think of the report Michelle just fucked up, I decide I need no further reason. Her ass can go too.

I move over to the desk and set my tablet down. Peter, the intern, tries to turn and scurry off.

"Don't move," I snarl. I then turn to Michelle. "Give me the phone."

I pick up the receiver and dial for the front desk. I don't miss that Peter won't look at me. I don't like this guy. Something about him rubs me wrong.

"This is Mr. Di Lorenzo. Have security come up to my floor. I would like Michelle McCallister and Peter"—I look down at my tablet—"Hall removed from the building. Make sure they turn in their IDs and passkeys. They aren't to be allowed back in this building as of today, they're both fired."

"Yes, Mr. Di Lorenzo. Someone is on the way."

I grunt and cradle the receiver. Michelle sits with her mouth hanging open, and all the blood has drained from Peter's face.

"For the record, you're not my type," I say to Michelle. "And if you weren't gossiping every chance you got, you would be able to do your work and finish in a timely fashion, or at least, you'd be able to do it properly."

I turn my gaze to Peter. "Her net worth is no one's business. I don't understand how you guys call yourselves fans but try to violate her life every chance you get."

"I…I…I—"

"Save it. My dead wife is none of your—or anyone else's—business. You shouldn't work for someone if you think they're questionable, so I'm doing you a favor."

Security arrives, and I turn to leave before I really lose my temper. I need to pull the proper reports and get on with my day.

Lizzy

"That's the one, Liz. You look amazing. You're going to take Dante's breath away."

"Yes," Denise sniffles. "This one is perfect. You look absolutely gorgeous."

I look in the mirror at the dress and it steals my breath away. I'll have to get back to my morning yoga religiously to tighten my tummy, but it's this one for the win.

The bodice gives the illusion that my top is bare, only a few intricate lace patterns cover my intimate places and scatter along my arms. The skirts are full princess layers with a petticoat beneath. The top layer is intricately beaded with sparkling lace.

I didn't know this was what I wanted. After I tried on a bunch of gowns that looked terrible on me, Nyla picked this one. It's the first gown that doesn't make me look old and frumpy.

I look like a fresh young bride. I place my hand over my chest and my ring winks at me. It's perfect. Tears come to my eyes.

"This is it."

"You know I love you. I'm so glad you found what you were looking for. I'll call you later, but I have to go," Denise says as she comes over to me.

I lean down and kiss her cheek and give her a tight squeeze. "I love you too. Thank you for everything."

"Anytime," she says and pulls away and turns to the bridal shop attendant. "I'm paying for the gown. Here's my card."

"Auntie Denise, no. This is the most expensive one I've tried on. There's no way I'm allowing you to pay for this."

"Girl, it's been years since anyone has allowed me to do anything. I'm paying and that's final. Elijah and I decided this morning we're covering the wedding. You do the planning and we'll cover everything else. I gotta go, love."

She rushes off and my heart swells with love for her and Dad. I turn back to the mirror and look down at my ring, then up into the mirror at the gown again.

"Oh my God, Ny. I'm getting married."

"I know," she says with trembling lips.

"Oh, no. What's wrong?"

"It's nothing," she chokes out.

I step down from the platform and rush to embrace my sister. I know her better than to think it's nothing. She's hiding something.

"It's not nothing. Ny, I'm here. Talk to me."

"I'm so deep in this I don't know what to do. I don't even know what I want or what I'm doing anymore."

"Is this about Gio?"

She nods.

"Okay, so what's with that? I don't totally understand him or his lifestyle. Like, that's the one off-limits topic between us. How are you fitting into all that?"

Nyla shakes her head. "No, this day is about you. We don't have time for me to explain it anyway. We need to get to your cake tasting appointment."

I purse my lips and frown. I can see she's shut down on me just that quickly. I sigh and nod, turning to change back into my street clothes.

I'm dressed quickly and we race to make my appointment. I'm trying to get as much done today as I can. Denise and Dad offered to get me a wedding planner, but I want the experience of doing as much as I can for myself. Nyla and I will meet with a few planners next week.

"So, are you going to ask the girls to be bridesmaids?"

I smile, thinking of my roller derby team. We've become close over the years. I would love to have them as a part of the wedding. They all get me.

"Yeah, I think I will. I liked the pink dress you tried on. I think you all would look nice in that one," I say to Nyla as we walk up to the cake shop.

Her phone rings and she answers me distractedly. "Yeah, I liked that one too. Um, Liz, give me a sec. Go on in without me."

I look at my watch to see we're running late. I go to pull the door open and enter alone. I step in and crash into someone.

"I'm sorry," I say as I look up from my watch.

I'm surprised to look up into the eyes of none other than Jacob. He gives me a small smile. I look around for an escape route. I do not want to talk to this asshole.

"Hey, Lizzy," he murmurs. "I wanted to talk to you. I don't understand what happened. We were fine, and suddenly you're not answering my texts or calls. You totally ghosted me. When I call the office for you, I'm always told you're not there."

"You call the office?" I shake my head. "You know what, never mind. Things weren't working out, and then…"

I huff and frown, holding up my hand. "I moved on. There's really nothing to talk about."

"So that's it?"

I go to step around him, but he blocks my way. He lowers his voice and leans into me. "Listen, do you know what you're getting into with that guy? You should be careful. I'd hate to see you get hurt."

I narrow my eyes at him. "Is that a threat or something?"

He throws up his hands and looks at something over my shoulder before he turns his attention back to me. "It seems you've made your choice. I guess I got what I needed. You be safe, Izzy."

I don't like the way he says my name. As a matter of fact, all of his words rub me wrong. I turn to see him brush by my sister on the way out the door. I don't miss the glare she gives him.

Asshole.

CHAPTER FORTY-SIX

For My Man

Lizzy

Dante has been tense since he arrived home. I wanted to share my progress with the wedding with him, but his sour mood made me change my mind.

After putting Bella to sleep, he kissed my forehead and disappeared. I'm not in the mood to game, but I text Ny anyway. When she told me she couldn't, I went in search of Dante, but he's nowhere to be found.

I pull out my phone and text him. I just want to make sure he's okay. I hate not having been at work to help him through the day.

Me: *I can't find you. Did you leave the house?*
Dante: *No. I'm on the rooftop.*
Me: *Oh. Okay.*

I have a little pang in my chest, knowing that's where he goes to get away from everyone. I get ready to mope to our room and go to bed when my phone pings with a message.

Dante: *Come up. Your thumbprint will work. I had it programmed.*

I blink a few times, remembering him asking me to place my print on his tablet a few weeks back. With a smile, I practically jog to the door that leads up to the roof. I squeal when the door pops open as I place my thumb on the pad.

I find Dante seated on one of the large ottomans just inside the glass doors. He leans back on one hand as he sips from a tumbler with the other.

He gives me a smile as I slip indoors. Pointing the glass at me, he lifts a brow.

"You were live?"

"No, I'm not feeling it. I think you're right; I need a break."

"Have I ever told you how much I love those little outfits? It's the thigh-high socks and tiny ass shorts. You're like one of my teenage fantasies. I swore when I got to college, all the girls would be dressed like you. I probably never would have gotten married if they were." He snorts and takes another drink.

"So let me get this right. You dated her in high school. Went to college and then traveled for two years? You two married after you came back."

"Yeah." He nods and winces at his glass. "You know. Now that you say it, I think Nonno was trying to stop me from making that mistake. I wasn't going to go to college. She wanted to get married senior year. Nonno put his foot down and paid for all four years of college and donated a shit ton to my college for a gym I never played in."

I laugh. "Yeah, Nonno was definitely trying to tell you something. They say the biggest lessons in life can be the most expensive."

"Tell me about it."

He places his glass down on the floor beside him and opens his arms. "Come here. I missed you and I didn't get to ask you about the planning. I'm sorry."

I move closer and he pulls me into his lap. I run my hand through his hair and peck his lips.

"How was it? Did you find a dress? I know that was your biggest concern."

"Yes, I did. It's out of this world. I couldn't have found a better dress. I felt like a real princess."

"That's because you are." He takes in a sharp breath. "I can't wait to see you in it."

I cup his face. "Do you want to talk about it? What can I do?"

I look deep into his eyes and see the stress there. He shakes his head and tugs me in for a kiss. It goes from a soft, gentle kiss to an all-consuming one. My toes curl in my socks.

I get an idea and slide between his legs. I rest on my knees and reach to release him from his slacks. He's already barefoot and his shirt is sitting open, displaying that hard body beneath. I lick my lips in anticipation. Reaching into his pants, I pull him free.

In usual Dante fashion, he bends to kiss me hard. I stroke him while he has his fill of my mouth. I moan as he sucks my tongue into his mouth. He bites my lip and pulls, releasing it with a hiss.

Without taking his eyes off me, he leans back on his elbows. I lower my mouth over him and seal my lips around him. After bobbing up and down a few times, I release him from my mouth and suck in a breath through my teeth.

"Ah," I breathe.

He grasps my face and tugs me back to suck him. I spit on it before taking him in. He lifts his hips and guides my head as I bob.

"Fuck," he hisses.

I gag and choke as he holds my head down and keeps his hips lifted. When he finally allows me up, I smile up at him as saliva drips down my chin.

Covering him with my mouth, I stand while folded in half. Dante tears my shorts in half and tosses the silky fabric once he rips them from each leg. Spreading my cheeks with his palms, he teases my lips with his fingertip. I moan around him but don't stop sucking and slurping.

"I want to eat you, come here."

I smile around him. Instead of obeying his command and lifting my head to turn to offer him my pussy, I decide to teach Dante a little something about me.

I settle my shoulders on his strong thighs and kick my legs up, opening them to offer him what he's looking for. He inhales sharply but catches me around the waist and buries his face in my honey. I bend my knees and hold them out to the sides as I wind my hips and grind my pussy into his face.

Dante groans while eating me out. Reaching for one of my legs, he claws his fingers down my inner thigh. The sounds he makes let me know he's a happy man. I moan as my stomach convulses. I lower my legs and come back up on shaky limbs.

Lightning fast, Dante wraps his arms around my waist and pulls me into his lap. I straddle his hips and sink onto him as he holds his dick up for me. His other hand is in my hair and his mouth is on mine like a starving man.

"You see how hard you make me?"

"Yes. Don't stop."

I ride him slow and easy as he thrusts deep into me from beneath. Suddenly, he flips us, so I'm lying across the ottoman. He pulls out, rolls me onto my side and gets behind me. I cry out as he pushes back into me while holding my leg up. He tears my off-the-shoulder T-shirt down the front, then pulls my bra cup down and palms my breast.

"Yes, baby. Take what you need. You feel so good," I say.

I throw it back at him and take all of his long, hard dick. He latches onto my neck and sucks on it. The sound of him moving in and out of my wetness fills the air. I'm creaming so hard for him.

"You're so wet for me."

"Always for my man."

"Say that shit again. For who?"

"For my man. Only for you, baby. Always for you."

He tightens his grip on my inner thigh and pushes my leg back, opening me wider for him. I look out toward the night sky and it's like I'm flying into the clouds. If this is what being married to this man will be like, I'm ready to get married tonight.

"I love you so much, Liz. You make everything better, baby."

"You too, babe. You too."

CHAPTER FORTY-SEVEN

Helpful Stalkers

Lizzy

I had no idea Dante fired Michelle until this morning when I was asked to man the reception desk. He wouldn't tell me why. He only said she was incompetent and messed up the reports yesterday. I was okay with that until I found out Peter was fired too. I can't help but wonder what happened.

"Hey, rumor is Dante fired those two for gossiping about you guys. You would think they'd stop gossiping around here. I just got two versions of the story in the break room." Nyla rolls her eyes.

I laugh. "I told Peter about that mouth of his. He sort of gave me the creeps. You know he watches the channel."

"Speaking of creeps and watching the channel. Jacob was in my chat last night."

"Really? Why? Wait, I thought you weren't going on." I frown and fold my arms over my chest.

She returns the frown. "I wasn't. Something came up. Anyway. He wanted to know if I knew what happened." She shrugs.

"What did you say?"

"I don't owe him anything. I said nothing."

"Oh, thank God. Izzy, I need to talk to you."

Looking up, I find a frantic guy with shaggy brown hair and glasses rushing toward the reception desk. I look him over. I know all the maintenance guys and I've never seen this one before, but he's wearing the uniform.

The backpack he has also seems out of place. Not to mention, he's just called me Izzy.

He licks his lips and looks around. "Your fiancé is probably going to kill me this time, but I had to do something. I had to say something."

"What are you rambling about?" Nyla bites out. "Spit it out."

Just then, Dante walks up. He lifts his head and does a double take as he takes in the lanky guy who's cowering away from him.

Dante narrows his eyes. "Why the fuck are you here and how did you get in? I told you to stay away from her."

"Yes, I know. B...but...I didn't listen and now I'm glad I didn't. I need to talk to you both. It's about Bella."

Dante lunges at him so fast I yelp. He has the guy by the collar dangling him in the air. "How do you know my daughter's name and what the hell do you need to talk to me about?"

"I heard Izzy call her that at the skate park. Li...listen, man, I told you, I'm a huge fan. I would never hurt Izzy or anyone important to her. Someone's been posting more of Izzy's personal deets, I got worried and started to reverse hack them and I've been following Izzy with my drone to keep my distance like you told me to.

"When Bella's school was posted this morning. I followed her, not Izzy. Man, we have to find her. Someone took Bella off the school grounds after your guys left. Please, I'm here to help."

Just then, Jace and Gio come rushing out of Gio's office. They take in the scene before them and the frowns on their faces deepen.

"Who is he?"

Dante drops him and takes a step back.

"The man I'm going to kill if we don't get our daughter back," I reply.

"Jeez, what's with you people?"

"Start talking, or I'm going to kill you either way," I seethe.

"I tried to follow them, but I lost them. My drone fell out of range or was scrambled or something."

"When I reverse hacked the person doxing Izzy, I got some shell company's info. I hit a wall there. I can give you a description of the car and pull pictures from the drone of the person who took her."

"Come with me," Jace orders.

The guy turns to me, with a small smile, he says, "My name is Aaron, Izzy. It's so nice to meet you."

"Not now, kid. Find my daughter," I reply.

"This day just keeps getting better," Gio snarls.

"What's that supposed to mean?"

"I found your mother-in-law."

"Where is she?"

"Her head is in the freezer at your in-laws' home."

"What the fuck?"

"I don't know, but that can wait. Unless you have something to tell me."

Dante shakes his head. "You already know what I know about all of that."

Gio nods. "Yeah, that's what I thought."

Dante's phone rings and it's like all the air is sucked out of the room. He pulls it out and places it on speaker.

"Hello."

"You want your daughter back. I want money. We trade. I'll text you the address. No funny business. I see a single cop and it's all over."

"You're going to wish the cops were there, you son of a bitch," Dante snarls.

The person laughs. "Twenty million. That's change to you."

"Let me talk to my daughter."

There's a small pause. "Daddy," Bella whimpers.

"I'm coming for you, sweetheart. Be brave for Daddy."

I look to Gio as the call ends, my chest heaving. "Her necklace. The teddy bear is a tracker. I'll call Denise to track it."

Dante

I can't stop pacing the conference room we're in. So many thoughts are going through my head. After watching the video, Bella will never return to that school again and they'll be lucky if they can keep their doors open after I'm done with them.

"How the fuck did this happen?" I roar.

No one can get me answers. We still don't know where my daughter is. The tracker isn't working. We think it's being scrambled like the kid's drone.

All we know is that it's Peter fucking Hall in the pictures Aaron pulled from his drone. I'm going to pull his spine from his body while his heart is still beating.

"How can we help?" Elijah says as he and Denise enter the room.

"Any luck with unscrambling the tracker?" Nyla asks.

"No, I tried the whole way here," Denise says sadly.

"Guys, this isn't adding up. It looks like Peter has only been getting the information from the forums like me. His accounts say he doesn't have the type of money he would need for a scrambler of this magnitude, and he hasn't had funds in the last six months.

"Dude is broke as fuck," Aaron snorts and shakes his head. "Don't you guys pay really well?"

"He was an intern," Lizzy grumbles. She looks at me with tears in her eyes. "I'm so sorry, Dante. This is all my fault."

I walk over to her as she sits at the conference table, bouncing her leg and wringing her hands. I cup the back of her head and press my forehead to hers. "This isn't your fault. We're going to get her back."

"His apartment is empty," Gio informs me as he hangs up his phone.

"Fuck," I bellow. "We keep hitting walls. I need something I can use."

"The guys found maps from several old malls and abandoned buildings. I have them checking all of them."

"I can help with that. I just need to find the tower that call to Mr. Di Lorenzo pinged from and match abandon locations and cross reference those with the area I lost signal in," Aaron says from his laptop. He types frantically on the keys of his laptop. "Bingo. I have it."

My phone pings at the same time. "So do I," I growl as the text comes in. "We have two hours."

"I'm downloading the blueprints from the city archives," Aaron says.

"I might be starting to like you, kid," Gio says.

Aaron pushes up his glasses and grins. "Cool, I totally work for hire."

"Don't push it," I mutter.

"Just saying." He shrugs.

At that moment, Dario walks through the door. His gaze scans the room for me. When we lock eyes, he gives me a nod.

"What do you need?"

"He's giving me two hours to get there. I need all of the men we have and someplace to bury the pieces of this fuck after I'm done with him."

"Let's go. I have all of that covered," Dario says.

"We can help," Elijah says as he and Denise step up.

"I'm coming with you," Lizzy says and stands.

"No, you're not."

"Dante, don't," Gio says firmly. "Let her come. We may need her skills."

CHAPTER FORTY-EIGHT

Flash Mob Lunatic

Lizzy

We're on the top deck of the mall Peter has Bella in. All of our teams are getting ready. Aaron has proven himself to be useful.

"Aaron and I will be everyone's eyes and ears. We want to get in and out without a hair on that baby's head being harmed. I have a sniper on the rooftop across from the building already," Denise says.

"Does she have eyes on them yet?" Gio asks tightly.

"Target in view, but I don't have a shot." Comes through my earpiece.

Denise nods. "Yes, we have sight."

I snap my thigh holsters on and ready my guns to slide them in place. Dante comes over and spins one of the wheels on my blades slung over my shoulder. I look up into his eyes.

"None of that badass shit. Get our daughter and get out. I've got him. I'll meet you at the car. Be safe in there. I don't like this, something feels off."

"We're the best at what we do. I'll get her out."

He leans in and pecks my lips. "I love you. My life means nothing without you two."

"You'll be making us ice cream and painting our nails within a few hours. I got this, babe."

I wink at him, and he walks off to lock heads with Gio and Dario. Peter is going to shit a brick when he sees those three coming. They'll be going in first with the case that supposedly has the money.

A few friends and I will roll in as a distraction and get Bella out. Once we have Bella, Dante has his own plan. I sit on the bed of Dad's pickup and put on my skates. As I finish locking the straps on my blades, my team rolls up and I hop up to roll over and huddle with them.

"Thanks, guys, this means a lot," I say as I look around at my roller derby team. We have a unique bond that goes beyond our paintball tournaments. "We're going to skate down to the lower level. We can enter the mall from there. Once the brothers come into view with the case, that's our cue to roll in and shake shit up."

"I'll get my baby out. You all make sure nothing stands in my way."

"We've got you," Ming says.

I nod and look around at the women I trust with my life.

"Let's move," Gio calls.

I clap my hands. "Showtime."

My team starts to glide toward the ramp that will take us down. We move into formation and take the first turn together, I lean into the turn and drop a hand out as I glide smoothly. We bend the next turn together as well.

The entrance comes into view, and I get low and pull it open. One by one, we roll in. We're still a few levels above Peter. Dante, Dario, and Gio come into view, and we speed up.

We need to be closer. I start to skate faster and take the ramp that dumps us onto the level Peter is on. I pull the pin on the smoke bomb I have in my hand. Out of the corner of my eye, I see the others pull their pins as well. I toss mine and glide right into the smoke.

I have my arms wrapped around Bella and I push off to get us out. Peter chokes and starts to yell. Simultaneously, music starts to play and a shot rings out.

I wrinkle my brows as the sound of the EDM music plays. I'm almost to the parking exit on this level when all hell breaks loose. Bella clings to me tightly with her face buried in my neck. People are rushing into the mall and begin to surround us and they're coming in the way we're trying to exit.

"You're not going to believe this—" Aaron says through the earpiece. "I'm sorry, guys. I was so focused on the mission I missed a text for a flash mob at this location. They promised a sighting of Izzy and a rave. Fuck, there are people swarming in the place at every entrance."

"I have Bella, that's all that counts."

"Guys, this text is coming from that company. Either Peter has help, or someone else is watching all this and interfering," Aaron says.

Dante

The goggles Denise gave us allow me to see the moment Liz has our baby in her arms. Peter moves to go after them, but I lift my gun and pull the trigger, hitting him in the shoulder. At the same time, music starts to play throughout the mall.

Peter falls to the ground in a heap and that's when all the confusion starts. The doors fly open, and people start to flood the building. I'm frustrated as fuck as I look around.

Suddenly Aaron's voice comes through the earpiece, and it all starts to make sense. I put my gun away quickly and go to pick Peter's ass up off the floor. However, he's gone.

I clench my teeth and look around for him. "That motherfucker isn't getting away. Do we have eyes on him?"

"He's running for it. He's headed toward the parking lot on the north side. One level above you."

"Thanks, Denise."

I take off and my brothers are right behind me. I'm not letting this son of a bitch get away.

"I have the girls," Elijah says.

I breathe a little easier knowing Lizzy and Bella have made it out safely. The composed Dante slips away. I might not even heat up the chain breakers before I rip his spine out. It will make it more brutal.

We come out running into the lot. Tires squeal away from us. I turn to see an old Corolla speeding away and make chase. The adrenaline pumping through me pushes me forward.

I fire a shot, but it only takes out the back windshield. I turn the corner to the next level and freeze. My heart is in my throat as the scene before me plays out in slow motion.

Bella and Elijah are in the pickup. Lizzy seems to be fastening Bella in. When Lizzy closes the door, the Corolla heads straight for her.

My crazy fiancée doesn't jump out of the way. She starts to skate full speed, facing the car head-on. I watch as my woman skates up the front of the car, over the top, flips in the air, and lands in a crouch with her guns drawn.

Then time speeds up as she stands and fires through the windshield I blew out moments ago. I run up behind her and wrap my body around her. I think I just start to breathe again as I get her in my embrace.

"I thought I told you no badass shit. You could have jumped out of the way," I say against her lips as I cup her face.

"Not my style." She shrugs.

I laugh and take her lips. "You're always full of surprises. Best secret my brother has ever kept from me. Actually, the best hire he has ever made."

I kiss her passionately and smile to myself. I can live with who I have to be as long as I get to spend my life with this woman. I don't remember at what point she became my work wife, but I know I'm ready for her to be my wife for life.

Superhero Skaters

Dante

Six months later…

Phil Collins's "Take Me Home" plays as Liz and Bella glide around the rink in Wonder Woman costumes with crowns on their heads. I can't stop smiling. I've never seen Bella so happy in her life.

My baby is seven going on thirty. This party turned out to be everything she wanted and more. As you look around, you can see the love that was poured into every detail. Liz's skate team moves around helping the kids who can't skate as Bella shows off her skills like a little pro.

I'm proud of her. Liz did a good job teaching her. She's on her own blades now. My chest swells as I watch the two most important females in my life laugh together. I can't wait for the wedding. Three more months and I'll have the wife I was always meant to have.

I stand with my butt resting against the wall and my arms folded over my chest as Gio rolls over to me with a smile on his face. I can't help returning the smile. I was willing to lace up a pair of skates because my little girl asked me to. Seeing Gio in skates reminds me of how much love Bella has in her life.

It's been hard having her ask about her grandparents. While I could give two shits about her grandfather, I still don't know what happened to his wife. I believe whatever he and Bethany were up to cost that woman her life. Mitch and Jace have been trying to find me answers, but nothing has come up yet.

After the Peter incident, Liz decided to take a leave from her channel and the office. Bella is now spoiled rotten with attention. Liz takes her to her new school and picks her up each day.

While I miss Liz's face in the office, I love coming home to my girls after a long day to find them reading together. Lizzy now has all the time she wants to read. For the most part, life has been quiet, and I have more balance for myself.

"This is the way it should be. You're happy now," Gio says.

I look into my brother's eyes. He's smiling, but I can see he's not as happy as he would have us all believe. His life is so complicated. I don't even know where to begin to help him.

"What about you?"

He pulls a face. "My time will come. I still have work to do."

"You're not getting any younger."

"Neither is Nonno."

"But that's Dario's problem, not yours."

He snorts and reaches to pat my cheek. "There's always a bigger picture, Dante."

With that, he skates off. I watch him scoop up a laughing Bella and stand wondering what hand Gio is playing this time. I turn my attention to Liz, and she locks gazes with me and rolls over to me. I stand up straight as she rolls right into my arms.

I wrap her in my embrace and peck her lips. My hands land on her ass.

"Did you really have to wear this costume?" I groan.

She reaches to move my hands up to her lower back. "It was what Bella wanted. Besides, I'll be hanging up my skates and the costumes for a while."

I knit my brows. "Why?"

"Come on, Mr. Di Lorenzo. Why else would I need to stay off skates for eight to nine months?"

I take in a sharp breath and plant my hands back on her ass to tug her into my body. I take her lips in a passionate kiss. When I break the kiss, I run my nose up the bridge of hers and place my forehead to hers.

"Are you saying you're pregnant, baby?"

She nods with that adorable smile. "Yes, I confirmed it this morning. We're having a baby."

I cup the back of her neck and kiss her again, hard.

"I don't deserve you," I breathe against her lips.

"Yes, you do. And I, you. We deserve all of this happiness, babe and we're going to take it."

"Wait until Bella finds out."

I go to kiss her again, but Dario catches my attention as he looks around the rink frantically.

"Hold that thought, baby," I murmur.

I release her and skate over to my twin. I reach him at the same time as Gio and Jace.

"What's going on?"

"Have you guys seen Carleen?"

"She was sitting with Denise and Elijah just a little while ago," Jace replies.

"They both said she told them she was headed to the bathroom, but no one has seen her since," Dario says, looking pale.

I wave Liz over. She skates toward us with a wary look in her eyes.

"Can you ask Ming to check the cameras to see if she spots Carleen?"

"Sure, is everything okay?"

"No, she's not answering my texts. I don't know where she is," Dario says. It's clear he's losing his shit.

"Where's Matteo?" Liz asks.

"He's with Dad."

"Okay, give me a sec."

Liz rolls away and I place a hand on my brother's shoulder. I can feel the rage rolling off him. I'm not ready to admit it, but I feel like something is very wrong.

I turn to lay eyes on Liz and she's waving us over. I tap Dario's shoulder and gesture for him to follow me. We move over to the counter where Lizzy and Ming are and the first thing I note is the grim look on Liz's face.

She narrows her eyes and leans into the monitors. "What the fuck? You guys are going to want to see this. Who is that guy?"

Dario rounds the desk. His face clouds over. My blood runs cold as my brother releases a bloodcurdling roar.

Fuck, I should have known it was too quiet.

ACKNOWLEDGMENTS

This book was a must write for me and then it turned into a series. I'm so excited about this series and I love these brothers. I can't wait for you to get to the end. I love, love, love Lizzy and Dante, but Gio…*Baby*!

This was me finding my way back to loving what I do. I fist-pumped so many times during this book. It just spoke to me. Thank you for sharing this journey with me. I appreciate you.

Thank you for your patience with me as I heal and get on track. A big thank you to all of my readers. I have found my way back to loving what I do and I'm glad to have you with me. As always, thank you for every email, message, and post. Love you guys for all of the support.

A huge shout-out to my husband for listening to me ramble about these books. Love you.

To God be the glory. It is a blessing to do what I do the way I do. I thank God for this gift. With all I am, I thank you. Thank you, Lord.

Next! Dario in My Best Friend's Wish. Back to work.

ABOUT THE AUTHOR

Blue Saffire, award-winning, bestselling author of over thirty contemporary romance novels and novellas, writes with the intention to touch the heart and the mind. Blue hooks, weaves, and loops multiple series, keeping you engaged in her worlds. Blue is a hybrid author, writing for her own publishing company Perceptive Illusions as Blue Saffire as well as Royal Blue.

Blue and her husband live in a house filled with laughter and creativity, in Long Island, NY. Both working hard to build the Blue brand and cultivate their love for the artists. Creative is their family affair.

Blue holds an MBA in Marketing and Project Management, as well as a MED in Instructional Technology and Curriculum Design. She is also an NLP Master Practitioner.

Wait, there is more to come! You can stay updated with my latest releases, learn more about me, the author, and be a part of contests by subscribing to my newsletter at
www.BlueSaffire.com
If you enjoyed Unexpected Lovers, I'd love to hear your thoughts and please feel free to leave a review. And when you do, please let me know by emailing me TheBlueSaffire@gmail.com or leave a comment on Facebook https://www.facebook.com/BlueSaffireDiaries or Twitter @TheBlueSaffire

Other books by Blue Saffire
Placed in Best Reading Order
Also available....
Legally Bound

Legally Bound 2: Against the Law

Legally Bound 3: His Law

Perfect for Me

Hush 1: Family Secrets

Ballers: His Game

Brothers Black 1: Wyatt the Heartbreaker

Legally Bound 4: Allegations of Love

Hush 2: Slow Burn

Coming Soon...
My Best Friend's Wish
The Ones Left Behind
Lost Souls Book 4: Again

The Lost Souls MC Series
Forever
Never
Always

Blue Saffire exclusive on the
BlueSaffire.com website

The A Million to Blow Series
A Million to Blow
A Million to Stay
A Million Blown Coming soon...

Other books from Evei Lattimore Collection
Books by Blue Saffire
Black Bella 1

Destiny 1: Life Decisions
Destiny 2: Decisions of the Next Generation
Destiny 3 coming soon...

Star

Other books from Royal Blue Gay Romance
Collection written by Blue Saffire
Kyle's Reveal
Beau's Redemption

www.ingramcontent.com/pod-product-compliance
Lightning Source LLC
Chambersburg PA
CBHW070917260626
47162CB00007B/2708

* 9 7 8 1 9 4 1 9 2 4 1 4 3 *